TEMPTATION

She stood in the bath, her graceful, delectable body rising like a sea-nymph above the water.

A groan rose low in his throat, his body hardening. A soapsud clung to the side of her breast, another to her abdomen. He watched her, entranced.

"Garrick," she whispered softly, "don't send me away."

Oh, how he wished he didn't have to. His wanting was a physical ache, yet more than that. Standing there by her side, he could almost feel the crackling energy that bound them together and entwined them. For the first time in his life, Garrick experienced a want unlike any he'd ever felt. He wanted her now.

And then she leaned toward him, one wet hand coming to rest against his face. "Love me, Garrick."

He closed his eyes, knowing he was a doomed man.

"Damn you, Lucy," he groaned just before he crushed her to him.

She raised her head for his kiss, accepted his assault willingly, drew his head down, and twined her hands in his hair. Their lips met, and suddenly everything spun out of control. Her mouth opened and every thought fled from his mind as he flicked his tongue inside her velvety wetness.

Sweet. God, she tastes sweet.

No, a voice inside warned him. *Don't do this. Don't risk it all. . . .*

Hi Kim!—
Surprise (!) Here's
my book. Cool, eh?

My Fallen
Angel

∞

Pamela Britton

Sorry I missed you
Fall man looks great!

Pamela Britton

HarperPaperbacks
A Division of HarperCollinsPublishers

🏛 HarperPaperbacks

A Division of HarperCollins*Publishers*

10 East 53rd Street, New York, NY 10022-5299

This is a work of fiction. The characters, incidents, and dialogues are products of the author's imagination and are not to be construed as real. Any resemblance to actual events or persons, living or dead, is entirely coincidental.

ISBN 0-06-101431-1

HarperCollins®, 🏛®, and HarperPaperbacks™ are trademarks of HarperCollins Publishers Inc.

Cover illustration © John Ennis

First HarperPaperbacks printing: February 2000

Printed in the United States of America

Visit HarperPaperbacks on the World Wide Web at
http://www.harpercollins.com

❖ 10 9 8 7 6 5 4 3 2 1

Acknowledgments

All of you know I'm crying as I write this, but then you know I cry at long-distance commercials, so here goes:

Thanks go to:

The best critiquers in the world: Cherry, Jennifer, Rose, Michelle, and Susan. I couldn't have done it without you. Sniff, sniff.

My family for always believing, especially Mom, who loaned me my very first romance novel. (It was Janet Dailey, *No Quarter Asked*, remember, Mom?) And to my adorable sisters: Patty, you're the best darn housekeeper in Regency London. LoLo, God willing I'll make good on my promise to make you my full-time copy editor. I love you all so darn much.

Georgia Adamson for teaching me to dot my i's and cross my t's.

The great gang at HarperCollins for having exquisitely wonderful, fantabulous taste.

Pat Teal, for sticking with me.

And to my racing buds ... from Winston Cup garages to the local track. Your support over the years has meant the world to me.

Barbary Coast
May, 1818

Garrick Asquith-Wolf was fighting for his life, and loving every moment of it.

Rain ran in rivulets down his face, his shirt a cold second skin. The ship lurched beneath his feet, making it difficult to stand. Yet through it all a grin split his face from ear to ear. He thrust his sword at his opponent, missed, drew back and thrust again. All around him men fought similar battles, but Garrick ignored the stench of blood and fear. Every muscle ached, his arms burned, sweat mingled with the rain trickling down his face. This was what he lived for, his mission in life: ridding the seas of pirate scum.

"Give up yet, Tully?" he jeered at his opponent.

Tully St. Clair, one of the most feared pirates on the Atlantic Ocean, sneered right back, his black eyes gleaming in the cloudy light. "I'll see ye in hell first, Wolf."

Fat drops of rain pelted Garrick as his grin widened. He swiped them away with a blood-spattered hand. "Let me know what it's like, then."

"You'll know first," Tully shot back, sword raised.

Garrick had just enough time to lift his own before Tully swung. His palms stung at the clash of the two blades. Once. Twice. Then again and yet again Tully lashed out. Garrick took a step back.

And slipped on the rain-slick deck.

His breath escaped him as his back hit the deck. He couldn't breathe, fought to take in even the tiniest sip of air. Tully grinned evilly. His blade glinted as he raised it above his head.

Garrick rolled. Tully screeched. The blade sunk into wood.

"Damn ye," Tully cried.

"It's you who's damned," Garrick managed to wheeze. Blade in hand, he pulled himself to his feet with a strand of frayed rope that hung from the mast.

They charged each other. Bits of sail and splintered wood littered the deck amidst the bodies of fallen comrades. Garrick pushed the images from his mind. Thrust. Swing. Parry. The rhythm blurred.

Then he noticed a subtle difference in Tully's fighting: His blade wobbled in the air, the hilt moved in his palm, the tip hung a little lower.

His opponent grew weak.

The realization was power. With renewed strength Garrick brought his blade down. Tully's eyes flicked with momentary fear as he was backed against the ship's rail. One more jab and Garrick had him bent over the blood-splattered wood.

"Arghh," Tully bellowed a heartbeat later. His free hand clutched at the ragged gash across his cheek. "Ye'll pay fer that!" But the fear in Tully's scurvy gaze belied the words. So did the blood on his hand. He knew he was a beaten man.

Garrick knew it as well. He swung his blade in a wide arc. The two swords connected with a bone-rattling crack and Garrick saw Tully's grip loosen. Wielding the sword with all his expertise, he closed in for the kill.

Tully's sword flipped through the air and disappeared over the rail to be swallowed by the frothing waves below.

Stunned disbelief contorted his opponent's face. Garrick threw back his head and roared with confident, victorious laughter. Drunk with power, he raised his sword above his head. Before he could bring it down, Tully grasped a piece of rigging, swung himself over the rail, and dropped into the churning sea.

Garrick's laughter turned full blown—it rang out over the white-tipped waves. "Let that be a lesson to you," he yelled at Tully, who quickly disappeared from view. Garrick's sword glistened above him. "No one can beat me! No one! I am invincible!"

The clouds echoed his bellow and a great clash of thunder rang out.

Only a few saw what happened next, and their words became infamous in the annals of pirate history.

Time and again the story was told of a luminescent bolt of lightning that streaked down from the heavens, captured the Wolf's upraised blade, then traveled down his arm and into his body—knocking him clean off the deck.

Apparently, the Wolf was *not* invincible.

Part 1

Two loves I have, of comfort and despair,
Which like two spirits do suggest me still;
The better angel is a man right fair,
The worser spirit a woman colour'd ill.

—*Shakespeare*

1

June 1818

Miss Lucy Hartford wondered at the wisdom of breaking into the Earl of Selborne's mammoth estate on such a cold and dank evening. More specifically, she questioned her degree of intelligence in general. Scaling a tree in the dead of night while somehow managing to hold a small lantern to light her way, all for the sake of helping one adorable, outspoken little boy named Tom, was certainly *not* one of her better ideas. And though the earl and his evil second wife were on holiday, she still ran the risk of discovery. In fact, she would rank this idea right up there with the time she'd disastrously experimented with gunpowder. Fortunately, the only casualty that day had been the chamber pot.

She grimaced as her booted foot slipped off the branch, knocking a combination of leaves, bark, and twigs to the grass-covered ground nearly thirty feet below. A gentle puff of wind caressed the branches around her and caused the lantern to sway and the candle inside to flicker. She held her breath as she waited to be plunged into darkness, but, with a hiss, the candle flared to life again.

At that moment she contemplated turning back. Contemplated, but decided against it. Her glance darted from the window that was her goal, to the ground, then to the window again. Her friends always told her she had more courage than sense. Lucy looked at her surroundings and grinned. They were right.

Still, that didn't change the fact that she knew this would be her one and only chance to gather clues, perhaps even evidence, proving Tom was really the long-lost son of the earl of Selborne. Unfortunately, in her experience, knowing something to be a good idea and actually implementing the notion were two different things.

Bother.

Leaves and small branches tangled in her hair, which she had tied behind her head. She swatted them away, then gasped as the hot lantern glass scalded her breeches-clad leg.

Rot and bother. There were at least thirty trees dotting the gently rolling hills that surrounded the earl's Tudor-style home, many of which looked far easier to climb—not that she could see much outside the rim of the light—but with her luck tonight, she'd probably fall out of this one.

No sooner had the thought sprung to her mind than something creaked. Undoubtedly the sound of her stays popping as her chest heaved up and down in agitation. Then she remembered she wore men's clothes. Her eyes widened. She heard one last, loud, ominous crack.

And screamed.

It didn't help, not that she'd expected it to. It felt as though she sailed through the air forever, colliding with something as she landed, a something which grunted in a very masculine way.

"Bloody hell," she finally groaned as she sat there, stunned, and took a mental survey of her limbs to assure herself nothing had broken.

"Not hell," the man gasped beneath her. "Not yet."

Lucy stiffened, suddenly realizing she sat across a man's chest as primly as a lady sat for tea. Good heavens. She pushed herself to her feet, too hastily as it turned out, for her foot thrust into him in the process. In horror she heard him gasp, then let out a long, agonized moan. She clasped her hands over her mouth, for it was the same groan her brother had emitted the time she'd accidentally struck him in his unmentionables with a billiard cue.

"Oh dear," she squeaked.

Something snapped. She turned toward the sound, her hair having escaped from it bonds to partly shield her face. She shoved it away impatiently.

Things went from bad to worse in that instant . . . very bad.

The grass had caught on fire.

"My lantern!" she wailed, watching as a great puff of smoke wafted overhead.

Flames shot up toward the sky like a bonfire on All Hallow's Eve. She clapped her gaping mouth shut and began to stomp, but the bloody fire refused to cooperate.

She stomped harder, broken glass crunching beneath her feet. Yet the flames grew bigger. She shrugged out of the coat she'd pilfered from her brother and tried to smother the inferno with the black superfine.

The fabric proved more flammable than the grass.

The coat caught fire. She dropped it to the ground and groaned as she watched the beautiful fabric turn into a textile torch which, in turn, lit a nearby shrub, which then set some dried branches aflame, and then started the trunk of the tree on fire.

It was the strangest thing about those flames, for they were quickly approaching gargantuan proportions when, suddenly, amazingly, they just disappeared. *Poof*. They were gone.

Lucy widened her green eyes in surprise as she stared first at the smoking embers on the ground and then up at the sky. She expected to feel raindrops on her face, but felt only the soft touch of ashes alighting on her cheeks and the persistent heavy dankness which always accompanies fog.

"What . . . ?" She turned back to her companion. "Did you see that?"

"If you are referring to the blazing inferno, then yes, I did catch a glimpse of it."

She ignored the sarcastic edge to his voice and turned back to the smoking embers. "It just disappeared." She scratched her head, absently tugging out a few stray leaves before dropping her arm back to her side. "Maybe it burned itself out."

"Perhaps so," the man grumbled.

She whirled to face him, suddenly realizing she had no idea who he was. "Well, thank you for your assistance Mr., er, ahh, whoever you are. I'll . . . I'll just be on my way now." She took a hasty step away from him.

"I don't think so."

"You don't?" she asked warily.

"No."

Lucy gulped as a truly horrible thought penetrated. What if he'd been hired by the evil Countess of Selborne to kill her because she knew who Tom really was? Indeed, if the countess had hired someone to kill Tom all those years ago so her *own* son could inherit the estate, what was to stop her from hiring someone to kill nosy Lucy Hartford?

She heard a soft rustle, and her terror increased as he got to his feet. For the first time that night Lucy wished she hadn't ventured out of her aunt's home alone. Never before had one of her "adventures" gotten her into such a fix. She dove to the ground, her hand searching frantically for something, *anything* to use as a weapon. When she felt the rough texture of a long-dead tree branch, she clasped it gratefully, then shot to her feet. She hefted the branch above her head and braced her booted feet.

Warily she eyed the dark form making its way toward her. A very *large* dark form, she amended. When she gauged him near enough, she swung.

Her victim never saw it coming.

It must have taken him a moment to realize what had happened for it was two swipes later before he roared, "Bloody hell, woman, put that branch down!"

He raised his arms in the air in an attempt to ward off her blows.

She may as well have been hitting an elephant, Lucy thought in alarm. She struck him again and again, feeling a piece of the brittle tree branch break off. With a growing sense of dismay, she realized that with each blow, her makeshift weapon grew shorter and shorter. Splinters flew through the air until all she had left was a short stub.

She threw it at him.

Turning, she ran blindly toward what she hoped was the back of the house and, more importantly, the cart and pony she had hidden there, but her leg connected with a hedge some demented gardener had trimmed to only knee high. She gasped as its prickly branches made contact with her skin.

An ironlike grip surrounded her right forearm and kept her from falling. She had no time to be grateful, for in the next instant he whirled her back to face him, clasping his other hand around her left forearm and effectively ending her flight.

"Let me go," she screamed, squirming in his grasp. "I'll not let you kill me . . . or . . . or . . . have your way with me!"

"Have my way with you?" the man questioned. "Have my way with you?" he repeated, his voice tinged with amusement.

For a long moment he said nothing and then when he did speak, exasperation was clearly evident in his voice.

"Calm down, wildcat. I'm certainly not here to harm you."

She said the first thing that came to mind. "No doubt that's what all henchmen say to their captives."

He snorted, or maybe it was a chuckle, but then she forgot everything as he said, "I promise, I'll not harm you." His voice was a low, seductive purr and his thumb began to rub up and down her arm in a soothing manner

"I d-don't believe you."

"I'm a friend."

His thumb continued to stroke her arm. Oddly enough it was having a strange, calming effect on her. She tried to see his face, but all she could determine was that he had light hair and shoulders the size of Sir Gilmore's prize stallion's. Lucy swallowed, her throat so dry she felt as if she were swallowing a desert.

"Are you a friend of a friend, or a friend of mine?"

"My name is Garrick Wolf," he answered, "and I'm a friend of the Duke and Duchess of Warburton."

"Adrian and Salena?" Lucy asked hopefully.

Salena Kent, Duchess of Warburton, was her dearest friend, other then Elizabeth Montclair, of course. She began to relax, then tensed again as she realized it could be a ploy to get her to do exactly that.

"How do I know you're not just telling me that?" she asked suspiciously.

"If I was truly out to harm you, do you think you could stop me?"

Lucy opened her mouth, then slammed it shut as she realized he had a point.

"Besides, the duchess suspected you might react in

this fashion," he continued. "She wanted me to tell you I am here to help you—let me see, how did she put it— 'keep chamber pots from exploding.'"

Lucy's fears wafted away like clouds on a warm spring day. Only a handful of people knew of that embarrassing incident, thankfully. Her heart rate returned to normal as reason began to assert itself. She breathed in a whiff of soggy night air, noting distantly that she could still smell the remnant of the fire.

"Goodness, you must be telling the truth." Tension drained from her shoulders. He must have felt it, because he gently released her. "But I wonder why Adrian and Salena never mentioned they were sending you?"

"I've no idea," the man responded.

Lucy nibbled her bottom lip. She supposed Salena thought she might get offended, which she might very well have. "How much have Adrian and Salena told you?"

"Everything, including the fact that you were told to keep yourself and Tom hidden at your aunt's."

Lucy grimaced in embarrassment. "I couldn't abide staying cooped up in the house for one more day. And when I heard the earl and his countess were on holiday, it was too good an opportunity to pass up. Why, there's no telling what I could learn by rummaging through their papers. Besides, I've never been one to stay meekly at home."

"Do you realize how dangerous it is for a lady of good breeding to venture out alone in the middle of the night?"

Lucy nodded. "Yes, I do, but is it not dangerous for a lady of bad breeding, too? And breeding aside, I simply had to do it. The earl's second wife has undoubtedly been paying that scoundrel Jolly blackmail money to keep him quiet about her part in Tom's disappearance all those years ago. If that is so, then I would reason she knows where to find Jolly. Indeed, he must have told her where to send the money, for I'm certain she would never deal with the man directly. And if we find Jolly, we'll be that much closer to proving Tom is the earl's son. Do you not agree?"

He grew silent again as he mulled over her words, then said, "You could have gotten yourself killed, or hurt."

Lucy rolled her eyes derisively. He was using that smugly pretentious voice males used when they didn't want to admit a woman could be as useful as a man.

"I assure you, sir," she said as firmly as possible, "I've climbed quite a number of trees in my time. I was in no danger of hurting myself."

"Yes, no doubt you're correct. I'm sure if you hadn't landed on me, it wouldn't have hurt a bit when you hit the ground."

"Hmm," Lucy conceded, unable to stop the laughter from tingeing her voice, "that *was* rather a stroke of luck, even though you are not much softer than the ground. Still, if you think the idea so silly, I give you leave to take yourself away from here. I, however, am getting into that house."

"Oh, no you are not," he countered. When she stiffened he added, "*I* will go inside, since you're so set on the notion."

Lucy wanted to insist she accompany him, but realized it would be useless. No doubt it was best to let him have his way . . . for now. She could already tell this friend of Adrian's was the obstinate, males-are-the-ultimate-sex, you-are-weak-woman type. She wondered briefly if she might have met him at Salena and Adrian's wedding. Yes. Perhaps that was the reason he seemed so familiar.

As the last of her doubts drifted away she said, "There was another branch below the one I used, sturdier, but at more of a distance from the window."

Before she could say another word, he'd turned away and headed back toward the tree. It was with a sense of amazed disbelief that she watched his dark form climb up the branches a moment later.

Why, he shimmied up that tree as swiftly as one of those monkeys she'd seen at the Royal Zoo. It didn't seem possible for a man of his large bulk to move so quickly, yet he did. To her absolute and utter astonishment he was through the half-open window within seconds.

She waited until she judged him well into the house before she took a last look around, then carefully followed. She'd never had any intention of simply staying behind. It was her one fault, she admitted ruefully, this desire—more of a burning need, actually—for grand adventure. It had gotten her into trouble more times than not.

It was the sad truth; she was something of a madcap.

The tree was a simple one to climb, as trees go, and the new branch was definitely much sturdier and far easier to cross than the last one, not to mention now she had no candle to impede her progress. However, the limb was a good distance below the open window.

"Blast," Lucy hissed, eyeing the dark opening. It looked impossibly far away.

As it stood, the only way she would make it inside was to jump for it. She mulled over the idea. It was risky, but she'd be damned if she just stood by and let Mr. Wolf have all the fun. This *was* her adventure.

Lucy took a deep breath and posed herself to jump. Grimly determined, she eyed the opening.

She jumped.

It wasn't a miscalculation on her part, really; it was more of an underestimation of the weight of her body. That and the fact that she hadn't planned on her arms feeling as if they were going to be pulled from their sockets when she landed. Her knuckles grew white as she clung to the sill. She let out a little squeak when she realized she was in trouble.

"Oh dear," she murmured softly, then, "Mr. Wolf," as loudly as she dared, in the off chance he was still in the room above. He wasn't.

Her grip began to slip.

Drop back to the branch, she thought, but then she realized sickeningly that she was too afraid to do so.

"Help?" she said a little louder.

Her hand slid ominously toward the edge.

2

Her fingers were just about to slide off the narrow sill when Mr. Wolf tugged her through the window and up against his wide chest. Her scream faded into a strangled gasp at being so quickly snatched from peril. She kept her eyes shut as she clasped her arms around him. He smelled like the sea, she noted distantly. She tried to stand. Her feet made contact with what felt like a hardwood floor, but her legs shook so badly he had to support her.

She hadn't fallen to a messy death.

Thankful for being rescued, she squeezed him harder, then almost completely lost her train of thought. Her breath escaped in a rush as she hugged him tighter, rather enjoying the feel of him pressed against her.

"Thank you," she murmured. "Thank you, thank you, thank you." She kept squeezing, just to make sure his muscles felt as firm as they looked, then said in a quavering voice, "I was too frightened to drop back down to the branch, and then I couldn't pull myself up, and when

I looked down I couldn't even see the ground, not that I could see anything what with it being pitch black outside, but I thought for sure I was dead . . ." She pulled back, her words trailing off as she got her first good look at him in the light.

Her breath escaped in an awe-filled rush as she studied the features candlelight illuminated to perfection.

He was beautiful.

No, beautiful was not enough; he was, well, *magnificent*. With his Nordic-like cheekbones, golden hair, white lawn shirt, sea blue eyes made even more blue by the copper color of his skin, and his buff-colored breeches tucked into black boots, all he'd need was a patch over one eye and he'd be the spitting image of a high-seas pirate, a swashbuckling hero come to rescue her.

"Oh my," she breathed softly, a strange mushy feeling surging through her insides, the same feeling she'd gotten after drinking that bottle of wine she'd snuck into her room on her thirteenth birthday.

"What the devil do you mean by climbing up here?" he hissed, pushing her away from him.

"You left me behind."

"I told you to stay behind on *purpose*."

All Lucy could do was nod, still staring up at him in giddy bemusement. His expression grew thunderous. She gave him an undoubtedly wan smile in return. It was obvious by his lack of response that he couldn't see her face with the candles behind her. Those candles revealed what appeared to be a sitting room.

A sofa, its long back against a wall, squatted on clawfooted legs to her left; two matching rose and white chairs sat to her right. It was a feminine room with floral patterns on everything: the furniture, the wall hangings . . . good heavens, even around the perimeter of the hardwood floor. Mr. Wolf looked distinctly at odds with such a backdrop, still sinfully handsome, but out of place.

Suddenly he tensed, and before she knew what he was about, he stepped past her, reached for the candelabra on the floor behind her, and blew out the candles. Lucy wanted to protest. She would have been happy to stare at him all night.

When he tugged her away from the window, she didn't argue, happy to follow wherever he went. Not even when he scraped the sofa away from the wall, then pushed her down behind it, did she say a word. Actually, she was a tad bit disappointed he hadn't placed her *on* the sofa, then lay down with her. She'd always wondered what it would be like to be kissed by such a man—a man who was tall and masculine and virile, the opposite of her short and somewhat chunky soon-to-be-fiancé, Lord Harry Harrington.

She sighed. A man such as this would never want her, not with her clumsy nature. She'd been lucky dear Harry had agreed to take her on. Once again she squelched a familiar pang of longing to have been born tall and graceful and blonde. Perhaps then she would . . .

The door opened. "Who's there?" a voice asked. It served to snap Lucy back to the world of reality far faster than if a bolt of lightning had zapped her.

Secret fantasies forgotten, she tensed as boot heels clicked on the floor. A shadow flickered against the wall and her eyes widened. She heard a step, then another and another. When the footsteps got too close for comfort, Lucy turned and knelt on all fours, then hastily started crawling toward the other end of the sofa, grimacing at the layer of dust she could feel beneath her hands. Actually, she had rather a lot of experience skulking about in such a way. Apparently so did her companion, for he made hardly a sound as he followed behind.

The footsteps stopped and Lucy tensed, expecting to hear, "Aha, I have caught you," at any moment. Instead all she heard was a loud thud. It scared her so much, she nearly yelped in fright. Only when she heard the distinct click of a latch being shut did she realize it was the window being closed. She froze and waited to see what happened next, then rolled her eyes in exasperation when the footsteps sounded again . . . heading straight toward her.

She scrunched down, making herself as small as possible and jabbing her elbow into Mr. Wolf in the process. She heard him gasp and felt her cheeks flame in response. The footsteps receded, the light faded, and then there was the unmistakable sound of the door closing.

Silence.

She felt her rescuer stir. A moment later he stood, then grabbed her elbow and raised her up alongside of him. When he moved away, she followed his dark form, all the while hoping he wasn't too terribly angry.

Garrick Asquith-Wolf, former naval captain now turned reluctant guardian, was beyond angry, he was furious. No, he thought, even beyond furious, he was livid. He reached for the flint to relight the candles, wanting to see into the eyes of the dunderhead who had hung like a bat from a windowsill, tried to unman him, and used him as her personal landing cushion while falling out of a tree, a *tree* of all things. She was the most idiotic chit he'd ever had the misfortune to meet. He wondered if she looked as stupid as she acted.

He raised the candles high and nearly dropped the candelabra in his astonishment.

Good God. Anyone as accident-prone as she ought to look like a hag, not this . . . dazzling beauty with eyes as green as precious gem stones and skin as luminescent as moonlight. He nearly groaned aloud. With her lush curves and heart-shaped face surrounded by masses and masses of long, titian-colored hair, she put his former mistress to shame, even in breeches and boots. She was—he searched for the right word—temptation.

Garrick wanted to rail his fist toward heaven.

Now he knew why the angel who had sent him back had looked at him so smugly when he'd told him he would be human in every sense of the word. To think he'd actually scoffed at his vow to remain chaste.

They had called the vow a test.

It would be torment, Garrick realized as he stared down at the woman before him. More than that. His mission to prove the boy in her care the son of the Earl of Selborne would be hell.

"Perhaps the person's gone?" she ventured.

"'Twould appear so." He resisted the urge to continue to stare at her and forced himself to turn away. He held the candles high as he walked toward the doorway.

"Where are we going?" She stumbled after him.

He turned to glare at her, which was a mistake, for as soon as he met her gaze, he felt a blazing shaft of heat stab straight to his manhood, causing it to stand at attention like an ensign saluting an admiral. He put a hand on her shoulder to stop her from getting any closer. Another mistake, he realized the moment they touched. He had to squelch the urge to pull her toward him. He almost groaned, then jerked his hand away as if scalded.

Damn it all to hell. He hadn't had a woman in months, thanks to his last voyage at sea—the voyage which had ended his life—and now he was forced into the company of a woman who made his former mistress look like Prince George.

"Follow me," he snapped. "I was in the process of examining the countess's bedroom when your circus performance interrupted me."

She blinked up at him, her emerald eyes soft and gooey. Garrick turned away. As soon as he was through the door, he snapped it closed, trying his best to ignore the huge bed centered against a wall, and the almost irresistible urge to toss his charge onto it, preferably naked. God's teeth, he'd had no idea a man could feel so beguiled by a woman.

Calling himself a fool, he headed for the lace-embellished *toilette* located near a window to his left. The bed loomed large to his right. He told himself he'd get over his instant attraction. He told himself a multitude of things, none of which he believed.

There were only three drawers to examine, thankfully, for the sooner he was out of the bedroom, the better. He set the candelabra down and began to search. There was only an odd assortment of ribbons, bows, and brushes. He closed the last drawer muttering, "Damn," and stepped back, bumping into Miss Lucy who, he realized, was stuck to him like a fly on sap.

"Beg your pardon," she said sweetly.

The contact was too much. "Get away from me," he warned through gritted teeth, feeling as if he'd been scorched by the flames of hell.

As her eyes grew startled, he realized his words may have been a bit too harsh, but dammit, he needed her to stop looking at him as if he were a present under her Christmas tree.

She turned away from him, and Garrick thought he saw a glimmer of anger in her eyes. Good. Maybe if she was vexed with him, she'd stop mooning. He crossed his arms and watched as she grabbed a candle from the candelabra, then flounced back the way they'd come, her boots tapping militantly as she headed for the wardrobe closet near the doorway and the chest of drawers next to it.

She opened one, rummaged through it, then closed it with a snap. She did the same thing to the next drawer, only closed it a little harder. By the fourth drawer she was closing them with a full-fledged slam.

He turned away, content to let her wallow in her anger. As it turned out he didn't have a chance.

"Mr. Wolf?" he heard her call out only seconds later.

So used was he to being addressed as "Wolf" or "my lord," he almost didn't realize she was calling him. He turned toward her, noting the piece of paper she held in her hands.

"What do you make of this?"

He walked forward and took the slip from her. "'Tis the address of a solicitor."

"Yes, I can see that," she said impatiently, "but it was hidden in a drawer."

When he said nothing, she said, "It *must* be important. Why else would she hide it?"

Garrick had a hard time believing they'd stumbled upon a clue so easily, but for the life of him he couldn't squelch the feeling that they had. Not only that, but there was the oddest sensation as he held the paper, a tingling, very much like the feeling he got when he touched Lucy.

Where had that thought come from?

They both heard the footsteps at the same time. Lucy groaned at the exact moment Garrick stuffed the paper in his pocket, then extinguished the candles, secretly glad for the interruption. Darkness swallowed them.

"Phibbs, you're a dodderin' old fool draggin' me out of bed like this," they heard a man mutter.

Lucy felt Mr. Wolf tug her toward the wardrobe closet. Next thing she knew, he pushed her into it. In amazement, she felt him cram his big body in next to hers, somehow wedging in between what felt like ball gowns. The smell of cedar nearly overpowered her, and so did her fear, so she grabbed his hand and held it next to her pounding heart.

He tried to pull it away.

She wouldn't let him.

The wood creaked ominously, and she envisioned them dropping out of the bottom of the wardrobe like potatoes through a rotted sack. Miraculously, the closet held, though she felt as if she were a contortionist she'd once seen at a fair. She shifted. He grunted. Then they both stilled when they heard the bedroom door open and a voice with a Cockney accent just like Tom's say, "See? Nothing here," in disgruntlement.

"I tell you I heard thumping."

"Probably the sound of your brainbox trying to function," the other man grumbled in exasperation.

"Very amusing," a voice retorted. There was silence, and the obvious sound of a person rustling about. "Do you smell that?"

"Smell what?"

"It smells like a candle."

"You're holding a candle, you dolt."

"Yes, but this smells like an *extinguished* candle."

There was a snort. "I've had enough of this nonsense."

"But I tell you, I *heard* something."

"Then by all means, feel free to investigate. I for one am going back to my bed."

"Wait." There was the hurried sound of footsteps. "I refuse to walk through these hallways alone."

Lucy heard the door close and breathed a sigh of relief. "I think they're gone."

She shifted a little; her body rubbed up against his. She heard a gasp, and wondered if she'd stepped on him again. She tried to push past him, her breasts sliding up against his arm. Her cheeks stung with embarrassment. She heard him gasp again, then her thoughts fled like petals on a breeze when she felt a hand gently caress her side. Strangely, she didn't move away. She *should* move away. It was terribly disloyal to dear Harry to allow a man to touch her thus. Still, Mr. Wolf's touch made her feel so strange, like when she'd plunged off the roof of the barn and into that haystack, just before she'd stepped on the pitchfork. It was a funny sort of feeling, right in the pit of her stomach, as if . . . as if she couldn't breathe.

She stiffened when his hand trailed up her side, skirted around her breasts, traipsed along her collarbone, and up the side of her neck to halt at long last on her jaw. She felt him shift, realized he was going to kiss her, realized that she should tell him to stop, but then she felt the gentle caress of his breath on her cheek, and then . . . and then . . .

Heaven.

It was a kiss so soft, yet so . . . so *amazing*, Lucy was too stunned to move. Her legs weakened. She felt Garrick try to catch her wilting body, but they were so cramped in the narrow confines of the closet they could barely move. He grunted in frustration, and without removing his lips from hers, pushed past some petticoats and stepped from the closet, leaving her behind. It worked out perfectly, for their two heads were on level.

Lucy sighed in contentment, but then he did something so unexpected, so startling, she stiffened in protest. Still he continued to pull her shirt from the waistline of her breeches. She pulled her lips away, but he started trailing kisses down the side of her neck instead. That left her momentarily breathless and so she closed her eyes, but then he leaned back and before she knew what he was about, he touched her breast.

She pushed him away in shock.

He flew over backward like Hyperion falling from heaven.

And downstairs two gazes shot to the ceiling.

"Now, you tell me that weren't nothin'," one footman said to the other.

3

"*What* do you *think* you're *doing!*"

Garrick didn't want to open his eyes. Unfortunately, the voice which had spoken sounded all too familiar. Arlan Horatio Shuck, his "Heavenly Guidance Counselor." He opened one eye, then wished he hadn't. The white-robed figure staring back at him looked furious—livid, really. His wings beat back and forth like a hawk's hovering over its prey. The motion caused the papers on his desk to rustle. One of his feathers came loose and drifted to the white tiled floor.

"You've been alone with Miss Hartford for a half hour," he ranted, raising his hands in the air. "*A half hour,* and *already* you've nearly broken your vow. What? Do you *want* to go to hell?"

Garrick stared at Arlan warily. Arlan stared right back. The silence stretched on, the only sound the agitated flapping of Arlan's wings as they brushed against the room's walls, a room where everything was white: the desk, the ceiling, Arlan's hair. It was like being trapped in the middle of a blizzard. It gave Garrick a headache.

"Well, *say* something," the angel demanded.

"This is not a fair test."

"Oh." The angel's thin lips spread into a grimace, exposing teeth that would be better suited on a horse; his blue eyes narrowed into a squint. "Oh, oh, oh, I get it." He looked toward the ceiling. "He says it's not a fair test."

Thunder rattled the little room, and the angel squinted back at him, a look of disgust on his face. "That excuse didn't work for Adam, either."

"Then give me another person to guard."

"Sorry. This is the path you chose, Garrick. This here and this now. We can't undo what we've already done because you've changed your mind."

When Garrick didn't answer, he added, "Do you know what we went through to place that little boy in Lucy's care?" Arlan didn't wait for an answer, just raged on. "First the carriage accident. And then manipulating Lucy into offering to care for the child, not that that took much work. You simply cannot change your mind midway through the test. This is your one chance to go directly to heaven. If you don't, you must take your chances with the Well of Souls."

Garrick stared at the angel for a long moment then ran his fingers through his hair, muttering, "God's balls. I had no idea it would be this hard."

"God's *what*?" Arlan snapped.

Garrick stared at him in confusion.

The lightning bolt came out of nowhere.

It filled the room with its brightness, bounced off a nearby chair, ricocheted off the door, and found its mark on the left cheek of Garrick's rear.

"Bloody hell!" he yelled, looking over his shoulder to check the damage.

"All clear?" asked a muffled voice from under a desk. Garrick turned back in time to see Arlan peek out, breathe a sigh of relief, and then slowly stand. "Whew. Thought you were going to get hit harder than that. The Chief must be in a good mood today. Guess you learned *that* lesson." He dusted off his robe. "*Not* a good idea to say things like that around here. Now, where were we? You were asking for a different assignment and I had just told you no, but there was something else. Ah yes, I remember now." Arlan reached into his desk and pulled out a scroll that, when unfurled, was easily two feet long. "I was going to tell you how many penalties you'd incurred for touching Miss Hartford." He scanned the list. "Where is it, where is it? Kissing, kissing, kissing. Ah, here it is!" His brow furrowed as he read, "An automatic one-day deduction shall be incurred when a guardian kisses his client."

Arlan looked up. "See? You've already lost a day. And right below it says a deduction of two days shall be incurred should you touch a mortal's, er . . . ahh, private parts. That means you've lost three days in all, leaving you a total of twenty-four days to prove the identity of the little boy Lucy has in her care. Need I remind you, Garrick, that if you break your vow of celibacy, you go directly to the Well of Souls. It's simply not a good idea to waste your earthly energy on physical pleasures. Con-

sider it a stroke of luck that you qualified for the
Guardian Program the first time around. Granted, if you
go back to the Well, you might, and I stress *might*, get
another chance, but I doubt it. And if you don't, well,
you know where they'll send you."

"Hell," Garrick muttered.

"Well, at least you've remembered *that* much."
Arlan's eyes held a warning as they stared across at him.
"You must be circumspect, Garrick. Prove the identity
of that little boy within twenty-four days and you'll earn
your spot in heaven. Fail and it's back to the Well of
Souls to await a hearing. And do you have any idea how
long it takes to get a hearing? An eternity.

"My advice is to stay as far away from Lucy Hartford
as possible since you seem to be so, er, attracted to her."

"Garrick, please, please wake up."

If there was one thing Garrick had learned to hate it
was the way he was zapped from one location to the
other. The same thing had happened the first time he'd
been tossed from heaven. *Kapow* . . . and he was on the
ground watching Lucy Hartford's behind hurtle toward
him from above.

A tentative hand touched his shoulder, bringing him
back to the present. Was it his imagination or did that
hand linger? He opened his eyes, then wished he hadn't.
She was close, too close.

"Oh, thank God. I thought you dead," she murmured.

God should be so kind. "How long?" he mumbled,

throat dry. After the sunlike brightness of Arlan's room, the candle she'd lit seemed as dim as moonlight in comparison.

"Only seconds," she answered, "but we must leave. When your head hit the floor, you sounded like Goliath falling to the ground."

He nodded, then sat up.

"Garrick," she said softly. "You're not angry with me, are you?"

"No," he snapped, pushing himself to his feet, fed up with the whole situation: Arlan, Lucy, the bloody mess this day had turned out to be.

She stood up alongside of him, then tugged at his arm. Reluctantly, he turned to face her.

"I'm so sorry for pushing you away," she said hesitantly. "What you did just startled me so. Not even dear Harry has done that."

Dear Harry? Who the hell was dear Harry? Never mind, he didn't want to know.

He shook his head, furious with himself for losing control in the arms of an innocent—an incredibly responsive innocent, but still an innocent.

"And I suppose I should warn you that I'm not the world's most graceful person," she went on to say as he stood. "Things just seem to happen around me. I mean, I didn't *plan* for that branch to break earlier, but it did." She sighed. "My aunt says I'm as clumsy as a pig on ice. And dear Harry refuses to dance with me—"

"Miss Hartford," Garrick interrupted. "I assure you I will never touch you again."

He wouldn't? Lucy thought. Whyever not? But then she realized she shouldn't *want* him to touch her. She should want dear Harry—a man who was expected to propose to her—to touch her. She should be outraged, horrified, disgusted by Mr. Wolf's behavior. She should be stricken with maidenly affront. At the very least she should slap his face.

Instead she felt a brazen need to make him want to touch her again. She peeked up at him.

He glared.

Her heart sank. Just sank to the bottom or her dirt-stained heels. He didn't like her. That much was clear. A lump the size of Sir Wilmont's garden grew in her throat. She tried to swallow, nearly choked, then looked away. Heaven knows she should be used to such reactions from men.

Heaven knows she wasn't.

Turning, she blindly reached for the door, wanting only to escape. It was hard to say who was more surprised when she opened the door and came face-to-face with two servants—her or the servants. One man's mouth gaped open. His face filled with horror, the dim light of the lantern he held turning his features into a ghoulish mask. He crossed himself.

Unfortunately, the other servant wasn't so timid. "Thief!" he screamed, pointing at her.

"Well!" Lucy huffed, sniffing back her tears. "I never. Thief indeed. Why, I'll have you know—"

Whatever else she'd been about to say was unceremoniously cut off when Garrick jerked her back and slammed the door in the footmen's faces.

"Stop!" came a muffled voice from the other side of the door.

Garrick shoved the lock in place, then pulled her toward the adjoining sitting room. He tried the window, but it was closed now. She watched as he struggled with the latch for a moment, then gave up and tugged her toward the door.

They burst into the same hallway as their pursuers, and a cold gust of air blew out Lucy's candle. She dropped it to the floor, then glanced over her shoulder and saw that the two servants had spotted them.

"Stop, thief," one of them yelled, charging in their direction.

She faced forward again only to crash into Garrick's back a moment later. He almost tumbled down the dark chasm before them. A stairwell.

He hesitated a moment, then plunged down the steps; Lucy followed closely behind. They made it down with nary a misstep, only to meet up with another servant at the bottom.

Lucy, unable to stop her momentum, sent the man flying backward with an "oomph."

"Beg your pardon," she blurted, managing to stay upright only because Garrick had a vicelike grip on her upper arm.

"Stop!" ordered their first pursuer from the stairs above.

They headed for the front door, bursting into the chilly night air a second later. It was blacker than a witch's cauldron outside, but Lucy noted Garrick somehow knew instinctively where to go.

The sound of pursuing footsteps receded, but still Garrick pushed on, practically shoving her up a small knoll, which Lucy dared to hope was the same knoll where her cart was hidden. When they crested the rise, she wheezed in relief at the sight of her pony cart.

"We can't go in that," he immediately announced. The wretch didn't sound the least bit out of breath, she noted. "We'll take my horse." He pulled her forward, dragging her behind like a poodle on a leash.

Horse, what horse? But then her eyes opened wide upon spying the white horse tethered next to the pony. Where had that come from? And the sudden moonlight, too?

"Hurry, they're pursuing us."

Lucy heard the thrashing footsteps as well. "B-but what about my aunt's pony?" she asked breathlessly.

"Leave it."

"We can't," she gasped in a breath. "My aunt will be furious."

In response he quickly untied the pony's traces, then slapped the little animal on the rear. Lucy watched in dismay as her aunt's pony and cart rumbled off into the night like a mail coach on its way to London. Next Garrick untied his horse and quickly mounted. He held out a hand to her. "Hurry," he ordered.

"I can't."

Garrick looked from her to the two servants nearly upon them, one of them brandishing what looked to be a pistol. "This is no time for theatrics, Lucinda," he rasped. "Give me your hand."

"But I hate horses," she wailed.

She saw him frown just before he reached down and grabbed her by the back of her shirt and pulled her atop his animal. The breath was forced out of her as she landed face down over his thighs. He gripped her derriere, then kicked the horse forward.

Lucy forgot everything as she struggled to stay aboard the lurching beast. Something swung alongside her head and she realized distantly it was Garrick's leg. She clutched at it frantically. "Garrick! Let me down!"

He ignored her words.

Minutes later Lucy prayed fervently for Garrick's horse to throw a shoe, have a fit of horsy apoplexy, or drop dead—anything to put her out of her misery. The ground sped by at a distance far too close for comfort. Her hair all but dragged on the ground. Her stomach felt ready to purge itself.

And then the horse lurched. Lucy gasped.

Seconds later they both flew through the air.

4

"Are you all right?"

Lucy lay still for a long second, the breath knocked out of her from her collision with the ground. She sucked in some air, her mind refusing to comprehend the blessed relief of immobility. Never mind that she'd just tumbled from a horse galloping at full tilt. She'd fall off a hundred horses if it meant not having to ride a single one ever again.

"Miss Hartford?"

Slowly, she opened her eyes. A dark shape stood silhouetted against a star-infested sky, nearby trees even bigger blobs against the horizon. Tall, tall grass rose on either side of her. The smell of green blades filled her nostrils, almost as heady and rich as Mr. Wolf himself.

"I'm fine," she finally managed to say.

"Good," he grunted, turning away.

Lucy's heart plummeted. No soft words? No helping hand?

Squelching the sharp stab of disappointment that a

gentleman could dislike her so intensely after knowing her for less than an hour, she pushed herself to her feet. But all her disgruntlement faded when she spied the white horse on the ground some ten feet away.

"What happened?" she gasped.

"He's dead."

Lucy's mouth flopped open like a castle drawbridge.

"Fortunately, he staggered off the road before dropping to the ground."

"Fortunately?" she exclaimed. "You call that good fortune? Your horse is *dead*."

She could see the silhouette of Garrick's big shoulders shrug. She would wager the next county could see his big shoulders shrug.

"It happens sometimes," he said.

She looked down at the horse. Poor, poor beast, she thought. To die while carrying them to safety. What a valiant animal. She might hate horses, but this had been an outstanding equine beast.

"We need to bury it," she announced.

Silence. An insect buzzed by her face.

"At the very least we need to offer a prayer up to heaven for its safe passing."

More silence. And then, "Miss Hartford. That is a horse. One does not bury a horse."

She straightened, turning to him, noticing the way his blonde hair seemed to glow in the moonlight, the way his shirt defined the shape of him. "Why not?"

"Because," he said in the clipped voice of a man on the verge of losing his patience, "a horse is not a human."

"But it has a soul."

She didn't like the way he dropped into silence. As if he didn't trust himself to speak. But she refused to give in. Every one of her pets had had a funeral. Even the frog she'd accidentally stepped on.

"Fine. Then say a short, fast prayer," Garrick finally gritted out.

She relaxed, unaccountably pleased by his concession, though a bit disappointed by his attitude. Didn't he love his horse? Wasn't he attached to it at all? *She* might not like horses herself, but this was his pet. Surely he had some feelings for . . . Just what was its name, anyway. Thunder? Gray Fox? Silver?

"Horse," he announced after she asked.

Horse, she thought, feeling her brows rise. What kind of a name was that? She almost asked him, but then lost her courage. She had a feeling he was like that branch, ready to snap at any moment. She was used to people feeling that way around her, had even grown to accept the fact. But she didn't have to like it. She reached for his hand.

He gasped.

Her heart thumped. "Oh dear," she breathed, wondering if he'd been hurt in their fall. She held the limb up to her face and tilted it toward the moon so that she could inspect it. "Are you hurt?"

He didn't move. Didn't say a word.

Was he in so much pain he couldn't speak? "It's probably sprained. I'll wrap it when we get back to my aunt's house," she said with a gentle, reassuring pat, not releasing his hand.

Again he didn't speak. She looked into his eyes, barely discernible in the darkness.

"Lucy," he said softly.

She could have sworn she heard a kind of longing in his voice, then assured herself she was being fanciful. According to her aunt, she was always being fanciful about something. But since her parents had died in that fire, she'd relied on her imagination. She imagined them as they had been, all smiles and love. She did the same thing with John, her brother. She refused to imagine him fighting in the war. She preferred to think of him astride a gallant white horse, not unlike the one that had just died. Her fantasies were the only thing that kept her going. She supposed that loneliness was why she'd taken such a shine to Tom. He wasn't much younger than her eighteen years. She felt sorry for the boy, and sorrow was a word she understood.

But all sorrow faded as she stared up at Garrick. He was certainly nothing to be sorry about. In fact, he was ten times better than any fantasy she could have conjured. Even so, there was a loneliness to him, and a longing.

Holding his hand closer, she wondered what had happened to make him that way. Much to her surprise, he let her clasp his hand. Tiny scars crisscrossed the fingers, visible even by moonlight. She wondered where they had come from. Turning her face to his, she tried to discern the answer in his eyes.

Loneliness stared back down at her.

Her heart gave a soft little cough. "Oh, Garrick," she said softly, letting her own loneliness leak into her voice.

She wanted him to kiss her again. Wanted to kiss away his pain, his longing, the despair she'd glimpsed through the soul of his eyes. The thought became a chant in her mind. *Please. Please. Please. Kiss. Meeeeeeee.*

He lowered his head. She stood up on tiptoe.

"Lucy," he groaned.

"Yes," she murmured back, waiting.

"Say your prayer."

Her eyes snapped open. She rocked back on her heels.

He stared down at her, and even in the darkness she could feel the coldness emanating from his gaze.

Oh, Lucy, you silly, silly girl, she chided. *You're a fool to have thought he'd want to kiss you. He wants no part of you. That much is obvious.*

Defeat made her shoulders slump. She turned toward the horse, wishing . . .

Wishing for what? For things that could never be? For a man such as Garrick to fall in love with her despite her shortcomings? Impossible. She might as well wish for the moon.

Closing her eyes, and despising herself for letting the realization hurt when it shouldn't, she tried to gather her composure. So she wasn't what society considered a classic beauty, she could live with that. And what was so bad about being accident-prone? What she lacked in grace, she more than made up for in intelligence. At least, that's what she often told herself. Sometimes she even believed it.

She took a deep breath, buried the knowledge that men such as Garrick were far beyond her reach, and began her prayer.

"Dear Lord," she said in a husky I-refuse-to-cry-whisper. "We thank you for your kindness—"

Garrick released a breath that sounded suspiciously like a snort.

Lucy paused, opening one eye to peer up at him. He stood perfectly still. Must have been her imagination. She closed her eye again.

"I know Horse was only a horse, but he was a good horse. Fast. Easy to, ah, mount. That is, I think he was easy to mount. But I don't know for certain."

Garrick growled. Lucy hurriedly finished, her words running together. "I ask that You receive him into Your welcoming green pastures. Reward his valiant spirit." Garrick squeezed her hand. "And may he always eat golden oats. Amen."

She opened her eyes, determined to come back to bury the animal herself tomorrow, or at the very least, hire somebody to do it.

Garrick let go of her hand. Lucy felt like a ship suddenly cast adrift.

"Let's be on our way."

He turned. Lucy watched him walk away. And despite all her brave words, despite telling herself otherwise, she suddenly wished with all her heart he wasn't so beyond her reach.

Fifteen minutes later Garrick wished he was back on board his ship, fighting against his enemies instead of his own desire for Lucy.

He found himself following a barely visible strip of

road with a woman who was about to drive him to distraction, not to mention hell, plodding by his side.

He'd had no idea this would be so hard. For the first time in his life he realized one didn't need to see a woman to be aware of her presence. He could hear her breathe, feel the soft brush of her arm as she walked alongside him, smell her elusive scent. What was it? Violets? Lavender?

Roses. It was roses. He clenched his hands at his sides, tempted to stop, duck his head, and take a longer sniff.

But he didn't. He couldn't.

The realization made him angry. Anger was good. Very good. It helped to keep him focused. It helped him keep his emotions buried deep down inside where nobody could get at them, not even one little sprite of a woman.

She stumbled. Garrick reached out to help her. Their hips brushed. His chest seized up.

"Thank you," she mumbled.

Garrick jerked his hand away. It tingled, almost as if he'd immersed it in a pool of ice-cold water.

"I've been thinking," Lucy said. "We need to go to London."

And her voice. Never could he remember hearing such a voice: a low, husky alto that stirred his blood and made him think of warm beds and sweet, passion-filled moans.

But he would not let himself be attracted to her. He would treat her as he would a sister, even though he had no family. He would ignore the way her body spoke to him. He would ignore the loneliness he heard in her voice. And above all, he would squash this ridiculous admiration he felt for her reckless courage.

"Which means we have to break the news to my aunt."

She was nothing but a young girl. She had her whole life ahead of her, while he had only twenty-four days.

"And we should probably leave on the morrow in the event the countess connects our break-in to Tom."

The mention of the boy's name caught his attention. He halted. So did she. Years of adjusting his eyes to darkness allowed him to see her almost perfectly. Even in moonlight, he noted, her hair sparkled, a soft breeze causing it to shimmer like the gold braid of a uniform. He hadn't wanted to be nice to her, he admitted. But it wasn't her fault that fate had played such a cruel trick on him.

It wasn't her fault at all.

Garrick prided himself on being honest, and he was honest enough to admit he'd been a heel.

"Do you think that's a good plan?" she asked in a soft, little voice.

He had no idea what plan she was asking about, but there was a tentativeness to her voice, almost as if she expected him to yell at her. Ridiculous, he thought. He didn't yell at young girls. And she was young. Too young for him.

"We can take my aunt's coach," she added.

"Take your aunt's coach where?"

"London."

It took a moment for the words to penetrate. Just a moment. *"London!"* he roared.

She flinched. Actually flinched. And, hell, there was that look of hurt he'd begun to dread. She tilted her chin up, just as she had earlier when she'd wanted to say a prayer for that damn horse.

"Yes, London."

She held tight against his anger. He had to admire that about her. She was like a starfish, holding steady no matter how rough the seas.

"Well?" she asked, arching a red brow.

"I cannot take you to London."

"Why not?"

And there was that grim pride he'd seen before. "Because."

"Because why?"

Because she wasn't a girl, she was a woman, and he damn well knew it. Because he didn't want to think about being alone with her for six hours while they traveled to London. But mostly because he didn't trust himself.

Bloody hell.

"Garrick?"

He turned away from her. "It's out of the question."

He took a step and nearly fell when he stepped into a carriage rut. Only years of experience standing aboard a lurching ship enabled him to remain on his feet.

"Is it because you don't want to be with me?"

He stopped, faced her once again. She probably didn't intend to ask the question in a self-pitying way. No. After the way he'd treated her, and his surly attitude, she probably meant it as a genuine question.

"No," he growled. "I refuse to take you because it will be too dangerous."

If he hadn't been looking for it, he wouldn't have seen the relief that sailed through her eyes. But there it was. Suddenly, unaccountably, he wanted to comfort her more. She had a heart to match her courage, he realized, a heart a man could wait a whole lifetime to find. He turned away, only to pivot right back on his heel again. Almost of its own volition, his hand rose up to stroke her jaw.

Green eyes widened, then softened.

"Stay with your aunt, Lucy. It will be much safer. The boy and I will go to London." In London, he could keep an close eye on him and forget all about a red-haired sprite with emerald eyes.

She leaned her head into his palm.

Don't, he tried to tell her with his eyes, *don't like me. Because if you do, hellion, you will lose your heart, as surely as I will lose mine, and my soul.*

He stiffened, stunned by the realization.

"Garrick, what's wrong?"

It wasn't rational. He'd only just met her. "Nothing," he said, his voice clipped by years of concealing his emotions.

"Is your hand bothering you again?"

He almost laughed. If only it were that simple. Pain could be willed away. Fear could be controlled. Nothing could have prepared him for Lucy. Nothing.

They completed the journey in silence. Lucy wondered if she'd said or done something to upset him, but for the life of her she couldn't recall what. Their time on the road had been almost magical, like those mornings when mist rose up from the ground and swirled about her feet, making her feel as if she walked upon a giant cloud. She hugged herself. Truly, she would treasure the memory of this trip to keep with her when he was gone.

They rounded the bend of the road to her aunt's house, relieved beyond words that they had finally made it, only to crash into Garrick's back two steps later. She looked past his shoulder.

The place was lit up like Vauxhall Gardens.

"'Twould appear your absence has been noted," he drawled.

Anxiety made her voice tremble when she replied, "'Twould appear so."

And any hope that her absence *hadn't* been noted was banished the moment Lucy opened the front door. Garrick was momentarily forgotten as she peeked inside, light spilling like milk onto the porch to illuminate the mellowed granite steps she had paused upon.

She blinked, her eyes adjusting to the light, only to wish for the blackness to swallow her up again when she spied her aunt standing in the middle of the spacious hall. She leaned heavily on her silver-tipped cane, one foot tapping on the marble floor, an expression on her face akin to the look she wore the time Lucy'd been caught drawing eyes on the back of Lord Craven's bald head. He'd fallen asleep, and she'd been unable to resist the smooth drawing board.

She tried not to cringe. "Good eve, Aunt Cornelia," she said after a very long and awkward silence.

Her aunt's eyes narrowed and Lucy recognized the look on her face. It was her I-do-not-trust-myself-to-speak look and it meant Lucy was in deep, deep trouble.

Lucy's feet felt as heavy as cannonballs as she slowly stepped into the foyer. When her aunt spied the costume she wore, her nostrils pinched together and then released, much like an enraged horse.

It was perhaps fortunate that at that moment her Aunt Cornelia spied Garrick entering the hall, for she was positive that once her aunt found her tongue, Lucy's ears were going to be scorched from the tirade that was sure to follow. She glanced back, deciding to try a diversionary tactic.

"Ahh, Garrick, this is my Aunt Cornelia. Auntie, umm, this is Mr. Garrick Wolf."

"Garrick *Asquith-Wolf*," he corrected.

Strangely, Cornelia looked even more enraged when she heard his name. "My lord Cardiff?" she all but snapped.

"At your service." He bowed.

Lucy turned to face Garrick. *Lord Cardiff?* Good heavens, the man she had kicked in the family jewels, the man who had cupped her chin and looked at her so kindly, was the infamous Lord Cardiff? The most famous rake in all the Royal Navy? How amazing. How . . . disconcerting. How utterly wonderful.

Why, she imagined every virgin in the county had spun fantasies about the man, as she had, fantasies about what he looked like, what it would feel like to be held in his arms, always wishing he would make one of his rare appearances at a ball. He was a legend among members of the *ton*. He had scorned his title to fight for the king's navy. But, heavens, he was no rake and he was twenty times more handsome than her dreams had ever conjured.

She glanced back at her aunt, only to cringe when she noted the dark scowl. Not surprising since his *lordship* was the sort of man any chaperone in her right mind would beat over the head with a club. Lord Cardiff was called "Wolf," she suddenly remembered, and not because of his appetite for food. The thought brought her back to reality with a clunk.

"*What* are you doing with my niece, my lord?" Aunt Cornelia asked.

Garrick looked a bit flustered by the question. "I . . . ahh . . . I came to her rescue. I'm a friend of the Duke and Duchess of Warburton, you see."

That seemed to be the right thing to say, for her aunt relaxed her stance a bit, but she still didn't lose the distrustful look in her eyes. "And *how* did you meet up with her?"

"I followed her."

Cornelia resembled a bull the way her head rose with anger, then fell with suspicion, nostrils flaring for added effect. "You *what*?"

"I followed her. I've been watching your house, you see. As a favor to the duke."

Lucy's eyes widened. He'd been watching the house? How marvelous. He'd been spying on her. Perhaps he'd seen her in her undergarments. Oooooh, that would be something . . .

"I am waiting for an explanation, Lucinda. *Where* have you been?"

Lucy flinched, turning back to her aunt. She gulped, deciding that honesty was the best policy.

In an attempt to make light of the situation, she made her voice as offhand and as unconcerned as possible, announcing, "I was at the Earl of Selborne's."

It took a great effort on her part not to grimace as she waited for the explosion.

It was immediate.

"Lucy Hartford, you incorrigible girl! How dare you do something so impetuous!" Cornelia banged her cane on the ground for emphasis.

"I went because I'd heard the earl and countess were on holiday," she attempted to explain.

But, as usual, her aunt failed to be swayed by Lucy's outstanding logic. The matron's cap atop her head looked ready to blow off, and so Lucy added hastily, "I know it was risky, but even Garrick—ahh, his lordship, agreed the idea was sound. Didn't you, sir—ahh, my lord?"

She looked at Garrick, who remained traitorously silent on the subject.

She returned her gaze to her aunt. "And it was terribly easy to break into the earl's estate. In fact, we even discovered the name of the countess's solicitor."

Her aunt didn't say a word, merely stared at her. Lucy wondered what she was doing, then realized her aunt didn't trust herself to speak. She flushed, then busied herself with brushing off her breeches, which were covered with ash. Next, she fussed with her hair, then inspected her boots.

Aunt Cornelia must have counted to at least one hundred before she turned to Garrick. "The truth, my lord, if you please. And do not sugar-coat it. The odds of my niece sneaking into someone's estate without destroying something in the process are slim to nil."

"Aunt Cornelia!" Lucy exclaimed, looking at Garrick in chagrin.

Garrick bowed slightly, and Lucy could swear she saw his lips twitch. The movement brought his blonde queue forward and for the first time she noticed the small gold hoop hanging from his right ear. She tilted her head to stare at it curiously.

The adornment was forgotten, however, when he said, "You are correct, my lady. I believe tonight's casualties were a jacket, several shrubs, a large patch of the earl's lawn, and a few years off the life of some of the earl's servants."

"Tattletale," Lucy hissed.

"I was afraid of that," Cornelia murmured. "Well, I'd better hear the whole story." She looked from Garrick, to her niece, then back to Garrick again. "Follow me."

She turned away, her cane thumping as she crossed the polished floor, leading them toward a parlor Lucy had privately dubbed the Flower Room. Every piece of furniture, wall hanging, floor covering, and bric-a-brac had flower buds on it. Lucy took a seat on a particularly hideous looking sofa with the unfortunate combination of red roses and yellow primroses as its pattern.

"Proceed," her aunt announced, taking the chair opposite.

Garrick stood by the grate, one arm resting on the mantel. She became aware of him again, of the way the fire reflected in his eyes. How handsome he looked in the light. How he managed to look so unrumpled was beyond her. She had no doubt she looked like something the barn cat had played with and then left behind.

"I caught her as she fell out of a tree."

Lucy stiffened, her appreciation of him disappearing in a puff of pique. "You didn't catch me," she huffed. "I would have landed just fine without you."

Garrick quirked a brow at her. Lucy had the sudden urge to wire his mouth shut using the gold hoop in his earlobe.

He turned back to her aunt with a droll expression schooling his face. "We had to climb the same tree again to break into the earl's home." He paused, as if debating how much more to tell her. His gaze caught hers.

Not much, Lucy begged with her eyes.

He frowned, once more looking at her aunt. "Suffice it to say, it was a long night."

Thank you, God, she silently prayed.

"The good news is that we discovered the name of the countess's solicitor. With any luck the man will be the key to discovering where the boy's former guardian resides, but it will require a trip to London."

Cornelia's gray brows arched. She had the appearance of a woman who knew there was more to the story, but had decided she'd heard enough. Instead she looked between the two, rubbing her temple with a hand that shook. "Have you any idea how many years you've taken of my life, young lady?"

Lucy felt the familiar sting of a blush fill her cheeks. She looked at the floor as if it held the answer to getting back into her aunt's good graces.

"And what will Harry say when he hears of this

evening's fiasco?" She stiffened. "Dear Lord, what if he decides not to ask you to wed him?"

Lucy plucked at a string on her sleeve. That Garrick had to overhear this conversation fostered fresh waves of humiliation.

"No, I won't frighten myself by thinking such thoughts," Cornelia mumbled.

The thread grew longer. Suddenly Lucy realized why. Her sleeve came off. Just slid right down her arm and landed in a pool of dirty white at her feet. She looked up, hoping against hope that Garrick hadn't noticed.

He had.

For some reason, the realization made her want to cry.

She looked away. Nothing had gone right tonight, she thought, absolutely nothing. And her aunt was correct. Dear Harry would be furious when he discovered tonight's escapades, not that it mattered much to Lucy. Her aunt pressed the match. It had seemed like a good idea to Lucy, too, until she'd met Garrick.

"I can't thank you enough for your assistance tonight, my lord," her Aunt Cornelia continued. "I've no doubt my niece would be spending the night with the local magistrate if not for you. It was most wise of His Grace to ask you to watch over us, but you should have made your presence known to me long before now."

"I was afraid the duke's concerns might alarm you, my lady."

"Yes, I see your point. Still, it would have alarmed me *more* if I'd spied you skulking about in our trees. I suppose you're staying at the local inn?"

"Indeed."

"Hmm, well, at least it's clean, and you won't be staying there for long should you decide to go to London. I only hope your theory about the solicitor being the connection between the countess and Tom's former guardian proves correct, although I must confess, I have my—"

"But Aunt Cornelia, don't you see?" Lucy interrupted, biting back her irritation that her aunt gave Garrick the credit for something she'd discovered. Plus she needed to show Garrick how little his derision affected her. "The countess would never have associated with a man such as Jolly. She had to have hired *someone* to do her dirty work, someone she trusted implicitly. Why not a solicitor? Indeed, she wouldn't have to tell him what her business with Jolly was. Only order the man paid."

"Lucy, what happened to your sleeve?"

Lucy colored, momentarily thrown. She could have sworn Garrick laughed. "Er, ahh, nothing, Aunt. I must have gotten it stuck in the tree." She looked down, only to force herself to look up again. "As I was saying. 'Tis obvious we need to go to London to explore this lead."

"We?" her aunt spat out.

"Yes," she said firmly, looking at Garrick. "*We.* Although his lordship might beg to differ."

5

His lordship *had* begged to differ, although the next morning Lucy had cause to regret being so firm in her insistence on going to London. If anything, Garrick looked even more furious than when he'd left the night before. The chill in his gaze blew through her heart like a winter wind. She looked away, wondering what it was about the man that made her heart pound like a woodpecker gone mad.

"Good morning," she said softly. The fact that they were alone made her unaccountably nervous. Ridiculous, she told herself, trying not to fidget in her chair. She'd climbed trellises with jars of hateful spiders in her hands. Jumped off roofs with injured kittens in her arms. She'd even shot a person once. Of course, that had been an accident. The point was, Garrick made her feel the veritable ninny. As if she'd lost her wits. Like those silly women at balls who swooned when a handsome man strolled by.

She fixed her eyes on the tiny violets imprinted on her dress, determined not to let him see how her breath quickened when he stopped before her.

"Where's your aunt?"

Look up, Lucy, you can do it. And she tried, she truly did. Her gaze got caught on skintight breeches that revealed thighs of Davidlike perfection. Next they paused on the bulge in his breeches. A very large bulge, she amended, blushing. His hips were the next detour. Masculine hips. Everything about him was big, even the fists clenched at his sides.

She peeked up farther. His white shirt had parted to reveal a sun-bronzed chest. She swallowed. Good heavens, would she ever get used to looking at the man? And his shoulders, they were so wide. His neck so thick. His chin had a teeny-tiny cleft in it. His lips were so achingly sensual, she licked her own in appreciation. She steeled herself, looking into his eyes.

And blanched.

He was livid.

"Are you done?" he snapped.

Well, no, not really. She'd have liked to stare at his lips a bit longer. And that earring of his still fascinated her. "I'm sorry," she mumbled.

"I asked you a question," he clipped out. "Where is your aunt?"

It took a moment to gather her thoughts, mostly because she'd suddenly caught a whiff of him. Salt and man, that's what he smelled of, as if he had brought a bit of the sea into the room with him.

"She's above stairs, dressing," she finally croaked, her voice as raspy as Lady Hortense just before she'd keeled over and died.

"And the boy?"

"Above stairs, too, I should think."

"Fine. I'll wait outside."

"No, wait," she called, impulsively reaching for his hand. "How . . . how does it feel today?"

She smiled up at him, a great giant of a smile that was meant to ask him if he felt as giddy and as wonderful and as strange when he saw her as she did when she saw him. He didn't look away, and for second, just the tiniest bit of a moment, something burned in his eyes.

"How does *what* feel?"

She blinked, telling herself she hadn't imagined it. "Your hand."

"'Tis fine," he gritted, trying to jerk away.

She wouldn't let him, just held onto it like a lifeline to a ship. "Wait," she said softly, slowly standing up. She'd misjudged the distance between them, though, for he was far closer than she realized. Their bodies brushed. She saw his eyes widen. *Yes*, she thought. *There it is again.*

"I haven't thanked you for yesterday."

"No need."

Almost, she closed her eyes. His voice washed over her like warm water, pooling in her very soul.

"Yes," she contradicted. "There is a need. If not for you, I might be dead."

He didn't say a word, just stared down at her, his eyes so different when viewed up close. Color upon color blended within them—green, blue, silver, so complex they reminded her of a stained-glass window or the colors of the sea.

"I'm sorry I've been so much trouble."

He didn't respond, just continued to stare down at her. She waited for a reaction, any reaction. Perhaps a slight lift to the corner of his mouth. Perhaps a minor softening of his remarkable blue eyes.

She got nothing.

Disappointment almost made her look away. Almost. Was she so hopeless then? Were her feelings so totally one-sided?

And then she saw him tense. Saw him move an arm. A finger rose to her chin, tilted it up. Hope beat a rhythmic staccato in her breast like the flutter of a bird's wings as it soared through the sky. Her breath caught, held, then released in a soft sigh as he gently stroked the line of her jaw.

"You should be careful," he murmured, his eyes scanning her own.

He does *feel it*, she thought. *He does, he does, he does.* She hadn't imagined yesterday. Hadn't imagined a moonlit night and warm, mingled breaths.

"I wouldn't want any harm to come to you."

She nodded slowly, hardly daring to move, hardly daring to breathe, wondering if she were imagining the words, the moment. And then his head began to dip toward hers. *Yes*, her heart cried out. *Oh, gracious, yes. Thank you, Lord. I will never ask for another thing again. He likes me. He truly likes me.* Her eyes closed. Anticipating. Waiting. Dreaming.

Warm lips pressed against her on the forehead.

Her eyes sprang open.

He stepped back, then patted her on the head. "You see, I wouldn't want Dear Harry to get angry with me."

And with that he turned away.

Lucy watched him go, feeling wretchedly deflated.

• • •

It took Lucy nearly fifteen minutes to collect herself enough to fetch Tom. The stairs of her aunt's home creaked as she made her way up them.

She found the boy sitting on a window seat in his room, his knees tucked up under his elbows. His head—with its mop of unruly blonde curls—rested on his knees, the expression on his face as glum as she herself felt. He didn't bother to look at her. Not even when she walked up behind him did he glance up, which was odd, for usually he loved to bait her with a lecherous grin, loved to tease her in that cockney accent of his—an accent she'd done her best to rid him of, and failed, over the past two weeks that he'd been in her care.

"What's the matter, Thomas Tee?" she asked gently, using the pet name both she and her friend Salena, Duchess of Warburton, called him.

Tom turned to look at her, his violet eyes lacking their usual luster. He shrugged.

Misery loves company, she thought, and so she patted him on the knees, indicating that he should make room for her on the seat.

He sighed, then dropped his feet to the floor and scooted over. "I dunno," he said at last. "I gots a feeling."

Lucy's brows rose, for when Tom got a feeling it usually meant he'd eaten too many sweets.

"What kind of feeling?" she asked warily.

He shrugged again. "Like somethin' bad's about to happen."

Lucy's eyes widened. "Bad? How do you mean?"

He seemed to mull her question over. "Bad like last night." He looked up at her, his normally cherubic face troubled. "You near 'bout got killed."

"Who told you that?"

"Wolf."

Lucy's brows rose. So he had met the boy? She wondered when. It must have been this morning, sometime before she'd gone downstairs.

"I never asked to be no bleedin' nobleman's son," Tom continued. "Always thoughts y'all a bunch'a crackpots, I did," he mumbled to himself, then suddenly looked up, obviously realizing what he'd said. "Except for you an' Salena an' Adrian an' Beth, o' course."

Lucy contained a smile. "Of course."

He was silent a moment, then said, "I s'ppose I'm just afraids that next time you really will gets hurt." He looked up at her in pensive admonishment. "You're 'bout as graceful as a drunken sailor, me loidy, you don't needs ta push yer luck by snoopin' around fer me."

Lucy tried not to take offense at his words. But it was hard. Especially when Garrick obviously felt the same way.

"Tom, I can take care of myself. You needn't worry. And now there's Garrick to look after us. You'll see. Things will be set to rights."

Tom worried his bottom lip, then took a deep breath and said, "I 'ope so."

"They will, you'll see. Now, grab your things and head down to the carriage. I'll meet you there."

A current of excitement raced through her at the thought of seeing Garrick again, no matter that he didn't seem to notice or care about her existence. She could *imagine* him taking notice. Her imagination was good. So much better than reality.

Tom's face lit up. "Yer bringin' the bird with ya?"

Lucy nodded vaguely. And she could imagine him kissing her, too, like he'd done yesterday, before she'd given him a foolish display of disgust by shoving him backward.

"Well, are ya?"

Lucy blinked, forcing herself to concentrate. "Er, of course. He goes everywhere with me, although Aunt Cornelia has insisted he ride with the servants."

"Ah, Luce, why can't he ride with us if I promise ta take care o' him meself?"

"Because me aunt—" She rolled her eyes at the boy's contagious form of speech. "Because *my* aunt says he can't."

Tom pouted. "That old battle ax is always gettin' in the way o' me fun."

"Tom," Lucy chided gently. "My aunt is not a battle ax. She is a very kind lady who is going out of her way to help you."

Tom looked down at the floor, his expression turning contrite. "It's just that I've been makin' so much progress teaching Prinny new words. I thought it might be fun ta practice some more on the ride to London."

"And drive us all crazy in the process," Lucy muttered, before her eyes narrowed suspiciously. "And just what have you been teaching him?"

Tom stood up, then said jauntily, "Oh, this an' that. You'll sees." With that he headed toward the door.

Lucy watched his retreating back, her eyes narrowing even further. Unfortunately, the only words Tom would likely teach her African Grey were the unsuitable kind, and Prinny *already* had a vocabulary totally unacceptable for a lady's pet. That was why she liked him.

She shook her head, wondering when the little imp had sneaked into her room for Prinny's "lessons," and what she would do without Tom when he was gone. She'd miss him terribly, she admitted, a deep sadness settling in her bones.

That sadness only grew worse when she spied Garrick outside. When Tom was gone, so would Garrick be. Then it would be back to her normal humdrum life. There would be no more swashbuckling heroes. No more dreams of being kissed by a fair prince. It was back to plain, silly, frumpish Dear Harry. The end of her adventure.

And back to the man she knew she could never love, or marry.

6

They arrived at the outskirts of London as dusk fell, the sticky fog surrounding them as they rumbled over Westminster Bridge. A few streamers of light poked golden fingers through the brown-gray haze, periodically illuminating the interior of the coach.

Lady Cornelia's town home was located on Arlington Street, near St. James Square, and as they drew nearer, Lucy felt her heart beat more rapidly. She'd been on edge for the duration of the trip, perhaps in response to Tom's dire words earlier, but more probably because of the discouraging sight of Garrick on horseback when she'd stepped out of her aunt's house that morning. She had no idea where he'd gotten the new horse, his other one having been buried that morning, but she'd been so depressed and hurt at his obvious attempt to avoid her company that she'd been tempted to tell him not to kill this one, too.

She hadn't, of course. Instead she'd held her tongue, telling herself he didn't hate her, he just didn't feel *anything* for her.

She pulled her navy blue cloak more tightly around herself, as if it could ward off her somber mood, and focused on the reassuring sight of her aunt's town home as it came into view. The brick house had always held special memories for her. Happy memories of times past when her parents had brought her to London for a visit. She missed her parents terribly, but she'd grown used to the ache of the loss.

"It looks as if Lambert has been keeping things in hand."

Her aunt's words jarred Lucy from her mental ramblings and forced her to focus on the scene through the carriage window. Light spilled from the town home's front windows, a welcome sight indeed on such a chill and overcast day.

The coach rolled to a stop and Lucy sat up straighter, shooting a look out the window. Garrick reined in his horse. The man so handsome. So, so . . . heroic-looking. She sighed. He'd insisted on staying with them, the better to protect them, he'd said. Would that it had been his own insatiable desire for her that had made him offer such a thing. A wistful feeling descended over her, the same wistful feeling she got whenever she thought of him near her. Her hand rose to her cheek. She closed her eyes; if she imagined hard enough she could still feel the soft touch of his finger, the warm kiss of his breath. A smile lifted the corners of her mouth, a smile which faded when she opened her eyes and caught her aunt staring at her.

Lucy jerked her hand away and tried to hide her consternation.

A footman came forward to hold Garrick's horse, but Garrick swung a booted leg over the horse's neck and jumped down before the servant arrived. *Goodness,* Lucy thought, *he even dismounts like a swashbuckling hero.*

Her reverie was broken when one of her aunt's servants opened the carriage door, blocking her line of vision. Tom practically bounded from the coach, the coachman jumping back just in time to avoid being landed upon.

"Thomas," Lady Cornelia barked.

Tom skidded to a halt, then turned back, a pained expression on his face as he jigged from foot to foot. "Gots ta empty me pisser, me loidy." He crossed his legs to demonstrate his point.

Lucy put a gloved hand to her mouth to stifle a laugh. She glanced past Tom to Garrick, who had just walked up behind him. Garrick emitted a noise sounding suspiciously like a snort.

"Well, goodness, boy. Be on your way," announced Cornelia, waving her hand imperiously.

Tom looked relieved, then turned and charged toward the door. Fortunately, Lambert opened it just as he reached for the handle, the butler doing a remarkable job of looking unfazed when the boy streaked by.

Lucy looked back to Garrick, struggling to contain her amusement.

He smiled, just a tiny bit of a thing that faded as quickly as the sun behind a cloud.

Lucy felt as if the coach had overturned.

Her heart fluttered. He looked away. Lucy wanted to cry, to scream out, *Don't! Don't turn away from me!* But she didn't. She blinked, trying to understand the tumultuous emotions that made her belly flop like a land-locked fish, that made her wish for the hundredth time that she'd been born someone other than Lucy Hartford, the disgrace of Sanderton County. She glanced at her aunt, and gulped at the expression on her face.

Her aunt glared, "I will speak to you about this later."

Lucy looked away. The coachman politely held the door. She seized the opportunity to escape.

The smell of climbing roses assaulted her nostrils as she neared the doorway. The flowers splashed their color against the brick facade of the house. There were hundreds of blooms making one last stand against the approaching fall. The smell mixed with the odor of beeswax and lemons filling the hall. What remained of the evening light shone off the hardwood floors and wood panels of the foyer. Lucy glanced left, comforted by what she saw. Her mother's picture still hung on the hall, a younger version of Aunt Cornelia. Her father's still hung in the morning room to her right. She glanced up the stairs directly in front of her, knowing that her room would be exactly the same as she'd left it: lemon-colored drapes, fluffy lace coverlet.

"Good evening, Lambert," her aunt said as she sailed through the front door.

"Good evening, my lady," the butler replied, a bland expression on his face. But when he turned to Lucy, he smiled.

"Good evening, Lambert," Lucy said, smiling back. There was an answering gleam in the butler's eyes, for the man was more like a family member than a servant.

Lucy turned to Garrick, trying to control her breathing as she stared at him. "Lambert, this is a friend of Lady Warburton, the Marquis of Cardiff." She ignored the frown her aunt shot in her direction for introducing a guest to a servant.

"My lord," the butler replied, and it was obvious he tried not to gawk. His eyes nearly boggled when he caught sight of Garrick's earring.

Completely oblivious to the assessing look, Garrick merely stared right back. Lucy looked between the two. All Garrick needed was a rapier and a red scarf and he'd be the spitting image of a storybook pirate. She stopped a chuckle midthroat. Garrick chose that moment to glance at her. Unable to stop herself, she smiled at him again. She didn't expect one in return, so she was stunned when the right side of his mouth tipped up.

She felt giddy. She felt like dancing. She felt like crying in delight.

"My lord," her aunt said, breaking the spell. "I dare say your staying with us will not be considered *quite* so improper if you share a room with Thomas." She turned to the butler. "Lambert, please show his lordship to the boy's room."

The butler nodded, and Garrick bowed toward the ladies before turning to follow the servant.

"We dine promptly at eight, my lord," Cornelia called, her eyes narrowing as she added, "Please do not be late."

Garrick looked over his shoulder and nodded, but Lucy noted he didn't look at her again, not even once.

• • •

"I will not have you developing a tendré for the man," Lady Cornelia said as she paced back and forth in front of Lucy, the powder blue skirts of her evening gown rustling like the sails of a battleship.

"But, Aunt, I've only known him for a day. How could I be developing a tendré for him?"

Cornelia stopped to stare down at her. Lucy clasped the arms of the pink-and-white chair she sat in and tried to appear unfazed, but her aunt must have known better.

"Don't try to bamboozle me, young lady. I saw the way you looked at him. What's more, I saw the way he looked back at *you*."

"You're mistaken, Auntie."

"No, I am not."

Lucy wiggled in her chair. If only her aunt were correct, but she knew she wasn't. The man didn't even want to ride in the same carriage with her.

"Lucy, I know how impressionable you are. It would be just like you to fall instantly in love with a man just because he came to your rescue."

Lucy's head snapped up. "Aunt Cornelia, I am not *that* bad."

"Oh yes you are, my dear."

"I am not. Why, why . . . look at what happened with Lord Washburn. I didn't become enamored of *him*."

"Really, Lucy, Lord Washburn is over twice your age and married to boot. And a good thing, too, for I'd hate to think what a young man would have done if he'd found you hanging from that tree limb. When I think back to what you looked like, your petticoats exposed, one slipper on the ground and the other dangling from your toes, I just cringe."

Lucy felt her cheeks flame with color. She really hadn't had much luck with trees lately. To this day she *still* couldn't believe her sash had supported her weight for so long, not to mention that tree limb. It had been a pity Lord Washburn had been the one to discover her, but at the time she'd been so relieved that help had arrived, she hadn't cared that he'd spent at least ten minutes doubled over in laughter before he'd gone to fetch her aunt.

"I assure you, Aunt Cornelia, I have *not* developed a fondness for his lordship."

Her aunt stared at her for an interminable minute, just stared at her. It was as if she looked at her through a spyglass, trying to see into the crevices Lucy tried to keep hidden. She'd never been any good at hiding her feelings, and it appeared she hadn't gotten any better, for her aunt said, "Yes you are, my girl. I can tell."

Lucy didn't move, didn't flinch.

Her aunt cupped her chin with an age-spotted hand. Lucy wished it were Garrick's hand.

"Lucy, my dear, sweet girl. You must face facts. A man such as Lord Cardiff is *far* beyond your reach. Don't delude yourself into thinking you can catch him."

The crushing words made Lucy want to look away. But she didn't. She ignored the sting in her eyes and looked her aunt square in the face.

"I know I'm being cruel, but I couldn't stand to see you hurt. Lord Cardiff will marry someday, I'm sure. And while you're certainly his social equal in birth, you are not . . ." Her aunt struggled to find the words.

"His type," Lucy finished for her.

"Exactly, my dear."

Lucy nodded, refusing to let her aunt see how deeply the words wounded.

"Harry is a dear, fine man," she said softly. "Dependable. Hard-working. Loyal."

"Perfect traits in a husband," Lucy mumbled. "Or a hunting dog."

Cornelia frowned.

"But I understand, Aunt. And I thank you for the warning."

Her aunt let go of her chin, then stepped back and stared down at her.

Don't let her see, Lucy thought. *Don't let her see that it is already too late*, for it was. As impossible as it sounded, she had already developed a tendré for Garrick Asquith-Wolf.

"I'm glad you understand, my dear. Very glad indeed."

Lucy looked away.

"Shall I see you at dinner?"

Lucy nodded, still not looking her aunt in the eyes. Aunt Cornelia stood in front of her, almost as if she sensed her deceit. Then she turned. Seconds later, the door clicked shut.

Lucy didn't move. Her heart knocked in her chest like the fist of an angry prisoner. Slowly, she got up from her chair, walking almost blindly toward the window.

How had it happened? she wondered. *When* had it happened? Was it the first time he'd touched her? When he'd kissed her?

She sighed, supposing it didn't matter. There was no use denying it. What she felt for Garrick was like chocolate compared to vanilla, like an orange compared to a lemon—so very different. She closed her eyes, rubbing her hands up her arms. An image of Garrick's face rose in her mind. So handsome. So . . . troubled.

Was that what drew her to him? Maybe the tendré was nothing more than compassion for a troubled soul.

She turned away from the window. She'd had more than her fair share of troubles in her short life, and she could empathize. It must be that which cried out to her. She sensed a kindred spirit in Garrick, his heart calling to hers like the keen of a lonely gull.

She would help to solve his troubles, she decided, and in the process perhaps win his heart.

7

Several hours after the confrontation with her aunt, Lucy realized how difficult a task she'd set herself.

The cold Garrick was back.

He didn't even glance her way as he entered the dining room, pulled a chair out, then took a seat; while she—an admiring breath leaked past her lips—couldn't pull her gaze away. Gracious heavens. If she'd thought him handsome in pirate garb, he was twice that dressed all in formal black. The color made him appear more bronzed, his eyes more blue, his hair more golden. No wonder Mary Crew had fallen all over herself when relaying the tale of how she'd spied him on the street last year. At the time Lucy had dismissed the girl's ramblings as slightly delusional, even going so far as to call her a twit. Indeed, Mary had only caught a brief glimpse of him, but if anything, Mary had severely *understated* Garrick's charms.

"Ahem."

Lucy started, then reluctantly tore her gaze away.

Aunt Cornelia stared at her as if she'd been caught with her petticoats down. Lucy looked away.

The seating arrangement for dinner had been chosen by her aunt, thereby putting Garrick on the opposite end of the table, Tom to her right, her aunt to her left. Cornelia'd thrown a tall epergne bearing roses and white tulips between them for good measure. It wouldn't be so bad except that even with all the table's leaves removed, the table *still* resembled a cricket field. She looked down its long length and tried not to squint. A spyglass would be helpful.

It was a sentiment which was to repeat itself as she strained to listen to any fragment of conversation which happened to drift on lazy air currents her way. She leaned forward, tilting her head to catch Garrick's response to her aunt's latest question.

"What . . . like to know . . . lady?" was his faint reply.

"Well, for one thing I'd like to know how you propose to find out if Mr. Barrow is actually the countess's solicitor. The sooner we return home, the safer I will feel."

Lucy heard her aunt's response clearly enough, which was why she thought she might have misheard Garrick when he replied, ". . . going to ask him."

"I beg your pardon?" Cornelia asked, setting her fork down with a *clink*.

"I'm . . . surprise the man into telling . . . "

"Capital idea," Tom pronounced, nodding in approval.

Lucy clenched her fork in frustration. She turned to Tom. "What did he say?"

"He's gonna visit the solicitasator tomorrow and pretend to be a runner."

Lucy relaxed a bit. "It's *solicitor*, Tom." She looked down the length of the table, the beginnings of a plan occurring. "That is a wonderful idea, my lord," she bellowed.

"Lucinda, please," her aunt snapped, "don't scream." She turned back to Garrick. "Well, I wish you luck. When will you visit the man?"

"Morning," came the faint reply.

Lucy turned to Tom. "When?"

"Tomorrow."

Lucy nodded, excitement buzzing through her veins. She could do this. All she needed was an excuse.

"Lucinda," her aunt snapped, and the look on her face would have done a magistrate proud. "You are not to go with his lordship, nor are you going to pester, connive, or bribe him to take you with him. Do I make myself clear?"

Lucy returned her stare, forcing a serious expression on her face. "I promise not to go with his lordship."

And she didn't.

She left *before* Garrick.

Which, as she would explain later, was not actually going *with* him.

She wiggled in her seat, firmly shoving aside the niggling sense of guilt flickering through her mind. Yes, indeed, desperate times called for desperate measures. She just knew she could help Garrick, and if she could do that, maybe, just maybe, it would help soften him up a bit.

"Do ya thinks he'll be surprised ta see ya?"

Lucy glanced at the boy, her "excuse" for leaving the house, Tom having been more than willing to come along. She bit her lip to stop a laugh from escaping. "Oh, I think he'll be *very* surprised."

The two shared a private smile. Lucy leaned forward and peered outside of the carriage. The clouds that had hung overhead had burned off, presenting a glorious day. Warm beams of light flickered in and out of the carriage like the flashes of a smuggler's lantern as they passed between the brick buildings. They would arrive soon, she thought, settling back in her seat and trying to quell her sudden nervousness.

Moments later they turned onto Catherine Street. A haze of dust rose up as their hired hack rumbled to a halt. Lucy pulled the hood of her black velvet cloak over her head in an attempt to keep the flecks of dirt out of her hair. When the coachman opened the door, she stepped down, then waited for Tom, checking the frogs on her cloak and insuring herself they were firmly fastened.

She walked with her head down, avoiding the eyes of passersby; the sound of the busy London street was a steady drone. She and Tom stopped in front of the next building down, a bakery, judging by the heavenly smell; even so, they both kept well into the shadows.

They didn't have long to wait. Less than two minutes had gone by when a coach drawn by a familiar pair of matched bays rounded the corner. She watched as her aunt's coachman pulled back on the reins, drawing the carriage to a flamboyant halt practically right in front of them. The hooves of the horses kicked dirt onto the walkway. One of the passersby had to take a step back when a lackey jumped off the coach directly in his path, opened the door, and all but bowed as Garrick stepped down.

But Garrick was oblivious to it all as he nodded to the servant and stepped down, mentally rehearsing what he had to say.

He straightened the cuff of his sleeve that hung just past his dark gray jacket, so engrossed in his thought he was positive he imagined the sweet voice that sounded in his ears, a voice that reminded him of soft flesh and moonlight.

"My lord?" the voice repeated.

He stiffened. God's balls. It couldn't be.

"Oh, Garrick."

It was.

He turned. She stood near the windows of the solicitor's office, red hair peeking in wispy tendrils from beneath a black cloak. A smile bright enough to be seen by passing ships was pasted upon her pixielike face. Worse, she had a partner in crime. Tom stood gleefully by.

Garrick cursed silently. He clenched his fists. He tightened his jaw. He did everything he could to keep himself from encircling the elegant, ivory column of her neck with his hands. Bloody hell. She was the most shameless hoyden he'd ever met. Still, he had to squelch a little stab of admiration for her tenacity.

"Get into the carriage, Lucy."

She looked a bit startled by his words. "I . . . What?"

"I said get into the carriage."

"But we want to help."

"The only way you will 'help' is if you get into the coach."

She looked momentarily hurt, but didn't move.

He lost all patience with her then. "Lucy if you do not get into that coach within the next ten seconds I shall tell your aunt you broke your promise to her."

"But I haven't."

"Are you going to tell me you and Tom just *happened* to be on this street?"

"No. We left *before* you. So, as you can see, I did not come with you, nor did I follow you. I just . . . preceded you."

He stiffened. Clever. He'd give her that. But that didn't stop him from turning toward the coach. When he halted at the carriage door and looked back to her, she smiled. He swept his hands toward the inside. The smile faded a bit, but she stayed put nonetheless.

"Get into the carriage," he repeated. His gaze shot past her to Tom who stood behind her. "You, too."

"Right away, mate," the boy retorted.

Garrick watched in satisfaction as Tom jumped into the open doorway. He looked at Lucy.

She stared right back. "Garrick," she said, determination coloring her emerald eyes, "please let me stay. I have an idea, you see."

"Which is exactly what terrifies me."

Her shoulders stiffened. "Well, I never. There's no need to be rude—"

"Get into the coach or I will put you in it myself."

Anger began to punctuate her stance. Her eyes began to flash like the queen's jewels. Her jaw looked as stubborn as a mule's. Good. Maybe if she was angry she'd stay away from him.

"If you force me, I will scream my head off."

"Fine." He strode forward, braced himself for the jolt that always accompanied contact with her skin, then clapped a hand over her mouth and half lifted, half shoved her into the coach. If touching her was Purgatory, convincing himself to let her go was hell.

Her scream of frustration died a swift death when he slammed the carriage door in her face.

Silly chit, he thought, turning toward the solicitor's door. If he weren't so irritated with her he would have applauded her cunning. He paused before the solicitor's front door. His whole body tingled from his contact with her, his manhood suddenly as hard a fishing rod. His frown deepened. Hell, he'd lost his *own* wits.

The door jingled when he entered; after the brightness of the street, momentary blindness dimmed his sight. Garrick stood for a moment, allowing his eyes to adjust and inhaling the smell of day-old bread and the musty odor of long-fallow books. Slowly, his eyes adjusted. Three windows lined the front of the shop, the blinds drawn to allow for wide bars of light to stripe the floor. A man sat behind a desk, his balding head beaded with sweat, his corpulent girth crammed into a too-small chair. He looked Garrick's fit body up and down, his eyes narrowing.

"What do you want?" he grumbled.

Garrick pinned him with his most commanding stare, a look that had sent grown men scurrying to do his bidding, a look that was guaranteed to intimidate. "I'm here to see Mr. Barrows."

The man's watery blue eyes narrowed. "Oh? Do you have an appointment?"

"No."

"Then go away."

Garrick's stiffened. Leave? Who was this little pea-ant to tell him to leave? Obviously, Mr. Barrows. "Sir," he snapped, "what I have to ask will only take a moment."

"I don't have a moment."

"Make one," he growled.

"Not if you were the King of England."

Garrick was just about to reach his hands across the desk and place them around the little rodent's neck when the door jangled.

He turned.

Lucy stood there, a Lucy who had removed her cloak to reveal a dress so tight he was sure she wore nothing beneath it. The fabric was red—red as sin, red as her painted lips, red as her cheeks as she stared right back at him. She straightened, pulling that pride of hers around her as if it were her missing cloak. Her breasts thrust out, big breasts, Garrick noted, lovely breasts. Their creamy skin bulged over the low neckline. He wanted to touch them, to see if they felt as soft as they looked.

And like a hound, he caught a whiff of her. His manhood tingled. Roses.

Bloody hell.

"May I help you?" Mr. Barrows asked.

Garrick glanced at the little rat, his fury increasing when he noticed the leer on the man's face.

"Why, yes, you can," Lucy said in a small voice that picked up strength at the growing look of admiration in Mr. Barrows's eyes. "I'm looking for Mr. William Barrows."

Mr. Barrows smiled. "I am he."

Two things irritated Garrick. One, Mr. Barrows had apparently forgotten his presence. Two, Lucy had apparently forgotten his presence, too. Not only that, but when she finally *did* recall it, it was to shoot him a look of satisfaction mixed with . . . hope?

"Oh, how lovely," she cooed.

Mr. Barrows nodded proudly, his eyes never straying from her cleavage as he slowly rose from his seat. "Can I help you?" he asked, coming around the front of his desk, his belly preceding his arrival.

"You certainly may," Lucy crooned.

Garrick wanted to shake her senseless, except he was afraid of dislodging the pea she had for a brain, or her nearly exposed breasts. When he eyed the low décolletage of her dress, his fury increased. She moved and the sweet swell of her breasts jiggled tantalizingly; the scent of roses filled the air to tease his senses. Unfortunately, he remembered all too well the feel of her flesh. He glanced at the solicitor again. The little weasel smacked his lips.

It was too much.

"*What* the hell do you think you're *doing*?" Garrick roared. How dare that little worm stare at Lucy in such a way? How dare *she* let him? He reached into his jacket, crossed the room to her side, and without even thinking about his actions, stuffed his handkerchief down the front of her dress.

Lucy gasped.

Mr. Barrows choked.

"How dare *you*, sir!" she spat, pulling the cloth out, her face reddening—if that were possible—even more.

Garrick tried to grab the fabric back so he could shove it home once again. She wouldn't let him have it. He pulled harder. She hung on to it as if it were the tiller of a ship.

Mr. Barrows looked between the two. "Do you two know each other?"

"No," they both exclaimed in unison, their battle having evolved into a full-fledged tug-of-war until, suddenly, Garrick let go. Lucy's eyes narrowed as he began to unbutton his jacket. She rested her hands on her hips and gave him a "try and put it on me" glare.

He answered her with a look meant to tell her he damn well would. He swung out of his jacket, having to clench his jaw to keep from bellowing at her. Little fool. Little idiot. Didn't she realize what a dress such as that *did* to him?

He took a step, determined to cover her up and put himself out of his misery. But just as he lifted the jacket, something popped. He paused. Lucy stiffened. They both looked down at the same time.

"Good God!" Garrick roared.

"Oh dear," Lucy moaned.

The dress had ripped, just peeled down the middle like an overripe banana. Lucy tried to clutch it closed. A flash of pink flesh caught his attention.

His eyes widened. Bloody hell. She *was* naked beneath.

Garrick glanced at Mr. Barrows. The sight of the corpulent man gawking at Lucy's naked flesh was the absolute last straw. He hauled back and punched the oversized rodent right between his ratlike eyes.

The man wilted toward the floor like a piece of dank rigging.

"You've killed him," Lucy screamed.

"Good!" he roared back.

She looked back up at him and swallowed.

Garrick stared back, fuming. He had the damnedest time refraining from touching her, whether in anger or some twisted form of self-torture, he didn't know. The sight of her standing there, her tousled hair framing her face in a wispy halo, her arms crossed in front of her like some sacrificial virgin, was nearly too much for his already over-taxed libido to handle. He turned away from her, ostensibly to check on the solicitor, but in actuality to stop himself from doing something foolish, such as pulling her into his arms and kissing her senseless. Damn fool.

"Cover yourself," he snapped, tossing her his jacket. He bent to ensure that the leech was alive. He was, more's the pity. When he stood back up he refused to turn around until he was positive she'd covered herself.

It was a few minutes later before he heard Lucy mutter, "You can turn around now," in a small voice.

Tom obviously sensed the tension between them, for he remained unusually quiet, right until the moment the carriage rolled to a stop in front of Cornelia's town home. And then, with his usual aplomb, he asked, "Ya gonna thrash her?"

"Thomas Tee," Lucy huffed.

Garrick ignored the child, stuffing the documents he had purloined from the solicitor's office into his coat pocket. When his eyes strayed to hers, they burned with anger.

Oh dear.

The moment they entered the house, Lucy tried to escape to her room, but a restraining hand on her arm stopped her. She looked up at Garrick and gulped.

"May I take your, er, coat?"

Lucy pulled her gaze away to glance at Lambert. She blanched at the wry look on the butler's face as he spied the latest addition to her wardrobe.

"Ah, no, Lambert, thank you. It's a bit chilly in here." She wiped the perspiration from her upper lip.

Lambert's brows rose, but he turned to Garrick nonetheless. "Would you like me to ring for some tea, sir?"

Lucy thought she heard him mutter something about a neck before he said, "No," in a tone of voice that made the butler's eyes widen.

Lucy was about to admonish him for being rude, but

then he grabbed her by the arm. She forgot everything as he all but dragged her toward a nearby sitting room.

The thud as the door closed was nearly as loud as the thud of Lucy's heart. She pulled her arm away and turned toward the door, a hasty exit in mind.

"I wouldn't do that."

She paused with her hand on the door.

"If you leave, I will tell your aunt the whole sordid story.

Lucy stiffened, then slowly turned to face him. "You wouldn't."

"I would."

She felt herself pale at the expression on his face, pulling her gaze away to stare at the white and blue Chinese rug covering the floor. When he continued to remain silent she had the distinct impression he was merely gathering steam, as a typhoon does before it roars ashore.

"My lord, please," she began, trying to head him off. She peeked up at him. "I know wearing that dress was incredibly silly, but all I wanted to do was hel—"

"Silly?" he interrupted, his expression turning thunderous.

She licked her suddenly dry lips. "Very well, *foolish*. But 'tis no reason for you to go off half-cocked. We can discuss this reasonably."

"Half-cocked?" Garrick said softly, taking a step toward her. "I'm more than half-cocked at the moment, my dear Lucy." He took another step toward her.

Lucy had the distinct impression he was being vulgar. She retreated a step, not trusting the look in his eyes, then tried not to panic when her rear came in contact with the back of one of two couches facing each other in the room. "Now, Garrick—"

"I am going to teach you a lesson."

Her eyes widened. "A lesson? W-what kind of lesson?" she asked, surreptitiously looking for an escape route.

He took another step, this one bringing him within inches of her. "I have decided to teach you what happens to young ladies who disobey me."

Lucy tried to dart around him, but a hand streaked out. He pulled her to him, his grip nearly bruising, her rear against the couch again.

"You're demented," she blurted. "And I didn't disobey y—" Whatever else she'd been about to say was cut off when Garrick jerked her roughly, almost violently against him.

Their eyes met, hers soft and pleading and sparking with just a touch of anticipation, his dark and promising.

"Garrick, I—"

She never got to finish her sentence. With the speed of lightning, his lips swooped down to cover hers. Lucy gasped, not in fear, but in excitement, for as Garrick's mouth angled down to cover hers she realized that this, this all-consuming passionate *need* to be kissed by him, this was what she'd wanted since the moment they'd met, was the reason why she'd allowed him such liberties. Yes, he was being a bit of an unscrupulous knave right now, but it was exactly that roguish air that drew her to him.

And if Garrick's lips were just a little bit hard and punishing as they ravished hers, she didn't mind. If his grip was a little too tight as he pressed her up against the back of the couch, she tolerated it. If what his eyes promised was punishment, she wanted to be punished for the rest of her days.

Her body began to tingle, delicious, shivery little tingles which rose the hairs on her arm. She sighed, then stood on tiptoe, leaning her weight against the sofa. Her breasts pressed up against him through the scratchy fabric of his jacket. The feel of it brought to mind his touch. The memory sent a flash of brazen need coursing through her.

Instinctively, her hands moved up his chest, over his shoulders, and to the back of his head. The silk ribbon in his queue entangled in her fingers. She pulled on it impatiently.

"Ouch," he grunted in pain when she tugged too hard. He tried to pull back, but she wouldn't let him, determined to feel his hair as it cascaded down around them. In a moment, it was loose, its soft, salt-smelling strands sliding up against her cheek.

She moaned. Garrick cupped the sides of her face with his own hands and tilted her chin up. She yielded to the sweet pressure of his thumbs and opened for him. A spicy taste flooded into her mouth.

She ignited on the spot.

His tongue touched hers, lightly at first, then growing more and more aggressive. Her front teeth bumped into his, causing him to draw back.

"Sorry," she mumbled through swollen lips, then quickly pulled his head back down toward her. Their noses bumped in the process.

This time she immediately opened her mouth. Garrick didn't. She tilted his jaw down as he had her own. He opened. Lucy sighed, reveling in the feel of Garrick's tongue when it finally mated with hers. She stroked his back, feeling terribly naughty, but glorying in his answering groan.

"Oh, Garrick," she murmured as he trailed kisses down the side of her neck, unbuttoning her jacket at the same time. She didn't protest at all when he parted the coat to reveal her flesh, didn't protest at all when he lifted her up so she could sit on the back of the couch, bringing her breasts closer to his mouth. All she wanted was to feel the warm heat of him touching her.

She felt his breath at first, hot and then moist as it wafted across her bare flesh. Then, with the softest of touches, his tongue touched her collarbone, almost like a feather. She arched into him, wanting him to lick lower.

He did.

Yes, she thought. *Oh, please*, she silently begged. *Please, please touch me there.*

He exhaled, his breath cooling her wet skin; her nipples turned into hard, pink pebbles.

And then he did it. He lightly nipped the tip. Sharp stabs of heat darted through her body.

"Garrick . . ." She leaned back farther, driven nearly delirious by the waves of pleasure coursing through her. Something jabbed into her calf. She moved her leg away as he continued to assault first one nipple, then the other. The thing in his pocket jabbed into her uncomfortably. She shoved it away with her foot.

One minute Lucy was leaning back in pleasure; the next she and the couch were falling forward; without Garrick to counterbalance it, the weight of her body was too much for gravity to bear.

She had a brief glimpse of Garrick, doubled over in pain, his hands clasped between his legs, before she squeezed her lids shut only to land a second later amongst a tumble of pillows at Garrick's feet. For a long moment she simply sat there, stunned, barely able to hear over the sound of her furiously beating heart.

"Cursed," she thought she heard Garrick mumble. Slowly, she opened her eyes. Garrick stood a few feet away with an expression of frustration and displeasure on his face.

"It wasn't—"

"Your fault," he finished for her with a scowl.

8

"Did ya thrash 'er?" Tom called from his sprawled position on the chaise when Garrick stormed into the sitting room that adjoined his bedroom. The boy's expression filled with curiosity as he pushed himself up into a sitting position.

"No," Garrick snapped, not wanting to be reminded about what had happened downstairs. How he'd managed—despite Arlan's dire warning—to lose precious days, just how many he had no idea. For the first time he found himself wishing he'd memorized that damn list and its ridiculous penalties, but at the time he hadn't thought it necessary. Now he knew how wrong he'd been.

He pulled the documents out of his pocket and threw them onto an oak side table with a flick of disgust. A few of them slid off the top to land on the rose and ivory Brussels carpet, not that he cared. Thank God she'd fallen. In fact, he was beginning to wonder if her "accidents" lately didn't have more to do with Arlan than the woman herself. It was possible. It was *damn* possible, he realized. Heaven's way of tampering with his life, not that he had a life.

"Brahh, typhoon a-comin'.'"

Garrick paused in shrugging out of his jacket to glare at the parrot.

The bird, seeming to sense his stare, ruffled his gray feathers and opened his massive beak.

"What's the buzzard doing in here?"

The bird stood up abruptly, ruffled his wings, and preened its feathers. Garrick could have sworn it looked offended.

"Pretty bird," it called, nodding its head up and down. "Pretty bird."

"Cornelia caught me visitin' him and booted me out. I sneaked him down here this mornin' when she weren't lookin.'"

Garrick eyed the bird with distaste. "It's not sleeping in here."

"I know. I'll return it later. Where ya goin'?"

"Out," Garrick replied, ignoring the bird and pulling off his shirt.

Tom gasped as he looked at Garrick's chest. Thin white lines crisscrossed underneath a mat of golden hair on his chest and arms. "Where'd you get those?"

Garrick paused in pulling on a clean shirt to examine his arms. He shrugged. "Here and there."

"Ya been in battle?" the boy asked excitedly.

He nodded.

The child's eyes widened.

Ignoring him, Garrick continued to dress. He

wanted only to escape, wanted only to leave. God's balls, he was hard. Not since that whore had tied him up in bed and made him wait for it had he been this hard.

"If yer goin' out wenchin,' I'm goin' with ya," Tom announced.

Garrick paused, leveling the boy a glare. The last thing he wanted was to be reminded of the fact that he couldn't go out whoring, not that he wanted one. What he wanted was Lucy. And he couldn't have her.

Ever.

Anger sang through his blood like a gale-force wind. "*If* I were going wenching," he snapped, "it would be highly unlikely that I'd bring a child with me."

The boy looked stricken. Garrick wanted to curse. Damnation, what was wrong with him? He'd turned into a heel. An absolute heel. He ran a hand through his hair. The ribbon tying it back was gone. Lucy. Bloody hell.

"But, Garrick," Tom pleaded. "I know the streets like me own hand."

Garrick had to force himself to soften his voice, force himself to smile. His face felt ready to crack. "Thank you, Tom, but no."

Tom looked away in disappointment.

"Sink your pisser, get a blister," the bird cackled cheerfully.

Tom looked up and then erupted into uncontrollable laughter. The parrot bobbed his head up and down and fluffed its wings proudly. Garrick turned away, determined to ignore them both.

• • •

"Absolutely not, Lucinda Hartford. How could you ask me to do such a thing?"

"Beth, 'twill only take a hour, perhaps two. And 'tis not as if I don't know where we're going. The address I saw on the papers Garrick pilfered is firmly imprinted in my mind. All we need do is hire a hack to take us there."

Lucy's tone was pleading as she paced back and forth in front of her closest friend, next to Salena, of course. Beth didn't look convinced. After ten years of misadventures, Lucy supposed everybody could reach their limit, even Beth, but that didn't stop Lucy from trying. Besides, there was simply no one else she could enlist for help. No one.

"Please, Beth," she begged again. Never had a man been as angry with her as Garrick had been, aside from Lord Montbank, of course. She hadn't spooked Garrick's horse with her swan costume.

"Were you planning on waltzing in there and simply asking to be taken to the blackguard?" her friend asked. "And how do you know that the address you discovered is not the same address Adrian already has?"

"I know because Tom told us long ago where he used to live. Beth, I am positive this is Jolly's new direction."

Beth pushed impatiently at a black strand of hair which had fallen from the knot atop her head. The wispy strands framed her heart-shaped face, the midnight blue day gown she wore making her eyes more blue, her hair more black. She looked like a china doll.

"And you simply propose to meander over to the most sinister location in all of London," Beth continued.

Lucy rolled her eyes. Here came the lecture.

"A place where even thieves think twice before venturing. A place called, of all things, the Barmaid's Tit." Beth pursed her lips in distaste. "And once there, your plan is to ask one of the patrons if they know of a man named Jolly, and if so, point him out to me, if you please?"

Lucy crossed her arms in front of her. "Exactly."

Elizabeth stared at her in dumfounded indignation. "You're insane."

The idea didn't sound nearly as good when Beth said it that way. Her ideas *never* sounded good when her friends repeated them. They had a way of over-dramatizing the danger. "I am going with or without you."

Blue eyes narrowed. "If you do, I shall tell your aunt immediately what you intend to do."

Lucy dared her with a look. "Oh? If you tell my aunt what I intend, I will tell your mother about the time we sneaked into Almack's two years ago."

Beth stiffened. "Lucy, you wouldn't dare."

"I would."

"I shall never speak to you again if you do."

Lucy shrugged in a manner of extreme indifference.

"And going to Almack's was entirely *your* idea," Beth added. "I wouldn't have gone at all if Salena hadn't convinced me she needed my help to keep *you* out of trouble."

"Yes, but that doesn't change the fact that we were

almost caught," Lucy countered.

"Because you tipped over the plant we were hiding behind."

"And you were almost seen by Lord Harrington."

"Because you forgot where the back exit was," Beth pointed out.

"And you almost jumped into the wrong coach."

"Because I was stupid enough to believe your brother when he said he'd be waiting for us by that lamppost."

"I'm going, Beth, and that's that."

"Why did I agree to this?" Beth moaned a half hour later. She hunched as far back into her seat as possible, eyeing the filth clinging to the walls and floor of the hired hack with distaste.

"You agreed to this because you're my friend and you care for me."

"Oh," Beth retorted halfheartedly, "is that why?"

Lucy nodded. But Beth ignored her. Lucy nibbled her bottom lip, then released a breath, worrying. There was a chance that this plan might not go very well. She glanced outside the carriage, noting the dilapidated condition of the buildings and the rough appearances of the people on the street. But she *had* to do this. What other opportunity would she have to impress Garrick with her cunning?

"I wonder how much longer?" Beth mused, her hands clenched in her lap.

Lucy sighed, her own hands clenched to stop them

from trembling. "Relax, Beth." Her voice came out a high squeak. She cleared her throat, then tried again. "We'll be there before you know it."

"That's what I'm afraid of."

Lucy looked away, refusing to let her friend see how nervous she herself was. The coach began to slow and then jangle to a stop. Both of them stiffened; Lucy peeked outside.

"I'm not going in there," Beth promptly announced.

Lucy didn't blame her. It looked as if it were a brothel, not a bar. "Then I shall go in alone."

Seconds later the coachman opened the door and let the rank air from the Thames into the carriage. The putrid breeze caused Beth to pull her blue cloak tightly around herself.

"Well, duckies, 'ere ya are. I'd offer to wait 'cept I values me 'ide too much . . . an' the contents of me stomach. Like ta see you two lookers waltz in there, I would." He cackled merrily, displaying rotted teeth.

"But you have to wait for us." Lucy said, trying not to breathe through her nose.

"Sorry, ducky."

"Then how will we get home?" she asked, her heart scratching at her chest even more erratically.

The coachman shrugged.

Beth covered her nose with her handkerchief and said, "Let's turn back."

"No," Lucy asserted firmly. She would not turn back. She had to do this. Not only did Tom need her help, but this plan was certain to impress Garrick. And she knew that if she could earn his admiration, she'd have a chance to win his love. She turned to the coachman. "Will you circle the block to wait for us?"

"Not in this neighborhood."

Lucy frowned. "How about coming back for us in, say, an hour?"

"An hour?" Beth exclaimed. "We will be dead within five minutes."

The coachman flashed his rotted teeth at them again. "If ya want's me ta come back in an hour, I'd be glad to. But I ain't waitin' for ya a minute beyond."

Lucy nodded, relieved, then pulled her green cloak up over her head and stepped down from the carriage. She took a deep breath of marginally less putrid air, hearing Beth do the same. A few moments later, she watched the coach rumble away, then peeked a glance at Beth. Her friend looked ready to retch.

"Well, I suppose we should enter," Lucy said brightly.

"Please, Lucy, I'm begging you to rethink this."

"I've quite made up my mind, Beth."

And with that she strode forward and pushed on the door with more force than absolutely necessary. The wood, being old and worn, was much lighter than it looked. As a result, it swung away from her and headed toward the connecting wall with the speed of a battering ram.

The boom as it collided with the supporting wall could no doubt be heard all the way to France. The rafters shook, sending a flurry of dust and grime onto patrons huddled around the tables. Lucy watched in horror as a piece of soot wafted down through the air like an errant snowflake and landed on the nose of an angry-looking man. It stayed there until the man reached up and slowly wiped it away, leaving a giant black streak in its wake.

Lucy pulled her gaze away from that streak only when the door started to close. She jerked Beth forward, nearly jumping out of her skin when it clanged shut behind her with the finality of a prison gate.

No one spoke a word.

She cleared her throat. "I, ahh ... May I, ahh ... may I speak with the owner?"

Silence.

"He's busy, mort," someone spoke at last. "But ya can come over 'ere."

Lucy smiled, growing even more nervous under the eyes of the bar's patrons. Beth shifted alongside of her.

When they didn't move, another voice boomed out, "Bet I could make 'er come."

The place erupted into laughter.

"Dickon, that dog'a yours don't even come. Maybe ya should keep practicin' on it afore ya move on ta something with two legs."

There were loud guffaws at this, some of the patrons even slapping the table with their big, callused hands. Lucy stared at the crowd, her face turning ten shades of crimson. She just *knew* they were being lewd. She gritted her teeth. *Think of Garrick. Think of a big smile on his face. Think of approval.*

She clutched the scratchy wool of her cloak, lifting up her gown as she picked her way around scattered debris, scuffed boots, and overturned chairs.

A burly man stood behind the counter washing

tankards. Lucy headed straight for him, ignoring the sudden thought that he looked as if he could rip her arm off and beat her over the head with it.

Still, she was unable to stop her nervousness from increasing enough so that her voice was a dry croak when she asked, "Are you the owner of this fine establishment?"

He didn't answer, just continued to stare at her through narrowed eyes as he meticulously washed the mugs with a filthy rag. Lucy glanced at Beth, who had shrunk so far back into her cloak, she looked like a monk on his way to a confessional. She turned back to the brute.

"I am, ahh . . . I am looking for a man named Jolly. Perhaps you could direct me to him?"

"Never 'eard of 'im."

At least he had answered her, Lucy thought. It was a start. She swallowed and tried again. "If you could direct me to the owner, perhaps he can help me?"

"What's a pretty lass such as you want with a blighter like Jolly?"

The voice came from behind her. Lucy whirled to face a table surrounded by four men. She wasn't sure which man had spoken, so her gaze encompassed them all. "I, ahh . . . I have something for him."

One of the men sat up straighter. "Aye, and what be that?"

Lucy stared down at the pockmarked and dark-haired man who had the mahogany skin tone of a sailor. "What I have is for Jolly's eyes only. However, if you know where we can find the man, it would be worth your while to tell me."

"'Ow worth my while?"

Lucy reached under her cloak and pulled a gold coin from her reticule. She threw it onto the table where it rolled to a stop against the pewter mug with a *tink*.

The man glanced at his companions, who eyed the piece covetously, then hastily reached out and scooped it up. "'E's upstairs."

Lucy caught her breath. "Goodness, upstairs?"

"Aye."

"Where?"

"Fourth room on the left."

Lucy nodded excitedly. "Thank you, sir." She grabbed Beth's arm and headed toward the stairs, oblivious to the loud laughter erupting in their wake.

Lucy stared at the battle-scarred oak door that was midway down the dark and narrow corridor, her brow furrowed in confusion as she listened to the sounds on the other side of the door.

"What do you think it is?" Beth asked for about the thousandth time.

They both listened to the rhythmic groans, lips pursed. "I've no idea," Lucy murmured. "It almost sounds as if he's hurt."

Beth leaned forward, but Lucy went so far as to place her ear against the door. When she pulled back, one eyebrow was quirked up in question. "Perhaps Mr. Jolly is suffering from indigestion?" she conjectured.

Beth shrugged and Lucy leaned forward again, her eyes opening wide when she heard the rhythmic thud-

thud-thud of something banging against a wall.

"Good heavens," Beth murmured, "he must be in need of help."

Lucy straightened, her expression almost panicked. "We have to go in there, Beth. We can't have Mr. Jolly die before we have time to question him."

She tried the handle, pushed on it with all her might, only to realize it was locked. Next she pushed on the door, then pounded on it in frustration when it wouldn't budge. She turned to Beth, growing more and more upset when the moans began to get louder.

"Step back," she said, an idea suddenly coming to mind.

"Why?" Beth's brow was furrowed in puzzlement.

"I have an idea."

"Oh no," Beth groaned.

"Move."

"But, Lucy—"

"Please, Beth. There's no time to argue."

Reluctantly, Beth did as asked. Lucy retreated, then eyed the door to Jolly's room with the grim determination of a knight storming a castle. Taking a deep breath, she charged.

The air whooshed out of her lungs like air up a chimney.

"Lucy!" Beth wailed as Lucy slowly sank to the ground. Her back slid against the door, splinters catching her dress. "You fool! I could have told you the door was too solid for such a stunt."

"Supposed to work," Lucy gasped. "Works in books."

"Ooooh," Beth huffed. "You and those books. I'm

going to burn them all by the time—"

Click.

Both of them stiffened.

Lucy looked up.

Beth stepped back.

"Good heavens," she cried a moment later, her eyes widening as she gawked at the man standing before them. She looked away, moaning, "Lucy, he's . . . he's naked. And he's got a pistol."

Lucy stared, transfixed, at the man's midsection. "Beth," she said slowly, "that is *not* a pistol."

9

Garrick listened to the sounds that came from the other side of the wall with half an ear. Thank God Jolly was done, for there was no way he could have taken much more of those all-too-familiar moans. Every minute had been sheer torture. Images of Lucy kept entering his mind. Lucy lying underneath him, her red hair fanned out around her, her face filled with longing as she gazed up at him. He would tease her mercilessly, bring her to a fevered pitch, and she would arch her head back and say . . .

"Let go of me, you pig!"

Garrick snapped back to the present.

"Beth, kick him!"

He shot up out of his chair. It couldn't be, he thought. Disbelief surged through him.

"Kick him between the legs!"

It was.

Lucy.

He charged toward the door, rage filling him, rage at one little mite of a titian-haired wildcat. All of his earlier fantasies were forgotten. They wafted away like so much fog under the heat of a blazing sun. *How* dare *she!* he thought. How dare she follow him again. What an absolutely foolhardy thing to do. He jerked the door open.

Jolly's room was in chaos. Even so, the sight that greeted him was one he would never forget. He stood there, his mouth gaping open, eyes disbelieving.

Lucy was perched atop Jolly's back, pummeling him with a fist, her petticoat-clad legs clasped around his bare waist. Jolly careened from side to side, naked as the day he was born. An outraged woman whom Garrick assumed was Beth kicked him with one ivory-clad, slippered foot, a pained expression on her face as she tried not to stare at his jiggling private parts. Jolly's mistress bounced up and down on the bed, her gigantic breasts swinging to and fro, her hands clenched to her rouged cheeks in agitation. When she saw Garrick, she screamed.

Garrick blinked and was suddenly, unaccountably, and thoroughly filled with hysterical laughter. He shook his head, trying not to let it escape, having to bite his lip to do so. "Stop caterwauling," he sputtered.

The mistress kept right on screaming and so he pulled a pistol from his belt and waved it in her direction; her scream died into a strangled gasp.

Lucy froze; her head snapped up.

Beth whirled, then yelped in fright when she spied the weapon.

Jolly was the only one who reacted with anything approaching logic. "Get the bloody bitch off o' me," he roared.

Garrick looked at Lucy, who immediately released her stranglehold around Jolly's neck and slowly slid to the floor, her expression filled with dismay and surprise.

"Garrick," she panted, "how, ahh, nice to see you."

Beth's eyes widened.

Garrick pasted what he hoped was a ferocious expression on his face, all the while fighting the laughter that threatened to erupt. The look must have worked, for Lucy took a hasty step back. He glanced at Jolly, still standing there, the paunch of his over-large belly hanging over his too-narrow hips. Lucy, the little hoyden, peeked glances at his rear.

"Stop staring," he snapped, some of his amusement fading. "Both of you come here."

Beth lost no time in complying, but Lucy dragged her feet as if she were a child as she headed toward the corner of the room. She looked up at him, her expression sheepish. "Garrick, I—"

"*Don't*," Garrick interrupted, "say a word."

Lucy swallowed audibly, then nodded.

Jolly continued to stand, his mistress staring in silence, a maroon-colored spread pulled up to her breasts.

"If it's all the same with you morts, I'd like ta pull on me breeches," Jolly said. "They're o'er by the chair." He pointed toward the corner of the room, then started shuffling in that direction.

"Don't move." Somehow, Garrick managed to keep his face straight as he looked at Lucy. "Hand him his breeches, Lucy. And keep your eyes off him."

Lucy blushed, then nodded. She was about to hand Jolly his trousers when Garrick stopped her by saying, "Check his pockets first."

Lucy's eyes widened, but she did as told. Her fingers searched first one pocket, then the other. She gasped when she pulled out a small pistol, palming it in a knowledgeable fashion. When she pulled the hammer back to see if it was loaded and primed, Garrick's eyebrows rose.

"It's loaded," she said in a small voice.

Garrick shook his head at Jolly. "Is that the only weapon?"

"Aye," he croaked.

Lucy squeezed the legs of the breeches and confirmed his words with a nod.

"Hand them back to him." He turned back to Jolly. "Get dressed."

Jolly pulled on his breeches with a hasty wiggle. When he was done, he and Garrick stared at each other, Jolly with fear, Garrick as if he were staring at a rodent.

"W-what'da ya wants?" Jolly stammered.

"Some questions answered."

Jolly seemed to pale. "What'da ya wants ta know?"

"Everything."

"Ever'thin'?" Jolly gulped. Then he tilted his head, scratched his scalp, a look of confusion crossing his pug-dog face. "Ever'thin' 'bout whats?"

"Tom."

Jolly licked his lips; his left eye began to tick. "Tom?" he croaked. "Tom who?"

Garrick took a threatening step toward him; Lucy and Beth stuck to his backside like barnacles on a ship.

"Quit repeating my words, Jolly. I know of your part in blackmailing the Countess of Selborne, so there's no need to play games. I also know you possess proof that Tom is really the son of the Earl of Selborne. I want that proof *now*."

"Yes, *now*," Lucy chimed in.

Garrick frowned down at her, but she ignored him.

"Don't know what yer talkin's about," Jolly stuttered.

"Liar," Lucy called.

"Lucy," Garrick warned. He turned to Jolly with an arrogant stare. "Liar," he pronounced.

Jolly, shifted; sweat beaded on his forehead.

Garrick slowly raised the pistol toward Jolly's head, drawing the hammer back with a fiendish grin. "Very well, if you won't tell me what I want to know, I've no choice but to kill you."

Someone gasped, Garrick guessed Beth. Jolly's mistress emitted a small squeak, and Jolly himself seemed to pale all the way down to his toes. He lowered his arms out in front of him in a gesture of self-defense. "I already told the gent what I knows," he whined. "I don't know no more'n that. So ya ken go aheads and shoot me. Rather that than a beatin' like last times. And I ain't told no one nothin', just likes I promised and if that ain't good enough fer ya, than so be its."

Garrick's brow furrowed. "What gent?"

Jolly looked confused again. "The gent what was here a month ago." When Garrick said nothing, Jolly said with a quaver, "Ya are from the countess, ain't ya?"

"No."

Jolly looked panicked. "I, well, I—"

Striding forward, Garrick placed a hand around Jolly's throat; Lucy and Beth hung back.

"The countess sent men asking questions?"

"Yes," Jolly gasped out.

"What did you tell them?"

Silence.

"What did you tell them?" Garrick shook him a little.

"I didn't tell them nothin.'"

Garrick had had enough. He aimed the pistol at the ground.

CRA-AACK!

"Argh!" Jolly bellowed. "Argh. Argh. Arrrrgh. Me toe! Me bleeding *toe*." He hopped up and down, clutching his injured foot. "'E shot me in the bleedin' toe."

"So I did," Garrick announced.

"You *bastard*. Ah, me toe. Me bleeding toe. I think it's gone!"

Garrick glanced down. "It's still there."

Jolly didn't look reassured. He peeked down, his expression clearing a bit when he realized the digit was, indeed, still attached. "So 'tis," he murmured.

Garrick took another threatening step. "Now. What did you tell the countess's man?"

It was clear Jolly was torn between spilling his guts and taking a chance Garrick wouldn't shoot him. Again. Fear won out. "I told 'im I didn't have no ev'dence." Slowly, gingerly, he set his foot down, wincing. "Semus was the one what 'as proof."

"Semus?" Garrick asked. "Semus who."

"Semus is the man originally hired to kill Tom,"

Lucy said in a small voice. "The man who never went through with the deed. According to Tom, he was killed by footpads last year. 'Tis how Jolly became Tom's guardian."

Garrick's gaze flew back to Jolly.

"The chit's right," Jolly agreed. "But he ain't dead. He only wanted everyone ta thinks so."

"But why?" Lucy asked.

Jolly shifted on his feet, wincing in pain. "'Cause, I tol' 'im I was goin' ta blackmail the countess."

Lucy appeared as confused as Garrick felt. "But hadn't you already been blackmailing the countess?"

Jolly looked up at Garrick. "Don't she never shut up?"

Garrick waved the gun. "Just answer the question."

Jolly frowned. "I didn't know about Tom bein' the countess's relation until last year. Semus don't hold his tongue so well when he's drinkin'. Seems me brother's loose lips were finally going to prove profitable for me."

Lucy gasped.

"I knew he'd once worked with the countess. When I found Tom weren't really 'is son, I saw th'mmediate possibilities. Semus'd be a rich man by now if'n 'e'd followed my advice."

"Where *is* Semus?" Garrick asked, trying to conceal his excitement.

Jolly looked up at them, his expression resigned. "Spain. He went ta Madrid."

10

"Spain," Lucy's aunt cried an hour later, her hands clutching at her gray dress. "We can't go to Spain."

Sunshine poured into the sitting room, the light refracting through the window to illuminate Aunt Cornelia's aging features as she sat in a high-backed chair.

"We have to, my lady," Garrick's deep voice rumbled. "We've no choice in the matter. If the countess has henchmen watching Jolly, they now know of our presence. Time is of the essence and, unfortunately, I can't leave you or Lucy behind."

Lucy absently traced an invisible pattern on her leg, hardly daring to breathe as she waited for her aunt's reply.

"You think they might come after us?" Aunt Cornelia finally asked.

"'Tis possible."

"Can we go into hiding?"

"You could," he said with an edge of frustration, "but I cannot stay behind to protect you and Tom."

Oh, Auntie, Lucy thought, *let us go. Let us go.*

"We could hire someone to protect us."

"I feel obligated to do the job myself. Besides, I believe you will be safer on a ship."

"You don't know my niece, my lord."

"No, but I *do* know ships."

Lucy winced, still not wanting to look up. If she did, she feared her aunt might see how very much she wanted this.

Her aunt was silent for a long moment. "'Twill be expensive."

"The expense will be covered by the duke, who has given me unlimited funds where the boy is concerned."

Lucy closed her eyes. *Please, God,* she prayed. *Please.*

"Very well," her aunt said.

Lucy almost jumped up. They were going. *Hallelujah.* She would have Garrick all to herself for weeks and weeks and weeks. Finally, she dared to glance at the object of her fantasies.

He glared.

Her heart fell to her toes, just dropped out of her chest and splattered at his feet.

"My lady, if I might ask for one more thing?"

He hated her. She could see it in the way his eyes tried to freeze her heart.

"What is it, my lord?"

"If I might have a word with your niece."

Lucy's gaze jerked up. Hope fluttered in her chest.

"Why?" Cornelia asked, suspicion hovering in her blue eyes.

"I have words I wish to exchange with her. Private words."

She held her breath.

"What words?"

Lucy didn't move. He loved her. *Please, please, please say you love me.*

"I wish to explain to her the pitfalls of dressing like a harlot and acting like a hoyden."

The breath gushed out of her.

"Ah. I see. I wish you luck, my lord."

Her aunt rose and left the room, and Lucy met Garrick's gaze bravely. Any hope that her plan might have impressed him a teeny-weeny bit fizzled in her breast when she saw the look in his eyes.

Don't yell, she thought.

I don't need to, his eyes snapped back.

And he didn't. "I'm only going to say this once, Lucinda," he clipped in a perfectly *awful* voice, "so please listen."

Lucy bowed her head. Her nails curled into her palms. It was worse than she thought possible. Worse than she'd imagined during the whole horrible ride back to her aunt's.

"When we board the ship I want you to stay far away from me."

She flinched, almost as if his words had shot an actual dart into her heart.

"*Far* away."

She tried to swallow, couldn't, and settled for closing her eyes. It didn't help.

"Do you understand?"

He was so close. She could practically feel the heat of his body. The urge to reach out and touch him was nearly overwhelming. *No*, her heart cried out. *No. I don't understand. I love you. I will always love you.*

"And if you so much as stir from this house while I make the arrangements for our passage, I will send you back to the country."

She finally managed to swallow. Her eyes burned behind closed lids.

"Do you hear me, Lucy?"

Open your eyes, Lucy. Open them. It can't be all that bad. Slowly, she lifted her gaze. A blurry blob that was Garrick shimmered. She blinked. Her vision cleared. A man stared back at her, a man she'd never seen before: cold, distant, uncaring.

"Do you?" he snapped again.

"Yes," she mumbled through a jaw aching to control her tears.

"Good."

He turned away. *Don't go*, she thought. *I'm sorry. So sorry for all the trouble I've caused you.*

When he turned and left, he stepped on her heart.

Part 2

Frailty, thy name is woman!

—Shakespeare

11

"Coo, ain't she a looker?" Tom breathed.

Lucy leaned back and peered up at the ship they were to sail on, a ship that looked like any other ship with its raised back end, thick rails, tall masts, and furled sails. She nodded as nerves, excitement, and determination made her shake like Lady Atherton's hands.

"Lucinda," her aunt called from behind her. "I want you to go to our cabin immediately. These Dover winds will chill you to the bone should you hang about."

Lucy nodded, watching mutely as her aunt directed the servants in the unloading of their trunks. A movement out of the corner of her eye caught her attention. Garrick. He stood near the rail of the ship talking to one of the crew.

A burning lump of dejection lurched in her stomach as she watched him. There was a sparkle in his eyes, a sparkle that fizzled and died when he caught sight of her. She tilted her chin, determined not to let him see how the memory of his cool and uncaring gaze burned in her mind.

"I'm goin' on board," Tom called.

Cool air whipped past her face as she nodded. The smell of brine and the rattle of the rigging lifted her spirits despite Garrick's coldness. She would have him alone for weeks. A captive audience. Surely he couldn't hate her forever.

"Land ho. Shiver me timbers! No prey, no pay. Move your arses, ya bloody curs. Raise the flag. Give 'im 'ell, mates."

Lucy turned, her brow furrowed. One of her aunt's servants came forward, the expression on his face pained as he held a cage out in front of him as if a rotten smell emanated from it.

"Good heavens, is that Prinny?"

The servant nodded, wiping at a wisp of his chestnut-colored hair which blew into his eyes. "Lord knows it ain't me. 'E's been like this since we pulled up behind ya. Saw the ship an' started singin' like a canary."

"Stow it," the parrot called, bouncing from his swing, to the side of the cage, to the floor. He flapped his wings at the breeze and broke into a song. "A sailin' we will go. A sailin' we will go. Heigh-ho, shiver me toes, a sailin' we will go."

Lucy felt laughter bubble up inside of her for the first time in days. "He must remember ships. His former master was a ship's captain, you know." She took Prinny's cage from the servant.

"Sounds as if he was a pirate," Garrick said from behind her.

Looking toward him, the smile still lingering on her face, she saw to her utter shock that he smiled back. A little bit of a smile, but a smile nonetheless. She clutched her cloak around her tighter, feeling almost giddy with delight. "I think you may be right."

"Lucinda!"

She shot a glance at her aunt, missing Garrick's pensive stare. The movement caused her cloak to whip about her violently, the green of her dress showing through underneath; the feather in her hat bobbed in the wind.

"The last thing I need is for you to take a chill," her aunt said, pointing at the ship.

Lucy pulled her cloak closed with her free hand. "I'm going, Aunt. I'm going." She darted another glance at Garrick, but he'd turned and walked away.

If possible, her spirits sank even lower than before.

"'Ave a safe trip, me loidy."

She smiled and nodded. "I shall try, Ben. Thank you."

Turning, she headed toward the gangplank, anxious to get out of the breeze. The ramp was pitching and swaying violently, and the ropes holding the ship to the dock creaked with strain. She eyed the vessel askance, then slowly made her way up the narrow plank.

"Trim the sails. Drop the anchor," Prinny called as he was knocked from his perch. His wings flapped angrily, his red tail shook, talons screeching on the metal floor as he tried to gain a toehold.

"I know, Prinny. I know." She breathed a sigh of relief when she reached the deck, then gasped when she was nearly run down by a ship's mate. Stepping back to the rail, she glanced at the coach. As usual, her eyes alighted on Garrick's tall form as he directed the servants to unload their trunks. She set Prinny's cage down with a *thunk*, then leaned against the railing, resting her chin in her elbow. She would be content to admire his rugged form for the rest of the afternoon. When she scooted closer to the railing, her toe crashed into Prinny's cage.

"Watch yer arse, bloody clodfoot," Prinny called, flapping his wings some more.

"Quiet, Prinny. I'm busy." Her eyes grew soft as she watched Garrick's every move. Wouldn't it be lovely if they could spend some time alone together on this ship? The familiar sting of humiliation filled her throat. She might as well wish for the moon. Garrick barely tolerated her. There was no sense in praying he might fall in love with her. No sense at all.

But she did.

Every day.

She sighed, her eyes catching on a carriage that pulled up alongside theirs. More passengers, she thought, then straightened in amazement.

"Beth?" she called to the blue velvet and ermine-cloaked figure who emerged.

Beth glanced around, then turned toward the ship. When she spied Lucy at the railing, she waved, said a few hurried words to the driver, and headed up the plank.

"Beth, 'tis you," Lucy exclaimed a moment later, opening her arms wide and pulling her friend into a fierce hug, both of them laughing, their bonnets colliding midair. When she leaned back, she couldn't conceal her amazement. "Goodness, whatever are you doing here?"

"I've come to say goodbye," Beth answered, grinning widely. "I know it sounds silly, but I couldn't go away without wishing you goodbye . . . and good luck, but then, of course you *would* understand. I dare say you get such urges all the time."

Lucy gave her another hug. "Well, I'm glad you did."

Beth glanced at Garrick, who was in the process of climbing up the ramp. "I haven't heard from you in two days, Lucy. What happened after the Tavern Incident?"

Lucy winced. Beth had a habit of labeling her catastrophes. The Chamber Pot Incident. The Barn Incident. The Byron Incident. It was no wonder a man such as Garrick couldn't love her.

"Lucy?" Beth asked softly.

She took a deep breath. "He was kind enough to keep what happened from my aunt, but he's quite upset with me." That was an understatement. She grimaced, staring at a knot in the rail. He was *very* upset with her. "There is good news, however. He actually smiled today."

Beth tilted her head. Lucy looked up in time to see an understanding expression in her blue eyes. "So he hasn't forgiven you?"

Lucy shook her head, clenching her jaw in order not to cry.

"You love him, don't you?"

She nodded miserably. Her hand squeezed the rail. Hard.

Beth was silent.

A white gull floated on the sea. Lucy watched it dance with the waves for a long moment before saying, "Does that surprise you?"

Out of the corner of her eye, she could see Beth shake her head. "No, Luce. I always knew it would be like this for you. Boom—you'd fall in love."

Lucy nodded, swiping a renegade tear. "I know. Isn't it wonderful?"

Beth shook her head. "If you say so. Though I must say, I always thought you'd fall in love with a stable hand or . . . or a chimney sweep, or the lamplighter."

Lucy swallowed. She refused to cry. Garrick might see her if she did.

"I never thought it'd be a man such as Garrick," Beth continued. "Someone who actually makes sense."

Lucy nodded, having to take deep breath to stop herself from crying. It was the kindest thing Beth had ever said to her. "Thank you," she affirmed, "for approving of my choice."

Silence again. Lucy became aware of the sounds around her. The gentle slosh of waves against the pier. The patter of sailors' feet as they went about their business. The soft clink-clink of the rigging as it waved in the wind.

Beth kept her silence, and her distance. She seemed to realize that if she touched her, Lucy would shatter.

"I love you, Luce, and I wish you luck," her friend said after a long silence. "You deserve him. I only hope he has the sense to realize that."

Lucy's lips quivered. A tear leaked past her lids to be

caught instantly by a cold breeze. It dribbled off the side of her face.

"*Shaaaaark!*"

Lucy stiffened.

"Shaaaark!" Prinny howled. "Shaaaaaark. Shark, shark, shark, shark, shark, shark . . . "

Lucy glanced at Prinny's cage, just in time to see a black cat pounce upon it.

"Oh my goodness," she cried.

The cage tipped over. The door swung open. The whole thing rolled against the rail and came to a stop. Prinny began to squawk furiously. The sound of the cat's cries interlaced with Prinny's terrified shrieks. Lucy intercepted the feline just as it was about to capture Prinny in its mouth. She pulled on the animal's tail, gasping in pain when the beast turned around and swiped at her with long claws.

"Ouch," she yelled, losing her grip in a flash. The cat turned back to Prinny. Lucy tugged on its tail again. It turned back and bit her this time. "Ouch!"

"Oh, Lucy. Get it," Beth cried.

"I'm trying," Lucy cried. She searched for a weapon, her heart fluttering as loudly as Prinny's wings. A row of fishing poles were secured to the rail. Visions of beating the cat with one of them rose in her mind, only to be instantly discarded. She stiffened when she spied a sharp-looking object right next to the poles. "Hand me that," she cried to a nearby sailor.

He followed her gaze and nodded, handing her a wooden staff with a hooked knife attached to the end. Lord knew what it was, but it would do well to kill a cat.

She turned, murder in her eyes.

The cat didn't stand a chance. It howled as she poked its backside, then started back out of the cage. Sparkling green feline eyes glared at her before attempting to do battle with the spear. A mistake. The blade turned out to be razor sharp.

"*Eeeeyow*," it screamed, shaking its paw in pain. Prinny squawked in his cage. Lucy could have sworn that cat shot her a look of promised retribution before it turned back to the cage, scooped Prinny up in its mouth, then shot toward the mainmast. It climbed the rope ladder that stretched the length of the mast.

"Oh no," Lucy wailed, giving chase.

With a flick of its long, black tail, the feline jumped halfway up the thick timber, Prinny squawking, "Man overboard, man overboard," the whole way.

Lucy followed after it. Bloody cat. She would kill it, kill it, *kill it!*

And as she chased after that cat, it became all the bad things that had happened in her life: the loss of her mother and father. Her brother joining the military. Garrick's refusal to love her. She swiped, swiped, swiped, following the cat up the rope ladder, her blade cutting into the lines like coral through a sponge.

"'Ey," a man called out and if Lucy had listened closely, she would have heard the panic in his voice. "Don't be doin' that!" Hell-bent on freeing Prinny, she didn't hear the warning in his voice.

She swiped again. The blade lodged into the hemp. She jerked it out and swung again, frustrated when the cat jumped to yet another rope. Grimly determined, she hacked at the next one. Victory swam through her when it broke in two.

Pandemonium erupted. Someone grabbed her arm, and Lucy turned to stare down into Garrick's furious eyes.

Twang!

Every person on deck looked up.

Twang! Twang! Twang!

People started to shout. Garrick pulled Lucy down just as another of the ropes she'd hacked at broke in two, and another, then another. They, in turn, caused other ropes to break. The frayed ends swung above their heads like the ribbons on a maypole.

Twang!

Rope whipped over their heads; the bottom half fell to the deck. Lucy sat up abruptly, pushing back her bonnet to see if Prinny was free. Her eyes widened at what she saw instead.

The mainsail was unfurling.

So was the main royal, the top gallant, and the main topsail.

The cat looked like a bell toller who'd forgotten to let go of his rope. Higher and higher it was lifted until suddenly, it let go of Prinny, then sprang toward one of the rope ladders paralleling the mast. It scurried down, jumped onto the deck, then ran down the gangplank as Prinny flew madly toward an open doorway.

Slowly, ominously, resolutely the sails continued to unfurl; immediately, the mainsail filled with a great gust of air. The ropes holding the ship dockside creaked, then groaned like rusty gates.

"Man your posts!" Garrick bellowed. The men jumped into action.

It was only then that Lucy realized what she'd done. Slowly, she pushed herself to her feet, thoroughly horrified as the sails began to fill with air. It was only a matter of seconds before all four were straining in the wind, as if the breath of God somehow blew into them. She turned. Beth had her hands to her face. On the dock, Aunt Cornelia stood by the carriage, mouth agape. Something creaked, the sound more like a loud moan, punctuated by a loud snap. Lucy looked down in time to see one of the lines tethering the ship disappear into the sea.

She glanced at Garrick. And blanched.

"*Luuuucy,*" he growled.

I know, I know, she thought. *I've done it again.*

The stern swung around. He looked away. "Cut the other line before the mast breaks," he yelled.

A sailor raced forward to do as he was told, the plank which stretched down to the dock falling into the sea with a loud, water-displacing splash.

"Dear God," Beth croaked from alongside of her.

"I know," Lucy groaned.

"Get below," Garrick ordered.

Lucy swallowed and nodded, but as she turned away, a thought suddenly gurgled to the surface of her mind.

No aunt, no chaperone.

She smiled, a great grin of a smile that must have looked odd considering the trouble she'd just caused. But she didn't care. She'd have Garrick to herself, at least for a few hours.

There was a God.

• • •

"What am I going to do?" Beth cried four hours later. Her blue-black hair swished from side to side as she paced in front of Lucy. "My father doesn't even know I'm gone."

"Does now," Tom announced.

Beth glared at the boy.

Lucy stared at them both from her position atop one of the cabin's two beds. "It's all right, Beth," she said brightly. "I'll speak to the captain about turning around just as soon as I see him."

"Can't do it, me loidy," Tom answered cheerfully, swinging his legs back and forth and rocking the hammock he was perched upon from side to side. The boy had his own cabin in the bow of the ship, but he'd been keeping them company for the last half-hour. "A man told me we couldn' turn back, what with the wind an' the tide's bein' against us. Strangest weather 'e'd ever seen, he said."

"But they *have* to. Dear God, we could be *ruined*," Beth announced.

"Ruined?" Lucy echoed in disbelief.

"Yes, ruined, Lucy. We have no chaperone, no maid, not a single proper garment for attire—"

"But—"

"We're unmarried ladies on board a ship full of men," Beth continued frantically. "Once word reaches town, we're doomed." She turned back to Tom. "Are you sure they are unable to turn the ship around?"

"Positive, me loidy. The gent told me the wind is carryin' us out ta sea as surely as the tide lowers the Thames. Said every time they trim the sails, the wind changes directions on 'em. They've given up tryin' ta fight it." And the child fairly smacked his lips in delight.

"Oh, how awful," Lucy said in mock dismay. She almost squirmed in delight. She'd have Garrick to herself for a while longer. She bit back a smile, staring at Beth's hands as they alternately crushed, then released her yellow silk dress.

A wave pitched the ship violently, causing Tom to giggle. Beth dove for a small table anchored to the wall, clutching it in terror, blue eyes round with fear.

"Beth"—Lucy made her voice as encouraging as possible—"my aunt will tell no one what happened. I'm sure she'll see to it our reputations won't suffer. And sailing to Spain with us won't be so bad. You could use the color in your cheeks."

Another wave pitched the ship, the look on Beth's face reminding Lucy of a cat she'd once seen caught atop a moving carriage.

"And it's not as if we're going to be gone for very long," she continued earnestly. "Before we left, Garrick assured me the voyage would only last a month. We can make do with what we have until then. And I've an idea about how to resolve being unchaperoned—"

"And what do we have?" Beth interrupted, still holding on to the table for dear life.

Lucy blinked at her in chagrin.

"I'll tell you what we have," Beth continued. "We have one trunk filled to the rim with petticoats, and another trunk filled with hats and gloves. I don't know about you, but I do not find the idea of parading around in my shift and a hat all that appealing."

"We have stockings, too," Lucy mumbled.

Beth clapped a hand to her forehead. "Yes, the stockings. Goodness, how could I have forgotten those? I suppose if we add the stockings we *will* look much more the thing, especially if we complete the ensemble with gloves."

Lucy looked down at the battle-scarred floor, unwilling to admit that she'd been hoping to impress Garrick with her beautiful new gloves, all fifty-two pairs of them. Sighing heavily, she realized the idea she'd been about to share with Beth would never work. She'd be lucky if Garrick ever spoke to her again, much less marry her to save their reputations. What she wouldn't give to be able to crawl under the sheets of that bed and forget all about the horrible day she'd had. She looked up as the door opened.

"Aaaaa-tention," Prinny called from his battered cage in the corner of the room. He ruffled his feathers, many of which were broken, then tilted his head to stare at the new entrant.

Lucy stared, too; it was impossible not to. *Garrick.* Oh, gracious. Her Garrick. Body parts tingled as she observed his wet, white lawn shirt plastered across hard, sun-bronzed skin. Two dusky nipples peeked through the shirt, a shadow of thick hair in between.

She swallowed, then met his eyes, brought back to earth with a thump at the fury she saw glinting from their depths. When she looked away, she told herself to buck up. Besides, how angry could the man be?

"Miss Hartford," he growled.

Very angry.

"Garrick, where have you been?" Beth asked.

His eyes darted to Beth's. "Busy."

"Doing what?"

"Helping to sail a ship with half its crew, including the captain, still in England."

Lucy gasped.

"No captain!" Beth cried. "Good heavens, who's sailing the ship then?"

"Thanks to Miss Hartford, *me.*"

He was sailing the ship? Blast. That meant that he'd be too busy to spend any time with her. Then again, she could always go up on deck. She wouldn't even have to dampen her chemise since it was raining outside. . . .

"Is there any chance we can turn around?" Beth asked hopefully.

"None. In fact, I've come to give you warning."

Lucy looked up in time to see him grit his teeth.

"A storm is brewing off our port bow. It looks as if the wind is pushing us directly into it. One of the crew will bring you some dried beef for your dinner. It will have to do until it's safe to light the stove."

The ship lurched. Beth's knuckles grew white. Lucy clung to the bed. Tom grinned widely as his hammock swung to one side then the other with a creak.

Only Garrick seemed unaffected. He stood in the doorway as if his boots were cemented to the deck. When the boat rocked again, he looked at her with the most *awful* expression on his face. As if she'd burned down Buckingham Palace or something. "Garrick, it can't be that ba—"

"*Do not* say a word, Miss Hartford."

So she didn't. She'd a lot of experience with people looking at her thus. Sometimes it was better to hold one's tongue. Still, he didn't have to be such a tyrant. What was she supposed to have done? Let Prinny die in the jaws of that miserable cat?

The door slammed behind him. All three of the room's occupants jumped.

"Braaah, typhoon a-comin'," Prinny cried, shaking his red tail feathers.

Lucy looked at her bird, murmuring to herself, "I think you're correct."

12

Lucy tossed and turned for hours that night listening to Beth's moans from seasickness and the ship's creaks and whines as it fought the storm. She went over the events of the day, wondering what she could have done differently. But there was nothing. Garrick would just have to get over his anger.

"Lucy?"

Pushing herself up on her elbows, Lucy answered, "Yes, Beth?"

"Water," came a hoarse groan.

"You're thirsty?"

"Yes."

"Where is it?"

"We're out."

Lucy nodded. "I'll go get some then."

Beth didn't respond, and a flash of concern shot through Lucy. She sat up. All she had on was her chemise. The scratchy wool of her bed coverings had rubbed raw her exposed parts, but she clutched the cover around herself anyway. The wood floor was cold as she crossed the room to Beth's side and reached out a hand to feel her forehead, relieved when she felt no sign of fever.

"S'my nose," Beth groaned.

Lucy hastily pulled her hand away and wiped it on her chemise. "Sorry, Beth. I was trying to see if you had a fever. Here." She reached out again, this time finding Beth's forehead. "No fever, good. Just lie still. I'll go for the water."

Beth mumbled something unintelligible as Lucy turned and felt her way though the darkness heading toward what she hoped was the table draped with their cloaks. She yelped as her toe collided with a chair.

"Luce?"

"I'm fine," Lucy called as pain-tears clogged her throat. Blast. Nothing had gone right today. First the Prinny Incident, then Garrick, and now *this*. She shook her head, thinking she hadn't had such a string of rotten luck since the time she'd tried to invent a new style of curling tongs, only to all but scalp herself in the process. She reached out, her hand shaking with cold as she felt for her cloak.

In a matter of moments she stood before the door to the main deck. The heavy wood rattled ominously as great gusts of wind crashed into it and whistled through its cracks. The moment the heavy plank was unlatched, the galelike winds pulled it from her grasp and slammed it against the outer wall. Immediately, the sting of rain and the pitch black of midnight assaulted her eyes. Air swirled around her legs and blew a hank of hair into her face. She shoved it aside, terrified, then leaned over and pulled the door closed, nearly falling as it slammed shut.

When she turned around and leaned against the door, her chest heaved in fear. She couldn't go out there, not even if her cabin were on fire and the ship about to sink. She pressed her hand against her heart, feeling its frantic gallop, then headed back to her cabin. That Garrick was out there sent a shaft of fear through her. Dear God, what if he died? She would lose the man she had loved. She would die an old maid, living in some cottage on the outskirts of London, untouched, unloved.

She clutched her hand to her mouth. But, no, Garrick was known throughout society for his prowess as a ship's captain. Certainly he would be safe.

She frowned as her thoughts returned to her original problem. She needed to think about Beth, not herself . . . or Garrick. And there was only one other place there was sure to be water. The captain's quarters, to her left and up some steps.

A few moments later she stood before the oak door leading into Garrick's cabin, her heart doing its best to throw itself from her chest. She took a deep breath and knocked.

No response.

She knocked again.

Still no response. He wasn't there, which meant he *was* out in that weather. Fear once again reared is ugly head. What if he was swept overboard or . . . or caught a cold? She straightened. If he caught a cold she would nurse him back to health. Visions of a sick Garrick, his eyes filled with undying gratitude as she spooned him soup, brought the first smile to her face in hours, a smile that faded when the ship lurched beneath her feet, almost pitching her on her rear.

Oh, goodness—Beth!

She braced herself on the wall, the hurriedly opened the door, relieved it wasn't locked. The smell of tobacco, man, and salt greeted her.

She peeked her head inside. "Hello?"

Empty.

Disappointment followed by relief brought a frown to her face. She stepped inside.

Two lanterns, one to the right of the windows and one to the left, lit up the room as if she were at one of Lady Chesterly's balls. The flames sputtered and hissed as the ship rocked, the sides of the lantern glass splattered with wax. She blinked against the brightness; shutters which protected the wall of windows above the bed rattled as wave after wave hurled against them.

Best to get what she needed and leave, she thought. Especially after his dire warning that he wouldn't be happy to find her in his appropriated cabin. Discouragement clogged her throat, but she smashed it down. Beth, she must think of Beth.

She had only taken two steps, however, when she heard the door to the main deck open with a *bang*. She paused. Footsteps sounded.

It couldn't be, she thought. It wasn't . . . ?

"Oh, heavens."

It was.

Whirling, she quickly searched for a place to hide, her eyes alighting upon the trunk at the foot of the captain's bed. It was huge, big enough to . . .

There was no time to think, just act, for she knew with an absolute certainty Garrick would be furious if he found her. Absolutely furious. Just right now she didn't think she could take another of his stinging rebukes. She opened the lid. It was empty, thank God.

As quickly as she could, she climbed inside, then scrunched down, releasing a huge sigh of relief when the lid closed easily over her head. Darkness and the smell of old leather enveloped her. Footsteps sounded. They paused in front of the door. Lucy heard the knob turn and held her breath. Two seconds later he was in the room.

Oh dear. Oh dear, oh dear.

She tensed. More footsteps sounded. They passed in front of her, then paused. The bed creaked. The unmistakable sound of clothes being taken off followed. Her eyes widened. Shifting a bit, she lifted the lid just the tiniest bit, the hinges squeaking in protest. She told herself she only wanted to see where he was, but she knew better. She wanted to see him, wanted to memorize him. On those cold, dark evenings, with nothing but a fire to keep her company, she would think of this night. Think of her Garrick.

As it turned out, she needn't have bothered. All she caught was a good view of the wall opposite the trunk. Disappointed, she was about to close the lid when a blur of fawn-colored fabric blocked her vision, a blur which quickly materialized into breeches as the lid abruptly opened.

Garrick jumped. His dirty shirt fell to the floor.

Lucy sat up, her gaze sliding over his breeches-clad legs, oh-so muscular when viewed up close, to his naked chest. She just about swooned. Never, *ever* had she seen a man with a chest like Garrick's—not that she'd seen a lot of chests—but she was sure Garrick's was the most amazing chest in the history of chestdom. It had ripples in it, sinewy ripples coalescing into hard muscles that quivered and rolled when he moved. She released a soft sigh, having to force her gaze away to meet a pair of furious, snapping-blue eyes.

She gulped. "Good evening, Garrick," she croaked.

For a long, tension-filled moment he just stared, then he placed his hands on his hips, his blue eyes growing as chilly as Lady Selby's pond.

"Lucy, what are you doing in my trunk?"

That was a very good question, Lucy thought. She decided to try a smile.

He glared.

She brightened her smile. "I, ah, I was looking for water."

"In a trunk?"

"Yes."

He frowned, his eyes stating clearly that he didn't believe her excuse, not that she'd expected him to. As an excuse, it was a silly one. Slowly, she stood. But Garrick didn't seem interested in arguing the point.

He stepped back, his pupils dilating as she exited the trunk. So he wasn't as oblivious to her as he pretended. Good.

"Beth is ill," she said when he looked about ready to let his anger loose. She peeked a glance at him, just in time to see a smidgen of his temper dissipate.

Just smile at me, she thought. *Just one little smile.*

He frowned. "It's over there," he snapped, nodding toward a side table.

She narrowed her eyes, beginning to get a little irritated with his attitude. The man acted as if she'd sunk the entire English fleet. It wasn't her fault she'd been so intent on freeing her bird that she hadn't realized the consequences of her actions. And just how *would* she have known? She'd never been on a bloody ship before. She reached for the decanter.

The thing slipped from her fingers. She tried to catch it. Too late. It hit the floor and shattered.

Horror held her immobile for a long I-can't-believe-I-did-that second. She looked up.

Garrick scowled.

It was too much. She wanted to scream. She wanted to yell. She wanted to hit him. Bugger it. She *would* hit him. She took a step.

Pain shot through her leg.

"Ooouch," she gasped, clutching at something to keep her from falling.

Garrick lunged forward.

"Little fool," he muttered as he scooped her into his arms. "There's glass."

All her anger faded away at the feel of his arms around her. Her mind went slack. He carried her. Oh, gracious. She clutched at him, her arms automatically clasping behind his neck. His warm neck. His strong neck, the fine little hairs that sprouted from it like the softest down.

Her breath caught. Held. Then slowly released as she became aware of other things. His eyes, so dark as she stared up at him. His chin, so strong-looking with its slight stubble of beard and a little teeny cleft. The shape of his ear with its small gold hoop. She'd never seen a man wear an earring before. Well, she had, but they weren't men in the truest sense of the word. Garrick was a man's man.

He laid her on the bed, but Lucy didn't return to earth. It was with a great deal of reluctance that she released him, her hand catching his blonde queue and bringing it forward over one shoulder. She watched through slitted eyes as he drew back, then reached for her foot, raising it for an inspection, a delightful squint on his face as he studied it.

Sudden thoughts entered her mind. Crazy thoughts. Did her feet smell? Were her toenails clean? Did she still have that teeny tiny little corn on her big toe?

"You have a shard of glass."

Oh? Was that all?

"Here." His face scrunched into an adorable frown as he eyed the shard as if it were a battle sword. There was a small prick. She flinched, the pain restoring a small portion of her wits. A very small portion, for it faded the moment he flicked the glass away and met her eyes.

Oh, Garrick, she thought. *Don't you feel it? Can't you see the way I feel for you? You must be blind as a bat if you don't.*

He slowly lowered her foot. Lucy wanted to cry out when he released it.

"You better stay there while I clean this up."

Her heart pitter-pattered in her chest. She'd stay all night. Forever. He was being nice. Oh, heavens, he was being nice. She nodded, sighing and laying back on the bed at the same time.

He stood, staring down at her for a breath-catching moment. *I've lost my mind,* she thought. *I must have.* For a split-second she thought she saw a flash of something in his eyes. Longing? Desire? He turned away. She melted into the bed. Oh dear. Could it be? Could it really, really be?

She held her breath as she waited for him to clean up the mess. When he faced her again he'd mastered that look.

"You should go back to your cabin."

Yes, she should, but she didn't want to. "I don't think I can walk," she announced.

"I'll carry you."

Oh, would he really? He walked forward. He didn't appear angry anymore. As he stared down at her he appeared . . . perplexed.

She sank back into the bed even more, putting on her best I-feel-faint look.

"Garrick," she said softly, hoping, begging, praying, that not even *he* would kick a horse when it was down. "I'm so sorry for what I did earlier today."

She braced herself, praying that the cold Garrick wouldn't return. She watched as he shook his head. Her hopes lifted. His look turned to one of pained resignation. A breath she hadn't known she'd been holding steamed past her lips. *Thank you, God. Oh, thank you.*

"There's no need to apologize, Miss Hartford. I realize I've been a bit harsh with you. 'Tis I who should apologize. I realize your propensity for disaster is not intentional."

She stiffened.

"In fact, I would venture to guess that much of it is beyond your control."

"Oh, it is," she agreed, relieved beyond words that at last he understood.

"Which is why I've decided to lock you in the hold."

She sat up. "You've *what*?"

There was a look on his face. The oddest look. A look very much like a . . . She felt her eyes widen. It couldn't be. She tilted her head. It was. Oh, joy upon joy, he was *smiling at her. Thank you, God. Oh, thank you. I shall never, ever ask for anything again. Never. Not even that new reticule I've been admiring at Madam Sophie's.*

Unable to stop herself, she smiled back, a glorious, wonderful smile. A smile to end all smiles. A smile to tell him without words how grateful she was that he wasn't mad at her anymore.

And then the oddest thing happened. He stiffened. She watched as before her very eyes the emotion dribbled from his eyes, leaving behind a cold block of ice otherwise known as Garrick.

"Leave."

She shouldn't have smiled, she thought. "I beg your pardon?"

"You should leave."

She should? "I should?"

"Yes." He turned away, reached down for his discarded shirt, and then *he* left.

Lucy didn't know whether to laugh or cry. Laugh, she decided an instant later. Definitely laugh, because she'd seen it again, that look. It *was* desire. She was sure of it. Garrick wasn't as impervious to her as he liked to make her think. He might try to act like it from time to time, but he wasn't.

Miracles *could* happen.

She hugged her knees to her chest. Hope, as wild and uncontrollable as a Scottish rose, bloomed in her chest. She smiled. Just smiled like a child on Christmas morning, then fell gleefully back onto the bed. She could still smell him, salty and tangy. She could still feel the imprint of his arm against her back. She sighed. How quickly he'd scooped her up. So bold, so decisive. If she'd known he would do that she'd have dropped the bottle sooner. . . .

She sat up. "Oh my goodness," she wailed, clapping her hands to her cheeks. She'd forgotten Beth!

He was demented, Garrick decided the next morning. Absolutely and utterly demented. What other excuse could there be for the way he'd reacted? He should have stayed angry at her, but she'd looked up at him with so much hope, so much pained resignation that he'd felt instantly contrite for snapping at her. And so he hadn't yelled at her; instead he'd teased her. Teased her. What an idiot.

He shook his head, wondering for the hundredth time what he'd done to deserve this fate. Not only was he trapped on board a ship with a woman who refused to leave him alone, but that ship wasn't moving right now. He released a frustrated breath. Not moving one damn bit.

Was this God's private little joke? Had he been such a horrible person when he was alive? He certainly didn't think so. He'd been an honest officer. A good officer, only killing when absolutely necessary, and only those who deserved their fate. Certainly he'd had more than his fair share of women, but that came with the territory. Women were intrigued by his profession, if profession one would call it. It'd really been more like a hobby, his title and estate having precluded the need for money. He'd been a rich man made richer by his hobby. At least he *had* been a rich man.

Once again his thoughts returned to his charge. God's balls, her foot had been small. Too small to support such a walking mass of calamity. But it did. He scrubbed his hand down his face. And her hair. He'd seen it down before, but never so wild and untamed as it had been last night. For a moment, a couple of moments, he'd been tempted to reach out and touch it, to wrap it around his hand and pull her face close to his, but he hadn't and he wouldn't. They didn't call him Wolf for nothing. He could control his emotions, would control the longing that clung to his soul every time he saw Lucy. She was not for him, he reminded himself.

"Calico said we're not turning around."

He started, mortified to realize that she'd sneaked up on him.

"He said that you've decided to continue on to Spain in an effort to save time."

Bracing himself, Garrick turned to look at her. His hands clenched when he spied the picture she made in her green dress, her hair loose around her.

"Not that we're making much time now," she said with a laugh, "but I think your idea sound. I'm not sure my aunt would agree, though. She'll wonder what happened to us."

He looked away. He didn't like the way she made him feel. Not one bit.

"Then again, I suppose we can send her word when we reach the first port. If we reach the first port."

"Don't you have someplace to go?"

A brief instant of hurt dipped into her eyes, then floated away. She was used to being rebuffed, he thought. But she didn't let it break her. Instead she drew that pride of hers around her as if it were a battle shield. "Where would I go?"

He looked away. He would ignore her, he decided. She was his charge, nothing more. *Nothing more.* Never mind that her skin glowed like the finest of pearls. Never mind that her hair swirled around in little corkscrews that begged for a man's touch. Never mind that the smile teasing the edges of her mouth begged for his kiss.

He would not be tempted by those lips. He would keep control of himself. Would force the sudden tightness in his groin to go away. He would force *her* away, by God.

"I thought I told you to stay below."

"You did."

"And?"

She shrugged. "I felt like getting some fresh air."

"You disobeyed me."

"Yes, I know. And it's a lovely day to disobey someone, don't you think?"

He frowned. She didn't go away.

He scowled. She smiled.

He gave up. "Where's Tom?"

"Tormenting the crew."

He didn't say anything. He should have locked her in her cabin. But as appealing as the idea might be, just now he didn't trust himself to touch her.

"Actually, he's with Calico."

"Who's Calico?"

"One of the crew."

Again, he held his tongue.

"They call him that because the hair between his legs is three different colors."

He frowned. What had she just said? And then her words sank in, sank in because of the teasing way her eyes flickered over his face, the way her cheeks filled with embarrassed color despite her bold words, the way she smiled up at him impishly.

"And there's another crew member named Stubbs."

He couldn't speak, was held immobile by the mischievous light in her eyes.

"*I* thought it was because of the peg he had for a leg, but Tom says it's really because he has a small—"

"Don't," he groaned. Little hellcat. How did she know about such things?

"Do you want to hear about Long John?"

She was making it up, he realized. Bloody hell. He shook his head, unable to stop the smile that rose to his lips. "You, miss, you are a hoyden."

She nodded. "So I've been told."

She smiled up at him, her eyes sparkling nearly as brightly as the waves behind her. Garrick stared, telling himself to leave, telling himself to walk away now before it was too late.

"You need to smile more often."

"I beg your pardon?

Her own smile grew. "Smile . . . as you are now."

He was smiling? Hmph. So he was. He shook his head, refusing to be drawn in by her charm. What use had he for smiles? He was cursed, even if her gamine grin made him wish for things that could never be, things he had no business wishing for. The realization stung. Hell, the more time he spent with her, the more his lot in life—or death, as the case may be—stuck in his craw, niggled deeper and deeper into a place he didn't want it to be. He was fated to leave this earth, fated to leave the ocean he loved, fated to leave Lucy.

Her smile faded. He could see the questions in her expression.

Ah, hellion, he thought. *If only you knew.* He reached to stroke her cheek, caught himself in time, and forced his hand back to his side.

"You should go."

She tilted her head. "So you told me last night."

Last night. A memory of a dainty foot and a wondrous smile filled his head.

"As I recall, *you* were the one who ended up leaving."

If he hadn't, he'd have done something foolish, something that might have cost him his soul.

"I thought your backside might have been on fire."

He'd been on fire for her, all right.

"So I think I'll stay, if you don't mind. You, however, are free to leave."

She was baiting him, he realized. He couldn't remember the last time he'd been baited.

"If you're not too afraid." She raised her hands, made a scary face at him, then waggled her fingers like a witch casting a spell.

A laugh rose up in his chest. He changed it into a growl.

He told himself not to admire her courage. He told himself not to think about the hint of loneliness that shadowed her eyes. He looked away, fixing his eyes upon the horizon. Damnation, what was wrong with him? Why couldn't he view her as he did other women? Apparently, flirtatious smiles and silly games he could deal with, but one blazingly honest, thoroughly open chit of a woman managed to keep him completely off guard.

He shook his head and stared out at the sea. The sky was blue today, the ocean so calm only a few white-tipped waves coasted along its surface. He stared harder, trying to find solace in the ocean he loved so much, trying to force himself to observe other things. It didn't work. He'd rather observe Lucy's smile while he still had the time to observe it.

"Decided to stay, eh?"

He clutched the rail.

"Well, I don't blame you. 'Tis beautiful out."

"So you've said," he grumbled.

Out of the corner of his eye he saw her gaze rove over the ocean. They both dropped into silence. The sounds of a ship filled his ears, familiar sounds. The slurp of water. The clink of the rigging as it vibrated in the wind. The voices of the crew, what there was of it.

"Have you ever noticed that clouds have shapes?"

No, he hadn't noticed. He hadn't had time to notice such things.

"That one there looks like a squashed frog, and I happen to know what a squashed frog looks like." She pointed. He didn't look. "And that one there looks like a snail with a broken shell." She turned to look at him. "Have you ever stepped on a snail before? They make that horrible little sound. *Criiick*." She shivered theatrically. He said nothing. She gave up.

"Tell me about ships," she asked when his silence became too much for her to bear.

He'd rather continue to be quiet, but it didn't appear as if he would get his way. She wouldn't let him. He could remain silent and hurt her feelings. Or he could answer her, and what? Answer and make her feel less lonely. Loneliness was something he knew a lot about.

"What do you want to know?" he asked against his better judgment.

She turned around, leaning her rear on the rail. The movement made the dress she wore outline her breasts, her woman's mound, her thighs. "How hard are they to sail?"

"Hard." Almost as hard as his manhood.

"What led you to become a sailor?"

"My father."

Her brows rose, filling with an odd sort of romanticism. "Oh? Was he one, too?"

"No."

"Did he always want to *be* one?"

"No."

"Then why did you want to become a sailor?"

"I didn't. He bought me a commission in the navy."

The romanticism faded. "Did you want the commission?"

"No."

"Then why did he buy it?"

He crossed his arms in front of him, debated how much to tell her. "Because I'd just burnt the south wing down."

She looked startled, then amused, then sympathetic.

"'Tis a good thing they don't allow women in the navy, else I'd have been consigned to a life at sea long ago."

She said it with such endearing seriousness, Garrick was hard pressed not to smile.

"I suppose I should be grateful," Garrick added, surprising himself. "It was probably the best thing that could have happened to me. Sailing became my life."

Tom's laughter rang out, a sudden reminder that Garrick had no life.

"Is your father still alive?"

His jaw tensed, then released, his gaze once again meeting Lucy's. Best to remember he was an angel, one with limited time left on earth.

13

Lucy waited for his answer. He looked so serious all of a sudden. She tensed as she waited for his answer.

"He and my mother died two years ago."

"Oh, Garrick. I'm so sorry."

He turned away. Lucy stared at his big, broad back. They were both orphans, she realized, and being sad over the loss of one's parents was something she understood.

Filled with need to see the smile that had colored his eyes just a few moments ago, she vowed to help him forget his loss, at least for a short while. Gazing around, she looked down the length of the ship, thinking. She needed to find the child in him, find that little boy who missed his parent's love. Her eyes caught on the row of fishing poles.

An idea began to germinate.

"I'll be back in a moment."

He looked startled by her words, straightening from the rail.

Please, please don't leave, she begged with her eyes. He gave her an unblinking stare. She clutched at her skirts, turned and all but ran toward the poles. When she returned a few seconds later, a gust of relief blew past her lips to see him still standing there.

"Teach me to fish," she said, offering him the pole.

Blonde brows rose. "I beg your pardon?"

"I said teach me to fish."

He looked at her, just looked at her as if she'd asked him to lop off his head. *Do this for me, Garrick. Do this for us.*

"You do know how to fish?"

He stiffened. "Of course I do."

She smiled. "Well, then good. Teach me how." She offered him the pole again. He flinched. She held her breath. *Please, God. Please, God.*

Reluctantly, he took it from her. "With your luck, you'll probably catch a shark," he grumbled.

She didn't take offense. He was correct.

He undid the hook from where it had been secured within the spool of twine, checked the line, then expertly reeled in the slack. When he was done, he handed it to her.

"Now what?" she asked.

"You need bait."

Bait? Of course. How silly of her. "I don't suppose you'd like to volunteer for the job?"

He didn't crack a smile, not even a teeny-tiny one. She blew a hank of hair out of her eyes. She had her work cut out for her.

"I'll be right back." She handed him the pole, then turned, hoping, hoping, hoping he wouldn't leave. A few moments later, she returned triumphantly.

"*What is that?*"

"Cheese."

"*Cheese,*" he barked.

"Yes."

"You don't fish with cheese."

"Well, you do if you don't have any worms." He wasn't making this at all easy.

His eyes narrowed. After a second, he reluctantly held out his palm. She plopped a piece in it. When he was done baiting the hook, he handed the pole to her. She made sure their hands brushed. He didn't seem to notice. Her own trembled.

"Now what?" she croaked.

"Cast it."

"In what? Stone?"

Impatience flickered in his eyes. He had no sense of humor, she thought. None whatsoever.

"Miss Hartford, surely you've seen someone cast a fishing pole before?"

As a matter of fact, she had. But she still wanted him to show her. She wanted him to come up behind her and put his big, manly arms around her. Wanted him to clasp his warm, strong hands over her own. Wanted him to breathe instructions into her ear. She shivered in delight.

"Miss Hartford?"

"Oh, umm, yes. I have seen it done." *Stupid, stupid, stupid, Lucy. You need to concentrate.*

"Then try it," he enunciated in the tone of a man who had thoroughly lost his patience.

She nibbled her bottom lip, determined to do such a fine job of casting the pole he would be dutifully impressed and declare his undying love. Well, maybe not love.

There were miracles, and then there were *miracles*.

Turning, she hefted the rod. *I can do this*, she thought. *If old Ben Gardner can do it, so can I.* Old Ben was at least ninety.

She tensed. The end of the pole quivered. She flung the line.

The whole thing flew into the sea.

"Oh noooo," she gasped, clasping her hands to her cheeks.

The pole landed with a splash and promptly sank.

"I've never seen that technique before," Garrick drawled.

Lucy turned. She could feel the burn of embarrassment. But she forgave him. Especially as what he'd said came very close to a joke. Besides, she had suffered through similar humiliations before. Undoubtedly, she would suffer through more. She dropped her hands to her sides, raising her chin. "I didn't like that pole, anyway."

He coughed. Or perhaps it was a laugh. Lucy wasn't sure. She pivoted on her heel, and a moment later returned with more cheese and three more poles.

He cocked a brow. "Do you have enough poles?"

Ooooh, he *was* teasing her. "Yes, thank you," she said with her best smile.

He didn't crack one in return, but she just knew it was in hiding. "Are you sure?"

"Positive."

"Then would you like me to bait it for you?"

Her smile grew. "Certainly." She handed him the first pole, taking great care to let their hands brush again. Much to her disappointment, he didn't seem to notice. Again. Bother.

When he was done, he once again handed it back to her. "Would you like me to cast it for you?"

"No, thank you." She could do this. She was sure of it. And she did, watching in pleasure as the line sailed over the rail. The reel spun like a carriage wheel, the hook and cheese seeming to float on a current of air.

A white gull swooped down and caught it.

"Oh nooo," she cried.

She thought she heard Garrick cough, wanted to glance at him to see, but she was too busy trying to stop her line from peeling off. She jerked on the handle. Didn't help. She dropped the pole, catching the line in her hand. The bird faltered midflight. She tugged. The bird dropped from the sky like a rotten apple.

"Oh nooo," she cried again.

But at the last second it recovered. She watched, heart in her throat, as her line continued toward the sea, sans the cheese, the bird caa-caa-caaing its anger at her audacity in nearly killing it.

Garrick coughed again, only now she recognized the sound for what it was. A chuckle. Just one, almost as if he couldn't bear to let more than one at a time leak past his lips. She turned to him.

"*Now* would you like me to do it for you?" he asked again.

"No."

Her plan to make him smile was working splendidly. She'd look like a fool a hundred times to make him laugh. She bit back a pleased smile. It took her a moment to get everything organized again. When she was done, she lifted the pole, flung the line back, then let it loose.

Nothing happened.

What . . . ? She turned, confused as to where her hook had gone.

It had *gone* into Garrick.

He didn't screech, didn't even bellow, just stood there, arms crossed over his chest, the hook, the cheese, and the fishing line dangling from his ear like a mouse family's Christmas ornament.

"Oh my." She covered her mouth with her hand.

He reached up, and it was then that she realized it wasn't actually *in* his ear, it was caught on his ear*ring*.

And the sight of Garrick, a frustrated frown on his face, the fishing line trailing from his ear like a miniature tightrope, was more than her easily amused sense of humor could bear.

She tried to stop it, she truly did, but the laughter rose up in her throat. *No*, she told herself. *Don't do it. He'll get angry if you do.*

A giggle escaped. His eyes narrowed.

She bit her lip.

"You're laughing at me," he pronounced.

No. No. No. She wasn't.

"You *are*."

She shook her head. Her jaw ached with the effort to contain her giggles. He took a step toward her.

The sight of that cheese swinging to and fro was her undoing.

Laughter burst free like birdsong. She convulsed, just wilted against the rail and clutched at her sides.

"You *are* laughing at me," he all but bellowed.

"Oh my goodness," she gasped. Poor Garrick. He tried so hard to be studious and in command. A single piece of cheese brought him down to the level of a human.

Tears clouded her eyes, her shoulders shook. She wiped at her eyes, which was probably why she didn't see him reach out. All she felt was a warm hand against her shoulder.

And suddenly, so suddenly it startled her, the laughter faded. Well, not completely. One last chortle slipped out. She looked into his blue, blue eyes. He stood so close, the smell of him so . . . so sealike.

Oh, Garrick, she thought. *You need my laughter. You need my love.*

She reached out and placed her hand against his cheek. She saw his eyes widen. She moved her hand to the back of his neck. His gaze softened. She pulled his head down to hers.

He didn't resist. *Yes,* she thought. *Oh yes. This is what you need. This togetherness. This connection we share. Let it banish the demons in your soul.*

Her heart pulsed, then pressed itself against her chest. His lips were close. So close. She closed her eyes.

"*Bloody hell!*"

Her lids sprang open. Garrick cursed again. The ship creaked. Lucy looked up. The sails had snapped to life.

How?

And then they were both knocked from their feet as the ship tilted.

"Arlan," she thought she heard him murmur. "Damn his feathered hide."

It had been a narrow escape, Garrick admitted later that same evening. A *very* narrow escape. He swiped a hand over his face as another gust of wind tilted the ship. He reached for the wheel, though it was completely unnecessary to do so. The spoked hub had been securely fastened to a southerly heading, the salt-laden air blowing the *Swan* smoothly on course, thankfully. Now he could get on with man's work. Now he could forget about Lucinda.

But like the persistent brush of wind across his face, the memory of their time together returned. Damnation. It was driving him mad, this way she had of looking at him as if he could slay her dragons. He didn't *want* to slay her dragons. He wanted nothing to do with her. But every time he turned around, she was there. The solicitor's. The tavern. His cabin. It was as if he were cursed, as if God smote him at every turn.

Was that it? Was this some sort of punishment? Some sort of test? Send him out to sea with her when he hadn't had a woman in months. Make him want her. Then tease him mercilessly by making her think she wanted him? Because he knew she didn't really want him. She was probably under some sort of heavenly love spell.

"Tough, isn't it?"

Garrick whirled toward the voice.

"She *is* part of the test, Garrick. I'm surprised it took you this long to realize that."

He stiffened.

The man said nothing, just stared at him with black, fathomless eyes.

And Garrick knew. He knew beyond a shadow of a doubt that the being standing before him was the devil.

He was short, squat even, with eyes as black as smoke. His face was fleshy, so fleshy he looked more like a baker than a supernatural being. The face was covered with hair. That struck Garrick as odd, but what was odder still was the bright blue, knee-length coat with a stark white, multi-layered cravat he wore. That, combined with his fawn-colored, velvet knee-breeches and the six small pistols which hung from a strap slung over his shoulder, made him look like some of the men Garrick had battled with in the past. In fact, he looked distinctly like drawings he'd seen of . . . Blackbeard.

The devil swept his tricorn off his head and bowed low. "Actually, the name is Belial. Or Beelzebub. Or the Devil. Whatever. I've gone by many names in the past. Call me what you will." His eyes swept appraisingly around. "I say, Garrick, this a *fine* ship."

Garrick ignored his polite, almost cordial words. "What do you want?"

Belial affected a look of hurt. "Now, Garrick, is that any way to greet me?"

"Get off my ship."

"My, my. We're snappy today, aren't we? Must be all that abstinence." He shook his head in mock sorrow. "It's tough, isn't it. Nothing like the lack of a good ballbouncing to put you in a cranky mood, eh? They selected her for you on purpose, you know. Knew how irresistible you'd find her. Rather devilish of them, wouldn't you say?"

Garrick didn't say anything at all. He was exhausted, confused by the emotions coursing through him, and tired of dealing with beings who thought themselves in charge of his life. He almost snorted. Who was he trying to deceive? He didn't even have a life anymore.

Exasperated, he turned and walked away, leaving Belial by the railing.

"I'm not finished, Garrick."

"I've no interest in listening, Belial."

"Not even about the little game I've set into motion?"

Garrick's steps slowed. Game? What game? Slowly, he turned.

"You see, I've done the most delightful thing," Belial continued. "I've sent my own minion after the boy, and, with a little help from me, he should be upon you within the next twenty-four hours." He shook his head sadly. "I don't think I need explain to you what should happen if this person gets his hands on Tom."

Garrick simply stared, the ramification of what Belial revealed slowly sinking in.

"And so I've come to offer you a deal." The devil continued, taking a step closer to him. "I'll give you your life back. You'll be free to live out the rest of your days with whomever you choose. Mortal, as you are now. All you need do"—a slippery smile spread across the devil's face—"is give me your soul."

A gust of wind blew over the deck of the ship, the sails moaning eerily above him.

"But before you agree," Belial continued, "look yonder." He pointed to the horizon with one taloned nail. "Do you see that speck of white?"

Garrick indulged the devil with a glance. "What of it?"

"'Tis my friends."

"Excellent," Garrick snapped. "I'm in the mood for a good fight."

The devil arched a brow. "My, we really *are* in testy mood. You should indulge in some hot, steamy fornication, Garrick, it would do your soul wonders. Oh, but that's right—you're not allowed. Too bad. One more reason for you to agree to my plan. But here's another: that's not just any ship there, Garrick, it belongs to Tully. You do remember Tully, don't you? He didn't die when he jumped overboard. Oh no. He's quite alive, and quite anxious to repay you for the loss of his eye. So I ask you, Garrick. What do you think he'll do when he gets his hands on Lucy? She's just his type, you know. Spirited. Beautiful. *Yours.* Oh, I know she's not yours in the *truest* sense." The devil laughed mockingly. "But Tully won't believe that."

Garrick just looked down his nose, though the devil's words sent a chill down his spine, a chill he couldn't afford to feel. "He won't catch us."

The devil laughed again, a low, nefarious chuckle. "You're wrong, Garrick. He will."

"I've beaten Tully before, Belial. I'll beat Tully again."

"Ahh, but it's not just Tully on that ship."

"Oh?" Garrick asked mockingly. "Is the Countess of

Selborne on it, too? Will she beat me over the head with one of her coronets?"

The devil's eyes narrowed. "I'm beginning to grow impatient with you, Garrick."

"Good."

"Lucien St. Aubyn is aboard that ship," the devil continued. "And what Tully lacks in brains, Lucien more than makes up for in cunning."

For the first time, Garrick felt a niggling sense of unease. "The Duke of Ravenwood? What has he to do with this?"

"Nothing. Everything."

Garrick stared, wondering at this latest twist of fate. He'd heard of the duke. Who hadn't? The man had killed his own brother. Apparently the rumors of his dark soul were true. He shrugged. "When you decide which it is, let me know."

The dark angel's lids lowered into slits, his eyes turned red with anger. "Don't mock me, Garrick. If you decline my offer, I'll not give you a second chance. Do you understand what will happen if you don't prove the boy is the earl's son? You go back to the Well of Souls. And I assure you, when your number is called, it won't be to give you another chance down here. You will be sent to me. What do you have to lose by agreeing to my terms?"

"Why do you ask me that if you're so sure of my failure?"

Belial's eyes glowed with anger.

"I'll tell you why. I think it's because you know you're the one who's going to lose, Belial. Not me."

Belial leaned back, looking momentarily incredulous, then drew up to his full height, suddenly towering a foot over Garrick's tall form. "You're a fool, Garrick. See where your ego gets you when your soul is in my grasp. Your puny strength won't stop the torment of watching your precious charge die before your very eyes. Nor will it assuage the agony of your soul's slow death."

The devil stepped back a few paces and then was gone.

Garrick stepped back, too, blinking at the spot where Belial had been. If the devil wanted a fight, than a fight he would have.

14

A man's greatest pleasure arises from a woman's titillation of his manhood. To achieve this titillation, there are several methods one can employ. The first is with the placement of the woman's hand against the man's erection. To do this, one must simply stroke the length of his arousal. The other method is one most men prefer. That is to place one's lips against the hardened . . .

Lucy sat up abruptly. *Good gracious!*

"Lucy Hartford, what are you reading?"

"She's readin' 'ow to make the sheets sing."

"Thomas Tee," Lucy gasped, glaring at the boy who practiced making knots with a small piece of rope. She glanced at Beth, covering the title, *A Hundred Ways to Seduce a Man*, with her skirts of her green dress, hoping Beth didn't believe Tom. That was all she needed. Another lecture.

"It's that book again, isn't it?" Beth asked.

Lucy slumped. Rats. "There's nothing else to do while we wait for dinner."

Tom snorted from his perch in the hammock. Lucy glared. Beth gave her a look Aunt Cornelia would be proud of.

"Besides," Lucy said with a tilt to her chin, "it's a very, er, enlightening book."

"Indeed it must be, judging by the color of your cheeks."

"No needs to read about it when I'd be 'appy to share what I know with ya," Tom added.

Lucy rolled her eyes. "I hardly think—"

"I need to see you."

Lucy's mouth snapped shut. Her gaze shot to the door. A jolt of electricity zinged through her. *Garrick.*

"M-me?" she asked, pointing to herself. The book slid off her lap and landed on the floor with a slap.

He nodded, his enigmatic eyes never leaving hers. "Now."

The door closed. Lucy looked between Beth and Tom.

"Do you think—"

"No." Beth cut her off. "He is not going to ask you to marry him."

"That wasn't what I was going to say," Lucy sputtered.

Beth's eyes narrowed. Tom snorted again.

All right, so the thought *had* hurtled through her mind. "I'll be right back."

Beth got up with her, stopping her before she crossed through the door. "Lucy, wait."

Reluctantly, Lucy turned back. Tom looked on curiously as Beth pitched her voice low. "Be careful," she said.

"Of what, Beth?"

Beth's expression grew sympathetic. "Getting your hopes up."

Like the stab of a hat pin, the words pricked at Lucy's heart. She tiled her chin up. "My hopes are always up, Beth. You know that."

Beth frowned. "'Tis exactly that which concerns me."

Lucy placed a small smile upon her face. "Beth, one must always have hope. Always. Hope is what's gotten me through the darkest times of my life. I will always be an optimist. If I weren't, I would be asking myself to be less than I am."

Beth didn't blink as she stared up at her though wide eyes, eyes that softened when she nodded. "Luce, you make me proud to be your friend."

Lucy smiled back. "And I'm proud to be yours, Beth."

With those words and one last smile at Tom, she left, feeling very melancholy yet all the more determined to win Garrick's heart. She would prove to Beth that where there was hope there could be victory, at least in theory.

The door to Garrick's cabin was ajar and so she knocked lightly. Her heart skipped a beat when he called, "Come in."

She stepped into his cabin, her eyes immediately drawn to his tall form. He stood gazing out the window that lined the back wall of his cabin, his hands clenched behind him, his back so stiff she could bounce a ball off of it. And any teeny little hope that he might want to see her because he'd enjoyed her company disappeared like a wish on Christmas morning.

"Garrick, what's wrong?"

He half turned toward her, his queue curling in a question mark. The gold hoop in his ear glittered as it caught the last rays of pink, yellow, and purple sunlight visible through the windows.

"Garrick?" she repeated, her heat beginning to flutter in her chest.

"I've some bad news."

Her breath caught. He was leaving her. No, wait. They were on a ship. He couldn't leave her.

She swallowed. "What is it?"

Still, he didn't face her fully. She moved up alongside of him, terribly aware of the heat that radiated from his body like nebulous shimmers off a hot carriage roof.

"Pirates," he said at last.

"Pirates?" she asked, resting a hand on his arm, his skin beneath his white shirt so warm. She loved to touch him; it made her feel more connected to him. And he didn't draw away. She swallowed back a smile. "Piracy dies out in the seventeenth century."

"Not in some waters."

She felt her brows draw up, then lower. "But we're miles away from where those pirates roam."

He swung toward her. Her arm dropped to her side. Her teasing smile faded when she saw the look in his eyes. "Not this particular pirate."

Good heavens. He was serious. Her heart fell to her toes, then just as quickly jumped back into her chest, where it tried to beat its way out. Gracious. Pirates. A shaft of excitement rose in her. "What pirate?"

"Tully St. Clair. The devil's own."

The words made Lucy shiver for some reason, though the name Tully meant nothing to her. It probably should have, judging by the look on Garrick's face. She stared. He looked magnificent in the golden light—pirates or no—almost like a painting she'd once seen of the archangel Gabriel, spectacular in his fury. And he was furious. She'd been on the receiving end of that look enough times to recognize it.

"Garrick, surely we can outrun this Tully St. Clair?"

Silence.

"They can't be that close, for I saw no sails earlier."

More silence.

"And with hardly any crew on board we must be lighter and faster."

Still nothing.

"And if we hang out our hands and paddle, we'll be that much faster."

Not even a twitch.

"Then there's always the option of tossing people overboard to create less ballast."

He finally turned to look at her, though it was really more of a glare. "Lucy, this is no laughing matter."

So he *had* been listening. "Who's laughing?"

"If they catch you, do you know what they'll do to you?"

She tried a cocky smile. "Invite me to tea?"

"Lucy!"

She flinched.

"If they catch you, they will rape you and then kill you, if they don't decide to keep you for a few weeks."

This time it was she who grew silent. "Oh, is that all?" she finally said.

"No, it is not. Do you know what it's like to be forced by a man over and over again? I've seen it before, Lucy. 'Tis one of the reasons why I vowed to rid the sea of pirate scum. The women become shells of themselves, some refuse to speak, some simply never snap out of it. I can't . . ." He turned away. "I refuse to let that happen to you."

She swallowed. All right, so maybe being captured by pirates wasn't as adventurous as the *Gazette* made it sound. Still, the odds of them actually being caught were so slim, she refused to consider it.

She reached out and placed her hand against his arm again. "Garrick, do not fear. We must be far ahead of them—"

"I fear nothing," he snapped.

She patted his arm. "Of course you don't. And with you at the helm, how could they possibly catch us?"

He didn't say anything. She thought he might ignore her words, for not with a twitch of his cheek nor a flicker of his eyes did he respond. Then, slowly, so slowly she might have missed it but for the fact that she stared at him so hard, she saw his face relax, could actually feel his tension beneath her hand drain away like water in a tide pool. He shifted, his eyes meeting hers, such blue eyes, their color even more spectacular with the sun drifting through them.

"'Tis going to be difficult, Lucy."

"No more difficult than what we've faced so far."

"You might be captured."

"You'll keep me safe." She gave him a tremulous smile, hoping, praying, wishing, he could somehow hear what her soul was singing. *I love you, Garrick. And I know you'll keep me safe, no matter what happens.*

She wanted, oh how she wanted, to say the words aloud. But for the first time in her life she lacked the courage to say what was in her heart. She was afraid to reach for the moon. Afraid she might come up empty-handed. So she settled for telling him without words, moving her body closer so that it brushed against his. She saw the look in his eyes change: it began to flicker, then burn.

"Kiss me," she murmured.

He didn't move, just stood alongside of her gazing into her eyes as if he'd never look away. "Yes," he finally said. "I deserve a kiss . . . for luck."

For luck? Idiot man. Couldn't he tell there was much more to it than—

He jerked her to him. She gasped. He crushed his lips against hers.

Ahhh, Lucy thought. Maybe, just maybe, he wasn't such an idiot. She opened her mouth, just as he'd taught her to do. His tongue swept inside. She groaned, the taste of him was so sweet. He made her feel as if she were kissing a bit of heaven, as if she floated among the clouds. She wanted more of that feeling. She rallied her courage to do . . . that *thing*, the one she'd read about.

Sucking in a breath, she placed her hand against him, just as the book instructed.

He gasped.

She waited for something—what, she didn't know—something wonderful, something sure to be incredible, something she knew instinctively the book didn't explain. Just to be sure she got whatever it was, she stroked him. He gasped again. She stroked him again. This time he groaned, a long, wonderful groan. And then, yes, she was sure of it, he began to *grow*, to *harden*. Amazement made her stiffen. He stiffened, too. Realization of where her brother's stallion had gotten its fifth appendage suddenly dawned. And then thoughts of horses galloped away as he tilted his head, coaxed her tongue into his mouth, and sucked on it.

"Gawittth," she moaned, then all but fell to her knees as little tiny explosions went off inside her. Her mind, her breasts . . . gracious, between her legs. She hardly noticed as he pressed her against a wall, only wanted him to keep doing that thing with his mouth. She stroked him harder—and he responded by placing his hand between their bodies and stroking her back.

Things began to happen quickly then, things she'd only ever dreamed about, or perhaps half-known but never understood. Her body began to tremble, her ears to pound. Sensations pulsed through her body, left her aching, *burning*.

He drew away. Lucy gasped in a breath of Garrick. Bereft at the loss of contact, she stared up at him, panting. He gazed down at her, his big, manly chest heaving, too.

Slowly, she became aware of things, things that weren't Garrick. The sound of waves as they hit the side of the ship. The rocking beneath her. The moan of the wind through the windows.

She thought he would say something, was hoping he'd say something, but then he looked up sharply, almost as if something had caught his attention.

She turned, still befuddled by what had passed between them. Still thinking that she could reach her hand out and do it again, that he would, in turn, do *that* to her again, only this time she wouldn't let him stop.

A spot of white caught her attention. She stiffened. A gasp escaped past swollen lips.

Sails, their rectangular shape distinct against the rose-colored horizon, hovered in the distance. They looked to be less than a mile away.

"Go to your cabin," he ordered.

She turned back to him. Honest to goodness pirates were trailing their wake. And though she knew she shouldn't feel it, excitement once again surged through her. Oh, not the same kind of excitement she felt when Garrick touched her—this was different. "Garrick, don't make me leave. I can help."

"Shhhh, Lucy." He placed a finger against her lips.

She shushed.

"I need you to take care of Beth and Tom."

Her eyes widened. Well, when he put it that way.

He reached out and cupped the side of her face, the gesture so familiar, so dear. And as she'd done before, she tilted her cheek into his hand.

"Go. We'll talk about this later."

This, he'd said. Did he mean the "this" that pulsed in the air between them? Or the "this" that had happened when he'd touched her private parts, and she touched his? Lucy wasn't sure.

"Go," he repeated.

She almost said no, but he glanced beyond her, his eyes fixing on the pirate ship. And against her better judgment, she went.

All night long they tried to outrun the pirates. Still, the sails loomed larger and larger behind them, the moonlight seeming to set the sheets aglow.

"They'll catch us by morning," Calico mumbled despondently from alongside of Garrick.

Garrick nodded from his position by the rail, staring out over the stern of the ship as if he could will the enemy ship to perdition. Damn Belial. But he'd not give up without a fight. Not while there was a breath left in his body. Fear was unacceptable. Fear slowed your reflexes. Fear could lead to failure, and he refused to fail Lucy, Lucy who was magnificent in her courage, who kissed him as a woman ought, and who would one day, despite her propensity for disaster, make someone a fine wife.

"Too bad that bloody moon won't go away," the old sailor continued. "We could turn in another direction and be away from them like that." He snapped his finger.

Garrick nodded, then looked up at the offending moon turning the tips of waves into silver ribbons. Two mountainlike clouds flanked its sides. Unfortunately those clouds had yet to move in front of it, nor would they if Garrick didn't miss his guess. Not for the first time he wished he'd been sent back with some sort of special powers, but he had none. They'd sent him back as a mortal in every sense, a mortal forced to do battle with immortals.

Belial. The name hung on the tip of his tongue, softly uttered, never forgotten.

"What could they want, m'lord? They ain't never even got a good look at us, yet they're pursuin' us as if they expect we got treasure aboard."

"They're after the boy," Garrick explained.

"The boy?"

"Tom."

Calico looked stunned. "Tom? But why would they wants 'im?"

As quickly as possible, Garrick explained, Calico's eyes wide when he'd finished. "I'll need you to hide him when the time comes, Calico. The ladies, too, of course. Have you a place?"

"Aye, Cap'n. Been used a time or two before. Usually for the cap'n's good brandy, but I wager it'll work just as well fer the ladies an' boy."

Garrick nodded, his expression fierce as he turned back to stare at the approaching ship, his thoughts once again on Lucy. He would move heaven and earth to keep her safe, to live up to the faith she had in him, faith that he could save them all from the very devil himself.

"This waiting is interminable," Beth blurted.

"What's intermiteable mean?"

"It means unbearable," Lucy explained to Tom, exchanging an anxious glance with Beth.

They were all ensconced in the cabin, Lucy having obeyed Garrick's order to keep her eye on her friends. Beth sat in her bed, her blue gown so wrinkled it looked to be made out of crumpled paper. Tom sat in the hammock, his eyes narrowed on Beth. They'd been snipping at each other all morning, not surprising since none of them had gotten any sleep.

"Why didn' she just say so?" Tom mumbled.

"Hush, Tom," Lucy ordered when Beth looked ready to snap at him.

The boy didn't appear happy about it, but he dropped into silence, his feet swinging back and forth.

Lucy looked out the porthole, but she could see nothing. Absolutely nothing. Frustration rose within her. She was used to action. She was used to charging into things. She was used to handling problems, not avoiding them. Despite the pride she felt that Garrick had asked for her help, his insistence that they all remain in the cabin chafed like the bindings of a rope.

It continued to chafe, until, a half hour later, unable to stand it a moment longer, she shot up from the bed and crossed to the door. "I'll be back in a moment."

"Lucy, you can't go out there!"

"I'm goin', too," Tom called.

Lucy paused, hand on the door. "No, Tom. You stay here and guard Beth. She needs a man to protect her."

"Needs a man ta do more'n that," the boy grumbled, but stayed nonetheless.

"Beth, I'll be back in a moment. I promise."

She turned away, hurriedly closing the door behind her. The hallway beyond was as dark as a tomb. She took a moment to let her eyes adjust.

BOOM!

Lucy yelped, her heart jolting in her chest. Beth screamed on the other side of the door. The deck beneath them shuddered.

"Oh dear." Gulping, she firmly ignored the wild beat of her heart and forced her leaden feet to move. One goal centered in her mind. Garrick.

Outside, the deck teamed with chaotic activity. Off to her left, less than a quarter mile away, sailed the enemy ship, a Jolly Roger waving at them from its main mast. Lucy felt her stomach drop to somewhere about the level of the ocean floor. The pirates had caught them. Shouts rang out. Men, their expression frantic, scurried about.

Garrick stood amid them like a mountain rising from a turbulent sea. He bellowed at one of the crew members, his face red with anger, each of his words punctuated with a stab of his finger. The hapless recipient of his tirade stared down at the deck, misery written on his face. Lucy was in time to catch his hurried apology.

"Perhaps you'll think before you act next time."

"Yes, sir." The sailor snapped to attention.

BOOM!

Garrick turned. *"Port rudder!"* he yelled.

"Aye-aye, Cap'n."

Lucy felt her heart flip-flop in her chest. She flung herself down atop a knobby deck just as the wheel spun toward the left. Once again the deck shuddered beneath her, the sail creaking in protest. She covered her ears and scrunched her eyelids closed.

Silence.

Well, not silence, really. There were feet scuffling by, and in one case over her. A crew member yelled at another. Gingerly, she opened her eyes.

A pair of scuffed black boots stared back at her. She pushed herself onto an elbow and peered up.

Garrick glared down at her. He was not pleased. She knew that because he didn't say a word, just stared down at her as if he couldn't decide whether to throttle her or throw her overboard. It was a look she was used to seeing on her Aunt Cornelia's face.

"Lucy, what in the hell are you doing out here?"

"Cap'n," a burly sailor interrupted before she could get a word in. Garrick turned to face the man. "Cap'n, we've got the cannon ready to fire."

Garrick's face turned a vivid, molten red. "Well? What in the hell are you waiting for? Fire the damn thing!" He turned back to her.

BOOM!

Lucy didn't even think. She flung herself at Garrick.

"Port rudder!" Garrick yelled, his voice ringing in her ears like the bells of St. Mary's parish.

"Aye, Cap'n," came the familiar call. The boat creaked, the sails groaned as the bow of the ship tilted again.

It was a second or two later before she noticed the whistling. She reared back in surprise.

"Get *down!*"

Shocked, Lucy found herself practically thrown to the briny-smelling deck. The whistling grew louder. Out of the corner of her eye she caught sight of crew members throwing themselves atop the oak planks, the sound of their bodies hitting the deck echoing in her ears.

She could see nothing with Garrick's big body covering her, practically crushing her, really. Under normal circumstances she would have been delighted to find herself in such a position. Now her heart beat in fear wildly. She was somewhat relieved when he slowly moved off her, but when she looked around, her eyes widened. The rail was broken not five feet from where they lay. The edges of it smoked ominously.

Garrick became a flurry of activity as he pushed himself to his feet, tugging Lucy up with him. *"Haul of all port, now!"* He boomed. "Starboard rudder, *now!* Someone put that damn fire out!"

The men wasted not a second in complying.

Lucy watched, mouth agape, as they rushed to the lines angling above her head. Their muscles bulged with strain as they pulled, the giant sails above her slowly tilting to the right. Suddenly, the wind caught the sheets, and the effect was immediate. The *Swan*, groaning with strain, quickly pitched to the side; her bow pointed suddenly and with dizzying speed to the right. The world tilted crazily. Everything from empty sea barrels to coils of rope slid past her with screeches of protest, the ship's yaw so violent the view over the left railing was clear blue sky.

She gulped.

BOOM!

Lucy flinched, but was too frightened to throw herself to the angled deck, her fear of rolling into the sea greater than her fear of getting hit by a cannonball. Once again she heard the strange whistling. Just then a black streak whizzed into the blue sky on her left, exactly where the ship would have been if not for Garrick's quick maneuver.

"*Ease off!*" he bellowed.

The men quickly complied, and the deck started to slowly level. It was the most incredibly coordinated, amazing thing she'd ever witnessed. She turned to stare at Garrick, mouth agape. She forgot all about evil pirates and stray cannonballs as she gazed at the man she loved, a man who had undergone an almost frightening transformation in the last few minutes. He was magnificent. His blonde hair flew about his head like a golden halo; the breadth of his shoulders strained against his shirt. He stood giving orders, quickly, succinctly, and with absolute calm. He looked . . . invincible. That is, until he turned toward her—then he looked furious. "Get below, Lucy, *now!*"

She nodded, dazedly, not even flinching when another cannon blast sounded.

Smoke, its rank sulfuric smell emanating from the deck below, hung over the *Swan* like the lid of a coffin. The battle-scarred ship fluttered upon the water, a wounded bird struggling to stay afloat. The *Revenger* was so close now Garrick could see men scurrying about its deck like ants spilled from a bottle, many of them clasping weapons. He clenched his own cutlass and glanced at his men.

Calico stood alongside him, rivulets of sweat born of fear and anxiety making their way down his face. His eyes moved beyond him to the tense faces of his men. All were staring at the approaching ship, the deck unnaturally quiet; only the sighs of the ship and the rhythmic slap of the ocean could be heard over the rustle of the giant sails hanging in tatters above their heads.

Soon now, Garrick thought. Soon, they would be boarded. He looked back at the *Revenger*, then glanced up to the black and white skull and crossbones waving from its mainmast, a vivid reminder of the skill and cunning of his enemy.

They had tried to outrun the pirate ship for over two hours, but the *Swan* had been like a minnow with a shark chasing at its fins. Every move Garrick tried had been instantly countered with a skill Garrick had rarely witnessed. Lucien St. Aubyn. Obviously the duke knew how to sail a ship as well as he wielded a gun.

Garrick slapped his hand on the rail in frustration, furious at the fates which would test him in such a way, thus putting in danger a woman with more courage than a good portion of his crew. He was an angel, for God's sake, surely there must be *something* he could do! Unfortunately, his only option was to hope like hell he could survive the coming battle.

"Won't be long now," Calico grumbled.

Garrick nodded.

"John's hoistin' the white flag as we speak." Calico continued, brow furrowed. "Do ya think they'll fall for it, Cap'n?"

"It's worked before," Garrick grunted. "And the

Swan looks battered enough they might believe we'll surrender. 'Tis worth a try."

"At least the women and the boy are hidden," Calico mumbled.

The corner of Garrick's mouth tilted, not into a smile. He was too tired, too frustrated to attempt that. It was more of a smirk as he remembered Lucy's cursing when he firmly, yet gently shoved her beneath his bed, Beth and Tom piled in next to her. She had ranted and raved when he'd nailed the boards into place, her fury with him clear in the banging of her fists against the thick wood. Livid was a more apt description. She hadn't wanted to hide. She had wanted to help, and God help him, he had wanted to let her, but he needed Lucy to protect the boy. He only hoped it never came to that.

"She's a bonnie one, Cap'n," Calico said, seeming to read his mind.

"Aye, Calico, she is." Garrick's hand clenched around his cutlass so tightly he felt the leather hilt bite into his flesh. God help them if they fell into the enemy's hands. God help them all.

15

Lucien St. Aubyn studied the *Swan* for any sign that the white flag waving from its standard was a trap. Not that the *Revenger* would have a problem overpowering the smaller vessel were that indeed the case, but it seemed odd that there was a such a small number of men visible on deck.

"Stand to your stations, men," he called, following Tully's gaze. The pirate looked the quintessential rogue with his left hand tucked into a belt with six small pistols shoved behind it.

Nothing but the deck of the ship moved, the pirates waiting patiently to inflict their revenge upon the *Swan*. Lucien had watched over the last two hours as each member of the crew had grown more and more furious with their prey, the smaller vessel having done a remarkable job of inflicting damage upon them. Now they stood, hatred on their faces, greed lighting their eyes, their dirty and unkempt hands tight around the thick cords they held, the grapnels attached to the ends of the hemp swinging like pendulums.

It might have been better for the crew members of the *Swan* if their ship had been sunk, Lucien thought, but he'd ordered Tully not to do so. Despite the pirate's protestations, Lucien had refused to risk harming the boy. As a result, the *Swan* would now have to face the furious and incensed members of the *Revenger*, and judging by the looks on their faces, few would survive the coming battle.

"Boarders away!" Tully called.

With a *whoosh* they swung their ropes. The grapnels flew through the air with talonlike precision and landed on the rail of the *Swan*.

"Heave to!"

Lucien tensed. If the *Swan* was planning to attack, now would be the time, for the *Revenger* was at its most vulnerable while the crew tugged the smaller vessel into their clutches.

Almost as if the captain of the *Swan* read his mind, battle cries rang through the air. Gunfire called out. Lucien stood there, daring a bullet to hit him, wishing a bullet would hit him, but of course, none did. Wood splintered above and around him, but none splintered his rotted soul.

"Get 'em, boys!" Tully called, his voice filled with rage, blood spewing from a wound to his arm.

Lucien pulled out his own weapon, though he had no intention of helping Tully and his men. Let them do all the work. He would stand by and watch.

The crew of the *Swan* were obviously outnumbered, he noted, though one man in particular was doing more than his fair share of dispatching Tully's men. He was a tall man, with shoulder-length blonde hair and the best sword arm Lucien had ever seen. Unfortunately, his prowess with a blade could do nothing to stop the ball that sent him crashing to the deck, his legs shot out from beneath him. Still, he made a valiant attempt to rise, only to have the butt of a pistol smashed into his head.

The battle ended quickly, almost as if all the fight left the crew upon seeing the big man fall. Lucien felt elation surge through him. It was done. His mission was almost complete.

The smell of blood clogged the air as those members of the *Revenger's* crew who weren't on board the *Swan* took up where their crewmates had left off by once again pulling the ship toward them, until with a loud groan the two hulls collided.

With a precision which spoke of years of practice, the pirate crew herded the survivors of the *Swan* to the rear of the ship. Their wounded leader was dragged in their wake.

"Well, Yer Grace," Tully said, scurrying over the combined rail of the two ships a few minutes later. "Seems we caught 'em fer ya."

Lucien eyed the wound on the pirate's arm. "It would seem so, Tully, though not without bloodshed."

"This?" He looked down at the wound. "'Tis nothing. A mere scratch." He waved his arm in dismissal, then said, "Are ya comin,' or do ya wait till we find the boy?"

"Lead on, my dear Tully. Lead on."

Tully smiled, exposing a row of rotted teeth, then turned away and hopped over the rail.

Lucien climbed over the splintered rail, too, dropping onto the deck of the *Swan* an instant later.

The smell of gunpowder hung heavy over the deck, mixing with the brackish odor of salt and fear. It was quiet, the only sounds the shuffle of footsteps as the crew of the *Revenger* searched the ship, and the steady rush of the ocean against the sides of the two vessels; the riggings and giant sheets added their own melody to the cacophony.

"Where's Scabbs?" Tully asked as he came to a halt by the rail. "There ya are. Take a few men and see to it that the remains of those sails are furled. An' I want every foot o' this ship searched. We're lookin' fer a boy. Bring 'im back ta me unharmed."

"Aye, sir."

The pirate captain pierced one of his men with a glare. "Where's the cap'n o' this vessel?"

"I 'ave 'im 'ere," answered a gruff voice.

Tully turned toward the back of the ship, taking two steps toward the person who'd spoken, then suddenly halting in his tracks. The reason became apparent when the big blonde man said, "It's been a long time, hasn't it, Tully?"

Lucien's brows rose, watching the play of emotions cross Tully's face: rage, disbelief, and finally, glee.

Slowly, Tully crossed to where the big man stood on one leg, blood dripping down his torn breeches. "Hang me from the gallows," he murmured, blinking his eye as if he still couldn't believe what he saw. "Yer supposed to be dead. Saw ya fall off the deck with me own good eye."

spied him standing a few feet away. Then she tensed again, no doubt at the sight of the blood and bruises that covered him.

His heart filled with unaccountable pride as he watched her change from intimidated kitten to ferocious lioness in the space of a heartbeat. Not for her a cowering attitude. Instead, her eyes filled with inner fire, her shoulders stiffened, and if she'd had claws, Garrick would have bet she'd have unfurled them and directed them at her captors.

She was magnificent.

Tully seemed captivated by her, too. His lone pupil narrowed as it observed the touch-me-if-you-dare tilt to her chin, her chest heaving beneath her green dress. The only time his attention wavered was to glance briefly at Beth, dismissing her immediately. When he turned back to Lucy, desire, fascination, and possessiveness shone from his eyes.

A growl emerged from Garrick's chest.

His captors must have heard it, for they suddenly pushed him to the deck. His head struck the boards with dizzying force, a spasm of pain shooting through his leg. A foot landed in his back to hold him down, though he struggled to get back up. Through half-closed eyes he saw Lucy charge in his direction, the only thing that stopped her the handful of hair Tully grabbed as she darted by. The sudden yank caused her to fall at his feet.

"What do you say, men. Should I take 'er right 'ere?"

Rage such as he'd never known burned through Garrick's blood. It doubled when one of Tully's henchmen came forward and quickly bound Lucy's wrists behind her back at Tully's nod. Garrick growled again. He burned to protect her, to smash his fists through Tully's eye.

He tried to calm down, telling himself he would do Lucy no good angry. He needed to think. Tully's "boss" was the dey of Algiers, a man who had personally put a price on his head, a price which a leech such as Tully wouldn't hesitate to cash in on. If he was separated from Lucy his test would be over.

A second man emerged from the doorway, shoving Tom in front of him. The boy fell to his knees. Quick as a cat he got back up, darted forward, aimed, then kicked the pirate right between the legs.

The unwary man toppled to his knees.

His fellow pirates erupted into loud guffaws. A huge brute of a man came forward and grabbed Tom by the back of his white lawn shirt, picking him up off the ground and shaking him as if he were an errant puppy.

"Let me go, ya bloody bastard." Tom railed his fist at his captor, but the man just held him further away, so that the boy's fists flailed the air like oars out of water.

One of Tully's henchmen pulled Lucy to her feet. She shot Garrick one last look of concern, then turned toward Tully, who stared at Tom intently.

"Is this the boy?" Tully asked Lucien.

Lucien came forward and stared into Tom's angry, yet frightened eyes. For the briefest instant something flashed across the duke's face, but then it was gone, replaced by triumph. "Aye."

Tully nodded and turned back to Lucy. With one sweeping glance his eyes darted over her shapely legs

"The Pendertons!" Lucy exclaimed, the reason he looked so familiar suddenly surfacing. Good heavens, the man was the Duke of Ravenwood!

At her words those black eyes darted to hers. "Very good, Miss Hartford." He bowed slightly.

"Al'ays amazes me 'ow you gents seem ta know each other," Tully mused.

"I'd sooner claim knowing the devil than knowing this man," Beth shot, darting a glance at Tully.

The duke flung right back, "Really? I'm flattered."

Beth's face turned a bright, vivid red. "Undoubtedly you enjoy watching this pig wreak havoc upon innocent people."

"'Ere now," Tully warned. Prinny shifted on his shoulder.

"I'd *enjoy* tying a sock around that pretty little mouth of yours."

"And I'd enjoy stuffing my foot into *yours*."

"You seem to be good at doing that to your *own* mouth."

Beth sprang up from the chair. "I would never have said what I said if you'd not dragged me onto the dance floor in such an ignominious fashion!"

Lucien took a step closer to her. "And I would never have done so if you had behaved like a *lady* in the first place."

"Why, *you!*" Beth fingers all but curled into claws.

"*Silence!*" Tully roared. Prinny squawked, shaking his wings in admonishment.

Beth jumped in fright.

"Sit down!" Tully ordered.

Beth sat.

"Yer Grace, if ya want the wench, ya have me blessings. No interest in 'er, anyway."

Ravenwood quirked a sardonic brow in Beth's direction before saying, "Rest assured, my friend. Much as I would love to teach her a lesson for calling me a . . ." He pasted a politely questioning look on his face, a look which was anything but gentlemanlike. "What was it you called me?"

"Murdering whoremonger," Beth announced proudly.

"Ahh, yes. How could I have forgotten? A murdering whoremonger. I'd far rather leave her to her own charming devices."

"It turned out to be true," Beth snapped.

"Did it?" he asked, leveling her with a freezing glare.

"Ain't nothin' wrong with a man murderin' his brother if'n he finds 'im in the arms of 'is mistress," Tully said into the silence which followed. "I'd do the same." He shot Lucy a look of warning which was all the more chilling for its implied meaning.

"Sink your pisser, get a blister," Prinny announced.

Lucy stiffened. Tully did, too, but then he opened his big, cavernous mouth and let out a guffaw. In vain she tried to keep the revulsion from her eyes as she spied his rotted teeth, but apparently she was unsuccessful, for Tully's laughter died.

His eyelid lowered ominously as he came forward, Prinny fluttering his wings as he tried to keep his balance. When the pirate rounded the end of the table, Lucy looked at him head-on. Not once did she flinch, not even when he was close enough to reach out and give her hair a painful tug.

His smile grew possessed by pure, unadulterated evil, exposing huge gaps in his teeth nearly as black as his soul. "Yer gonna enjoy it when I sinks it inta ya."

She opened her mouth to tell him that she'd sink a knife into him before she allowed him to touch her when, suddenly, Prinny lifted his tail. Her eyes widened. The bird hunched his back. She groaned.

A huge, white-and-green piece of excrement landed on the pirate's shoulder.

The duke gave a snort of laughter. Beth choked. Lucy covered her mouth with her hand.

"Arrrgh," Tully bellowed, clutching for the bird. Prinny launched himself off the pirate's shoulder and landed on the back of a chair near the duke and the servant.

"Ahhhh, ha ha ha ha ha ha," the bird cried out, his human-sounding laughter filling the cabin. Lucy groaned again. "Ahhhhhh, ha ha ha ha ha ha."

"Mousad!"

"Yes, sahib."

"Kill that damn bird."

"No," Lucy cried, shooting up from her chair.

Tully pushed her back down. "Tell cook ta stuff it fer dinner tonight."

"You tell him that and I'll have *you* for dinner," Lucy snapped.

"That can be arranged," the pirate leered.

But the servant didn't move. He stood, his black eyes unblinking as he stared at his master.

Tully turned back to him with an impatient stare. "Well, what are ya waitin' fer? Grab the damn bird."

The dark-skinned man's gaze didn't waver. "Perhaps sahib has forgotten?"

Tully stiffened in anger. "Fergotten? Fergotten what?"

"The cook is dead, sahib."

"Dead?" Tully roared. "Whadda ya mean dead?"

"I believe," the duke interjected, "what Mousad is referring to is your order to have the cook fed to the sharks last night, in the hopes that he would . . . let's see, how did you put it? Ahh, yes, I have it. In the hopes that he would make a better meal than those he served."

Ravenwood turned toward the black servant. "Am I correct, Mousad?"

Lucy's brows rose, her eyes darting from the servant, to Prinny, to the duke, to Tully, then back to Mousad again, who bowed to his master. "His Grace is most correct."

Her gaze swung back to Tully, who scratched his head in a monkeylike confusion. "I did?"

"Yes, sahib."

"Hmph," Tully mused, his brow knitted in confusion. "Seems maybe I recall now, though the drink clouds me memory a bit. The soup were cold, weren't it?"

"Yes, sahib."

Tully shrugged, then turned toward the duke and winked at him. "Guess that'll teach 'im, eh?"

He started guffawing again, the duke looking him up and down as if he were a rare and bizarre species of animal.

Tully's laughter faded when the duke failed to find as much amusement in the situation as he apparently did. He turned back to his servant. "Find another crew member to take his place, *then* cook the bird."

"You'll not cook my bird," Lucy huffed, rising from her chair again. Tully shoved her back down. She landed on her rear with a teeth-thunking clunk.

Mousad didn't meet his master's eyes as he replied, "I have tried, sahib, but no one will take the job."

"Won't take the job! Why in Blackbeard's name not?"

"If I may interject again?" the duke asked as he fiddled with the cuffs of his sleeve; he looked ... well, bored. "Perhaps their reluctance has something to do with the fate of your last three cooks?"

Tully considered his words, his one brow lifting into an arch. "Aye. Could be yer right." But his consternation faded. "No matter. The women 'ere can cook fer us till we get inta port."

"I'll not cook my own pet!"

Tully reached out a grubby, scarred paw to tilt her chin up. "You'll cook whatever I tell ya to, lassie."

"No, I will not."

His grip tightened, painfully so. "If ya please me, I may take it easier on ya tonight, and if ya don't, I'll make sure ya makes it up ta me in other ways instead o' throwin' ya overboard."

He chuckled softly, one of his fingers stroking her chin, his skin so callous it felt like stone.

Lucy was not amused.

17

As it turned out, Mousad was never able to catch Prinny, Tully having pulled out his pistol to shoot the bird before the duke stopped him and offered to buy Lucy's pet from him. Lucy had no time to be grateful, for in the next instant she and Beth had been hauled off to cook for the hungry crew. The result was that now they both stood over a boiling pot of . . . something.

She could see nothing beyond the yellow-orange glow, the deck of the *Revenger* so dark the inky blackness was broken only by the light of the fire. But she could feel the crew's lecherous and lascivious glances as they went about their work. It made her feel as if she were standing in a pit of snakes.

Both she and Beth stood near the center of the ship loosely termed the "galley." Really, the only thing which gave it the appearance of such was the stove brought up from below. Certainly the smells hanging in the air didn't give rise to the notion. No, the combined odor of beef broth and dank timbers brought to mind the smell of Tully's breath and cow pastures instead of fine dining.

"Are you almost done?"

Lucy turned to Beth, ignoring the hulking presence of Mousad, whose dark skin was nearly indistinguishable from the night air surrounding him. She wrinkled her nose. "I'm not sure. Would you like to taste it and find out?"

Beth shook her head emphatically. "No."

Lucy looked back at the pot of stew, surveying it with a dubious glare. "I don't blame you." She sighed, then dipped her wooden spoon into the boiling contents. A moment later she grimaced in distaste. It was horrible. Worse than horrible, it was ghastly.

"H-how does it taste?"

Lucy frowned. "Like the insides of Garrick's boots." The mention of Garrick's name made her heart thump painfully. Where was he? Was he all right? And what about Tom? Was he alive?

"Perhaps if sahib adds some vegetables?"

The voice, coming unexpectedly out of the darkness, startled both girls. Lucy swung around to face Mousad.

"I . . . ? Vegetables?" she asked.

"It is common to add such things, is it not?"

Beth took a small step in Lucy's direction, then leaned toward her ear. "He's correct, Lucy," she whispered. "I distinctly recall seeing vegetables in soup before."

Lucy pushed her lips out in thought, considering for a moment. "And where would I get such items?"

"From the hold below, sahib. They were loaded from your ship to ours."

That must have been before they'd sunk it, Lucy thought, a depression settling over her nearly as black as the cloudless sky above. Images of Garrick's bruised and battered face flashed through her mind. As best she could, she shoved them aside. "Will you show me?"

"As you wish, sahib," the giant answered. He turned, grabbing a lantern hooked conveniently to the side of the stove and headed toward a dark rectangle which obviously led below.

Less then five minutes later they stood in a room so black the darkness outside the glow of the lantern was like a physical presence, thick and heavy. The acrid stench of moldering vegetation rose up around them, that and stagnant seawater; the smell nearly gagged her. Bags and an odd assortment of bric-a-brac lay about, the ribs of the ship curving around them like the skeleton of a whale long since stripped of its flesh. Lucy shivered and wrapped her arms around herself, though it was far from cold in the humid hold.

"I'm scared." Beth murmured softly.

"I know, Beth. But we'll be all right. I'll think of something."

A pause, and then, "I'm not sure if that reassures me or terrifies me."

"It better reassure you because I'm your only hope."

"Now *that* terrifies me."

Lucy shook her head. If Beth was up to sarcasm, she must not be *that* scared. She watched her friend head toward bags of produce with narrowed eyes, all the while reviewing her options. She needed a plan, she thought desperately, and a good one if she were to succeed.

Think, Lucy, she ordered her sluggish mind. *There has to be a way out of this.*

She had just thrown out the notion of pummeling Mousad with some well-aimed potatoes when the subject of her thought said, "Not that one, sahib," in a deep rumble.

Lucy started, Mousad's voice erupting so suddenly out of the darkness she dropped what she had just blindly grabbed from one of the bags. A quick survey revealed the strangest vegetable she'd ever seen. It looked like a carrot, but it was white and far longer than an average carrot. At least she thought it was white, but it was hard to tell in the darkened hold.

"What is it?" The words escaped her mouth before she realized how ridiculous it was to ask one's captor what kind of vegetation one had held in one's hand, especially when one was contemplating how to knock that same captor senseless with said vegetation.

Mousad seemed impervious. "That is dandelion root, sahib."

Her brows drew together in surprise. "Is it edible?" She caught Beth's glance. Her friend was shaking her head at her in an obvious attempt to tell her, without words, that she should keep quiet.

Mousad nodded. "Though I would not recommend it, sahib."

"Why not?" she asked, ignoring Beth's frown, the servant having piqued her curiosity.

"It is for loosening one's bowels, sahib."

"Bowels?"

"Yes. A herb of great power."

Lucy's eyebrows rose. *Good heavens*, she thought. She'd nearly brought new meaning to the term "poopdeck." Her breath caught, the import of what she held in her hand suddenly sinking in.

Mousad merely eyed her with an unfathomable look. She darted a glance down at the root, then back at Mousad again before reluctantly turning away.

Telling herself to be patient, she busied herself grabbing assorted vegetables from other bags, all the while peeking sideways glances at Mousad. But it was fully five minutes later before he turned away from her. Not wasting a second, she quickly scooped up some dandelion root, then grabbed a few more in the off chance she didn't have enough.

"You will need many more than that if you wish to infect the entire crew, sahib."

Lucy jumped, dread causing her stomach to clench as if she'd eaten some of the root herself; fear sent her pulse rate skittering out of control. Slowly she turned and faced her captor. "I . . . I . . . I don't know what you're talking about. There's nothing in my pouch but carrots and . . . and onions and such."

The servant's lips tilted into an ever so patient smile. Lucy wondered at it for half a second before he said, "I am speaking of the root you put in your pouch, sahib."

"What root?" Lucy asked, giving him what she hoped was an innocent grin. "I didn't put any root in here."

Still, she was unable to keep her eyes from widening as Mousad strode forward, reached into her pouch, and pulled out a long, thin, white object.

"Ohhh, that root."

Mousad smiled, though Lucy didn't find the situation the least bit funny. Not the least little bit.

"Yes, sahib. That root."

They stared at each other for a long, endless moment until Lucy couldn't take it a moment longer. "Please," she said frantically, her shoulders slumping. "Please don't tell Tully."

"Lucy, what have you done?" Beth asked, fear sharpening her voice into a shrill yell.

Lucy ignored her as she stared up at Mousad.

"Sahib misunderstands. I have no intention of telling my master."

Lucy couldn't believe her ears. And when Mousad's hulking form moved alongside of her, and then he began to scoop more of the root into her pouch, her mouth dropped open. She glanced at Beth, who looked equally incredulous.

"W-what are you doing?" she finally managed to choke out.

"I am helping you, sahib."

"But . . . why?"

He straightened from his task and held out his wrists; the metal bands gleaming around them were almost as bright as his smile. "I have much to gain by your success, sahib."

Lucy watched with apprehensive eyes as Tully took a hesitant sip of the brownish liquid.

They all sat around the table, a parody of a dinner party. Beth sat to her left, the duke across from her.

Tully hunched over in his chair like an old crone directly opposite Lucy.

The knob of the pirate's throat bobbed up and down as he swallowed. A ghostly trace of steam cycloned up from the bowl and toward the skull archway above, almost as if pulled by invisible, evil forces.

Lucy had to blink, she stared at the pirate captain so hard, then clenched her hands in her lap in an effort to contain her nervousness. Forcing her expression to be blank as possible, she watched Tully take another slurping sip. Her own throat swallowed reflexively along with him.

Tully looked up, catching her staring at him intently. "It'll do," he announced in a gravely voice.

That was the cue for Mousad to begin serving. The duke, who sat at Tully's left, was the first, his presence the only thing in the room that didn't clash with the elegance of the table setting Tully had managed to unearth from God knows where. Mousad served her next, then Beth, who looked as if she were about to expire on the spot; her black hair had escaped in long hanks from her chignon, and her blue eyes were filled with fear.

Lucy gave her a tentative smile before glancing down at her food. When she looked back up at Tully, he smacked his lips together.

She tried not to gag as she made a great pretense of eating.

"Pour some wine, Mousad," Tully ordered, startling Lucy into dropping her spoon. It clattered into her bowl, sending a shower of brown spots onto her dress.

"Excuse me," she mumbled.

"Quite all right, Miss Hartford," the duke announced. Lucy looked up, surprised at the reassuring smile the duke sent her. "The stew is excellent."

Her mouth dropped open, no sound escaping until she mustered the courage to say, "Thank you," in a small voice. For the first time she wondered if perhaps he wasn't such a villain. Indeed, he'd saved her bird, too, though she had no idea where her pet had gone. But at least he wasn't floating belly-up in a cauldron of stew, she thought.

They continued to eat in silence, or in Lucy and Beth's case, pretend to eat, but much to Lucy's frustration there was no sign the root was working. Tully still looked as healthy as a horse on its way to Newmarket. When he was done, all he did was lean back in his chair in an attitude of extreme relaxation, pat his over-large belly, then open his mouth to release a great gale of a belch. Lucy concealed her revulsion only with the grimmest restraint.

"Well, Yer Grace," he said, "now that we've had our evenin' victuals, I fancy watching Wolf hang from the gallows fer entertainment. Whadda ya say?"

Lucy gasped.

Tully darted her a glance, then smirked. "Don't ya like me idea, me lady?"

No, she did not. Furious, she stiffened in her chair, knowing she should probably keep control of her temper, but she was tired of feeling helpless, of Tully's taunts, and of trying to ignore his lecherous stares. "I'll kill you first."

Tully merely opened his nightmare of a mouth and guffawed. "Will ya now?" he chortled, spit and chunks of soup flying out like a miniature hailstorm. "I'd thought ya'd be glad ta be rid o' him. I'd wager a little mite like you fair gets crushed every time 'e pumps ya." He looked at the duke, paused for a moment, then let out another burst of cackling laughter, slapping the table for added effect.

Lucy watched his evil, complacent face for half a second before something inside her snapped. Everything converged on her at once: their capture, Garrick's beating, the fear of what was to become of them. Enraged, she picked up her soup bowl and flung it at his stupid, crater-filled face.

She had the satisfaction of seeing his expression change to one of surprise just before the soup connected with a satisfying *splat*, the bowl clattering to the floor.

For seconds the pirate just sat there, bits of potatoes, carrots, and beef clinging to his face like mud. But then he gave an earsplitting bellow of rage, swiped one grubby paw over his face, and charged to his feet.

Lucy froze, torn between throwing something else at him and darting for the door. She glanced at the room's other two occupants. Beth stared at her in horror, the duke looked amused.

Lucy glanced back in time to see Tully's hand whip out to capture her chin in a hard, punishing grip, forcing her gaze upward.

"Let her go," Beth cried.

Tully leaned toward Lucy. His black eye gleamed evilly as he brought his nose within inches of hers. His rank-smelling breath filled the air in a putrid cloud and made her gag.

"Ya'll pay fer that," he said softly.

Lucy's heart beat so loudly, she almost missed his words. "I . . . I think not."

His grip tightened. He pushed his mashed nose closer to hers. "I'll enjoy tamin' ya in bed."

"Never," she squeaked.

He released a bark of laughter.

Lucy jerked her chin out of Tully's grasp and turned her head away, trying hard not to breathe. "Too much onion," she wheezed.

Abruptly, Tully's laughter faded; his hand streaked out to capture her chin again, jerking her face toward his. "I'm lookin' forward to tamin' that tongue o' yers, too." As if in anticipation, his tongue snaked out to wet his lips.

Lucy decided, nothing ventured nothing gained. "And I'm looking forward to cutting *yours* from your head. And . . . and other body parts, too," she added before she lost her nerve.

He chuckled nastily and straightened, releasing her chin with a painful flick. "Think ya could hack off somethin' that big?"

Lucy slowly looked toward his crotch and said, "I've seen splinters that were bigger."

She started as the duke let out a shout of laughter. Tully didn't look amused at all. He leaned toward her, his breath touching her with its foulness. "That tongue o' yers is sharp, but we'll see 'ow much fight ya have left in ya after watchin' yer lover hang from a rope."

"You'd think they'd feed us more'n that little scrap o' bread. Me dinner pail's still rattlin'."

"I'd be thankful they remembered to feed us at all, Tom, though I'd wager it was you they were concerned with most."

"Well, if they was tryin' ta impress me with their hospi-toe-tality, they gots a long ways ta go."

Garrick smiled grimly in the dark hold where he and Tom and the rest of the *Swan's* crew were being held. Dankness surrounded them—it was in the air, on the floor beneath them, and seeping into Garrick's soul. He could still see Lucy's face and the terrified look in her eyes as she was dragged off to Tully's cabin.

He thought back to the time they'd shared, of her smiles, her laughter, and from that came the notion that perhaps if he hadn't been so enchanted by that smile, none of this would have happened.

He frowned. Once there, the idea haunted him and teased his conscience, making him vow to escape and save her.

"I think I 'ear footsteps again," Calico said.

The rest of the *Swan's* crew, all twelve of them, broke into murmurings which quickly grew silent when the door rattled, then was shoved open; a torch momentarily blinded them all. When Garrick held his hands out before him, the chains which bound his wrists rattled and the movement sent a spasm of pain through his wounded knee.

"Which one is 'e?" asked a small-framed man with the evil grin of a felon.

"The big one," answered his companion, a wrinkle-faced brute with a red scarf tied around his head and a gold hoop hanging from his left nostril.

"*Saay*, ain't that painful?" Tom asked, spying the adornment.

The brute's response was to glare down at him. The smaller pirate came forward, a pistol held out in front of him. "I've orders ta bring ya above," he said to Garrick. "If ya give us any trouble, I'm ta kill one o' your crew, starting with that one." He pointed his long-barreled pistol at Calico.

Garrick didn't say a word as the pirate unlocked the chains around his wrists, tied his wrists, then motioned with his pistol for him to get to his feet.

"Garrick!" cried a desperate voice when they reached the main deck.

Garrick turned, blinking against the brightness of the deck. Lucy streaked toward him, one of the crew at her heels. Her hair streamed out behind her like a ruby standard. He winced as she slammed into his bruised chest. When she tilted her head back, there was fear in her eyes, more fear than he'd ever thought possible for such a brave and courageous woman.

"Garrick," she cried as she was pulled away. "Oh, Garrick, I thought you dead."

"Now ain't that touchin'," Tully said, using her hair to jerk her against him.

Garrick growled, rage such as he'd never felt before filling his soul. "If you touch her, Tully, you're a dead man."

"Oooh, I'm frightened, yer lordship. 'Specially seein' as how yer 'ands be tied."

"I'll use more than my hands by the time I'm through with you."

"Like ta see ya try, Wolf."

Garrick wanted to try. Now. The fear in Lucy's eyes was doing strange things to his insides. But he knew if he were to vent to his rage, Tully wouldn't hesitate to use the pistol aimed at his heart. The feeling of helplessness enraged him even further.

Tully, the bloody bastard, knew he had the upper hand. The expression on his face was one of a man who intended to enjoy every minute of his revenge. "What's the matter, Wolf? Afraid ta fight?" he taunted.

Lucy squirmed, swiped hair from her face and exposed aqua eyes filled with as much animosity as Garrick felt. "He's not afraid of you ... you ... you ... *walking soup bowl!*"

Tully's complacent expression vanished, replaced by one of pure nastiness. "Gonna let you lick it off a me ta'night, lovey."

Lucy screeched, her hands clenched into fists. Tully's grip on her hair tightened, holding her immobile.

"Don't provoke him, Lucy."

"But, Garrick, I—"

Tully jerked her again. "Listen to 'im, woman, afore I fetch yer friend Beth an' string 'er up, too."

"If you harm either of them, Tully ..." Garrick warned.

"Eh?" Tully asked, darting him a glance. "What're ya goin' ta do, Wolf, haunt me from the grave?" He chuckled. The sound turned into a gasp when Lucy's elbow slammed into his gut.

"*I'll* haunt you from the grave, you *worm*."

Tully, apparently, had had enough. He turned to the man who stood by his side. "Where's Scabbs?"

The man looked as if he was standing on shards of glass as he answered, "He's, ahh, he's sick, cap'n."

"Sick!" Tully boomed.

"Aye, cap'n. There's a few o' us here who don't feel too well."

"Argh, well, pussies be the lot o' ya. You there," he called to one of his men. "Get over here an' hold the wench." He thrust Lucy at the man, then turned toward Garrick.

"Well, Wolf, say good-bye to yer woman." He motioned for Garrick to be guided to the rope by two burly looking men.

Garrick waited until they were an arm's length away before he sprung into action. In a move which he'd perfected over the years, he ignored the pain in his leg and spun on one heel, kicking the pistol from Tully's hand. Lucy yelped, then pulled free from Tully's grasp. The pistol fired harmlessly into the air.

Arms encircled him from behind, but Garrick thrust an elbow into his assailant's gut. A whoosh of air was released, and the arms around him slackened. Garrick spun around, using one of his legs to kick the legs out from beneath his enemy. The man cursed as he fell to the deck with a grunt. Garrick's booted heel silenced him. Another man came out of the darkness to take up where his crewmate had left off. A quick, sharp kick to the man's gut left him gasping for air.

"Garrick!" Lucy screamed.

Garrick whirled.

Tully and Lucy were engaged in a battle over a pistol Tully had had tucked in his belt. Lucy's hands were clasped around his wrist as she tried to ward him off from aiming the weapon at his head.

Garrick charged. Hands reached out and grabbed him. Pain sent sharp spasms of fire through his insides and his knee as his assailant knocked him off balance and threw him to the deck. The pirate landed on top of him. For a second he couldn't breathe, his enemy's leering face grinned evilly from atop him, a pistol aimed at his head.

And then he was gone.

His assailant was jerked off of him and sent careening into a mast. The pirate's head connected with a thud, then his body collapsed into a heap.

Stunned, Garrick looked up and into the face of a man so black, his teeth were the only thing visible against the backdrop of stars. He bent down and helped him to his feet.

"Help your woman, sahib. I will go help her friend."

Garrick didn't waste a second. He charged at Tully, his hands reaching for his throat. Tully shot him a look of surprise which turned to shock when Garrick jerked the pistol from his grasp.

"Step away, Lucy."

Lucy nodded, her chest heaving from her struggles. She stepped back, but a hand materialized out of the darkness and pulled her against him. A gleaming knife was held to her throat.

"Let the cap'n go," a man said. He jerked Lucy up against him, moving the knife up her neck further. Lucy tilted her chin to avoid contact with the blade.

"Scabbs! Bless yer eyes. A promotion fer you, it is." Tully chuckled nastily, his face filled with smugness as he turned to Garrick. "Drop the pistol or yer woman dies."

Hope seeped out of Garrick like water through a sieve.

"I think not, Tully."

Every head swiveled in the direction of the feminine voice.

"Beth!" cried Lucy.

Beth stepped from the darkness, the pistol she held out in front of her shaking like tree leaves in a gale as she pointed it at Lucy's captor.

18

"Let go of her, you cur!" Beth ordered.

"Beth, oh, Beth," cried Lucy in delight. "I do believe I could kiss you."

"Release her," Beth ordered again when Lucy's captor failed to comply. She even went so far as to take a threatening step toward him. "If you don't release her, I warn you I shall blow a hole in your stomach."

"No," the man gasped, and his face seemed to turn green in the lantern light. "Not me stomach."

"Scabbs!" Tully took a step. "Damn yer eyes, Scabbs," Tully yelled, "if ya let 'er go I'll rip yer bloody throat out."

"Sorry, cap'n," Scabbs gasped just before he dropped to the deck, knife and all. Within seconds he was writhing on the ground, his arms wrapped around his abdomen, moaning in pain.

"Good heavens." Lucy cried.

"It's working," said Beth in equal astonishment.

"*What's* working!" Tully roared.

"We poisoned your soup," Lucy said primly. "You should all be dead by morning."

Beth stifled a laugh; Lucy heard it and began her own soft chuckles. It was a lie, but she wasn't about to tell Tully that. Let the worm wallow in fear. By the time he realized she'd not told him the truth, he'd be wallowing in something else.

"You poisoned the soup?" Garrick asked.

They both nodded.

"How?"

"Tully made the mistake of asking Lucy to cook," Beth answered.

"Bloody whores!" Tully announced. "Is that where all me men are?" He stomped his feet in childish frustration. "I should'a known better than ta let a red 'aired witch like ya onta me ship." He turned to Beth. "An' you! No better than her, ya are. A curse on ya. Ya hear! A curse on ya—"

"Silence!" Garrick roared, stepping forward and poking the nose of the pistol into Tully's ribs. He turned to Lucy. "What kind of poison did you use?"

Her grin turned into a full-fledged smile. "Dandelion root."

Garrick nodded, obviously familiar with the herb. "Lucy, hand me that line over there."

"Here, sahib."

Lucy whirled toward the voice. "Mousad!" she cried, "where have you been?"

"Detaining the crew, sahib." He held up the rope he had clutched in his left hand.

"Mousad! Damn yer black hide! Was it you what showed 'em 'ow to poison that soup?"

Mousad smiled. "It was, sahib." He bowed low and when he straightened, amusement filled his chocolate-colored eyes.

The words seemed to be Tully's undoing. His face grew positively blotchy. His eye patch looked as if it were about to pop from his head.

"Ya bloody whoremongers. Ya bloody *buggerin'* *whoremongers*! I'll get even with ya. If it's the last thing I do, I'll get even with ya . . . with *all* o' ya!"

Lucy didn't even see Mousad draw his fist back, but she heard it connect with a satisfying splat. Tully slumped to the deck.

Mousad's startling white smile grew. "I have been longing to do that for a great while," he observed.

Lucy smiled, feeling her heart bloom with happiness. She had done it. By God, for the first time in her life, one of her plans had gone flawlessly. She rushed forward, straight into Garrick's arms.

She felt him tense and thought he might have patted her back, but in the next instant he pushed her away. Lucy felt confusion stampede through her.

"Garrick, what—"

"Find me Ravenwood," he called to Mousad, turning away from her without a backward glance. Her last sight of him was of his white-clad back as it disappeared into the darkness.

Hours later, Garrick headed to Tully's appropriated cabin, his bones heavy with exhaustion, yet filled with an elation that made his steps light.

He'd found the evidence he needed to prove the countess guilty. Letters. At least ten of them, all of them addressed to the duke and all of them asking for his help in taking care of her "problem." And though the boy wasn't mentioned by name, the letters, combined with the duke's testimony, should be enough to convince the earl.

He smiled grimly. And the duke *would* testify. If he didn't, Garrick would deliver the bastard to the magistrate himself. And if it was a choice between swinging from the gallows for engaging in pirating or cooperating with Garrick, there was little doubt the duke would chose to cooperate to save his own miserable hide.

Of course, he would have liked to have killed the bloody bastard, but he'd taken great delight in pitching Tully and his crew overboard in his place. Lucy—his brave, courageous, incredible Lucy—had cheered from the rail as they were dropped into the ocean one by one.

Garrick's smile spread. Little hoyden. She was as fearless as she was clever and never had he met a woman more suited to his taste.

But he couldn't have her.

He clenched the handle on Tully's cabin door. The thought rose bile in his throat.

Blindly, he stepped inside the musty-smelling cabin. A huge table stood before him. He went around it, wanting only to duck beneath the skull archway and strip away his dirty clothes and try to decipher why he felt so bloody odd when he thought of Lucy.

"So you're going back to London?"

Garrick jerked around.

"And here I thought you might not succeed. I'm glad to see I was wrong."

Garrick's eyes narrowed. The voice belonged to Arlan, no doubt of it, but where was he?

"Over here."

Garrick scanned the interior of the cabin, his gaze landing on the table.

"Like my new outfit?" Arlan asked, ruffling his gray feathers, his claws anchoring him to the back of a chair.

Garrick blinked, then opened his eyes. The bird was still there.

"Birds are one of the few earthly forms guidance counselors are allowed to inhabit," Arlan explained. "Usually we choose doves, but I wasn't in the mood for cooing."

Garrick shook his head. If he'd been less exhausted he could have come up with some sarcastic remark. Just now he didn't feel like it. "What do you want?" he asked instead.

Arlan sidestepped a few paces, his talons click-click-clicking on the wood. "I'm here to give you a warning, Garrick." The words were uttered in a serious tone; unfortunately, the effect was spoiled by his head tilting to the left. Arlan raised a claw and tilted it back. "Hate when that happens. Braaah." A wing rose to cover his beak. "That, too."

"Warning? About what?" But he knew. Bloody hell.

Arlan turned so one eye faced him. "There. Now I can see. I'm here to warn you about your feelings for Lucy."

"I have no feelings for her."

Arlan squawked, his wings beating like a bird of

prey's. "Wrong, wrong, wrong," he cried when he'd gained control of himself. He pointed a wing tip at Garrick. "The Chief knows these things, Garrick, you can't lie. That's why He sent me. He wanted me to talk to you."

"Very well, you've talked. Now leave."

"I'm not leav—braaahh—" Arlan shook his head. His feathered chest expanded with an exasperated breath. "I'm not leaving until I've said what I've come here to say."

"Then say it."

"Fine. I will. Goodness, sometimes I wish I weren't an angel. Calling you a horribly crude word would feel good right now." He wagged a wing at him. "Don't try to deny it, Garrick. We know you're developing feelings for the girl."

"I am not," Garrick spat out, "developing feelings for her."

"Are too."

"Ridiculous."

"*Ridiculous?*" Arlan asked. "*I'm* not the one talking to a bird."

Garrick narrowed his eyes.

"Anyway, you didn't let me finish. We know you're growing fond of her." Arlan held up a wing. "Don't interrupt. Just let me finish. You're down to fifteen days—"

"Fifteen days?" Garrick protested.

"Yes. Now, I don't see any problem with restoring the boy to his rightful place in that amount of time. But, Garrick—and this what I came down here to tell you—if you don't watch yourself, you might find yourself distracted by Lucy. You can't afford to be distracted right now. Ignore your earthly feelings. Do what you came here to do, nothing more. And I mean *nothing*."

Garrick crossed his arms in front of him, refusing to say a word.

"Keep your distance from her. Don't let her near unless you absolutely have to. And above all, *don't kiss her again*." Arlan punctuated the end of his sentence with a pause.

"Is that all?" Garrick asked.

"Yes."

"Good. Leave."

Arlan wagged a wing tip at him. "I'll leave, Garrick, but I'm telling you to be careful. Lucy has a long life ahead of her. You don't. It's best you remember that she's fated for someone else."

Fated for someone else.

The words still echoed in his ears when a knock sounded on his cabin door not two minutes later.

"Garrick?" a familiar, tentative voice called.

Lucy. Ah, God, Lucy.

"Garrick, are you there?"

He almost didn't answer. He almost took the coward's way out, but he knew what he must do; delaying it would only cause more pain in the end.

Still, his feet felt heavy as he walked toward the door, and when he reached for the handle, his hand shook. He stared at his fingers for a moment before clenching them, then forced them to unfold and open the door.

"Garrick," she gushed, working through the crack and throwing herself in his arms. "Oh, Garrick, I thought you might be angry with me."

It was harder than he thought. Automatically, his hands lifted to stroke her back, only to fall to his sides. He clenched his eyes closed, knowing what he must do, hating to do so.

"Garrick, whatever is wrong?"

He opened his eyes. Lucy stared up at him, concern clouding her features. She worried her bottom lip.

"Lucy," he moaned. What to say? What to tell her? "You must leave."

A red brow arched. "Leave? Why?"

Because if she didn't, he knew he'd pull her into his arms and do something they'd both regret; because with every breath he took it grew harder to resist her; because, God help him, he loved her more than he thought it possible to love a woman.

"Because I need to plot a course to London."

Her face cleared. She smiled. "May I help?"

"No!" And if the word was a bit more strident than he'd meant to make it, so much the better. He watched as her eyes grew wide. Immediately, he wanted to apologize, but he didn't. If nothing else, his stay in the hold had made him realize how little time he had left. He would be gone soon, and the sooner he started preparing Lucy for that moment, the easier it would be on her.

"Lucy, please understand," he said, the confusion and hurt in her eyes was nearly his undoing. "I need to concentrate."

To his surprise, her face cleared almost instantly. He had no idea why, but he knew it most likely boded ill for him.

"So I distract you, do I?" she asked, taking a step toward him.

Damn, Garrick thought, *she* would *take it the wrong way*. He backed up, nearly groaning when her hips took on a seductive sway as she stalked him toward the bed. "Lucy, don't."

Her lips tilted in amusement. "Why, Garrick, are you afraid of me?"

Yes, he silently answered. God, yes, he was afraid of her, of how much it would hurt to leave the thoroughly engaging woman who was only inches away from him now, her sweet smell rising up to excite his senses. She was everything he'd wanted and more.

Her hand rose. He released a breath he hadn't known he'd been holding when she gently reached out and shoved a lock of his hair away from his face. But instead of her arm dropping back to her side, she playfully drew a finger down his cheek until she found his lips, her touch as light as a wisp of air. Gently, suggestively, she encircled his mouth with a soft finger. Their eyes met, hers blazing with an inner fire which he longed to be scorched by. "Lucy, I mean what I say."

"Oh, I don't doubt that you do," she whispered with a sly look. "But will you be able to stop wanting to touch me? *That* is another question entirely."

"You don't understand," he answered, knowing what he must do, hating to do it.

"Garrick," she squeaked as he reached down, scooped her up, and tossed her over his shoulder. She giggled, then said, "Now this is more like it." But her laughter slowly faded when, instead of turning toward the bed, he strode toward the door.

"Garrick—" she warned, obviously surmising his intent.

He ignored her and ducked under the skull archway, made his way around a chair, then came to a halt before the battle-scarred door. She started to struggle in earnest when he took a firmer grip on her behind and reached for the handle.

"Garrick, I warn you. I'll not forgive you for this."

The light spilling out from the open door allowed Garrick a perfect glimpse of Lucy's startled and furious gaze as he gently set her outside his door. Before she had a chance to dart to her feet, he turned and strode back to his cabin, slamming the oak door in her face.

It was without a doubt the hardest thing he'd ever had to do.

19

"Lucy, you are absolutely, positively the most insane person it has ever been my misfortune to know," Beth announced the next afternoon. The sun, which was beginning its descent into the horizon, cast a crimson glow over the ship, turning Beth's blue dress a vivid shade of purple which suited her pale complexion to perfection.

Lucy shrugged, ignoring the comment. How could she explain to Beth, who had been so very verbal in her disapproval of her behavior, that she was terrified that once they hit dry land, Garrick would run in the other direction? He had barely acknowledged her presence since their time in his cabin. She wasn't sure what she'd done to anger him so, but suddenly she was terrified that if she didn't seize this chance to find out, she might never get another opportunity.

"I'm doing this, Beth. And you can't stop me."

Beth's hopeful look faded. She nodded, then glanced around the deck furtively, as if searching for someone else to help convince her friend. But Lucy had taken great pains in timing the exact moment to strike. Currently, Garrick was engaged in holding the wheel; the only way he'd be able to see them was if he suddenly developed the power to see through wood, for he stood in a location not visible from where they were. The rest of the crew was engaged in their duties, the men far too busy sailing a ship twice the size of the *Swan*, with half the crew, to pay them much heed.

"You can't stop me, Beth. He needs me. I know he does. What's more I know he *wants* me."

Beth colored. "I do not even want to know how you know that."

"Practice."

Beth held up her hands. "I don't want to know, Lucy."

"And the book," Lucy added. "You should study the book, too. Might come in handy one day."

"The only book I shall study is how to pick smarter friends."

"And the next book I shall study is how to pick *supportive* friends."

Beth placed her hands on her hips. Lucy tilted her nose in the air.

"You're quite mad."

"About Garrick, yes."

"And what if he boots you out?"

"He won't."

"You hope."

"I know."

Beth released an exasperated sigh. Lucy ignored her, flicking her thick braid over her right shoulder and checking to ensure the knot around the rail was tight. The wind might pose a bit of a problem, she thought, but she didn't think it would jostle her around too much. Thank God the weather was fine, for she didn't fancy lowering herself down the back of a ship in surging seas.

"And what if you fall?" Beth refused to give up.

Lucy shrugged again, making sure the rope around her waist was tight. "I won't fall, Beth. And if I do, just tell Garrick to turn the ship around and fetch me."

"Fat lot, that."

Lucy looked up, and couldn't help but smile.

Beth saw it and glowered. "What am I supposed to do?" She pretended to tap an invisible person. "Excuse me, Garrick?" she asked, pasting a prim look on her face. "Lucy fell into the ocean while trying to sneak into your cabin so she could seduce you." She pointed with her thumb over the railing. "She's the bobbing head with the shark fin next to it."

Lucy snorted in laughter, then said, "Really, Beth. Don't be melodramatic. I've scaled worse than this at boarding school."

"Yes, but I hardly think this compares to sliding down a drainpipe!"

"Shhh. It won't take but a minute. And all you need do is hand me that grappling hook so I can break the glass, then lower me my pails of water."

Beth placed her hand against her forehead and closed her eyes. "If I were smart, what I would *do* is run to Garrick and tell him what you plan," she mumbled.

"Who said you were smart?"

Beth's eyes snapped open. "That does it! I'm leaving."

"No, Beth, don't." Lucy grabbed her friend by the sleeve and nudged her back around. "I was only poking fun. You know I need your help. The door to Garrick's cabin is locked. Not only that, but with the wheel so close, he's sure to see me if I try to sneak in. Please, just lower me down so I can perch on the ledge. It should take me no more than two seconds to break the glass, then enter."

"You'll fall."

"No, I won't."

Beth shook her head. "I do not believe this is happening. You want to throw propriety to the wind and seduce a man you're not even married to. Good heavens, Lucy, have you lost your mind?"

"Propriety be damned," Lucy spat. "You know I've never cared for it. Garrick is the man I love."

Beth eyes had widened, but then the look in them softened. "Lucy, please. I beg you. We'll be in London in two days. Try to soften his heart on dry land."

"I may not get the chance on dry land, so I'm doing this now." That said, she took a deep breath, peeked down at the sea below, then said a quick prayer that this would work.

The *Revenger* left a trail of foam in its wake. That trail seemed a long way down all of a sudden, Lucy thought. Wiping her sweaty palms on her breeches, Lucy turned back to her friend. "Remember, if anyone should ask, I'm helping Mousad prepare the evening meal."

"And what exactly do you plan to do if you reach your destination alive?"

"If I told you, you'd blush scarlet."

"I don't suppose it has something to do with the water you're heating on the stove ... water you want me to lower and which could be used for a bath?"

Lucy nodded determinedly.

Beth eyed her as a rector would a doxy. "Hmm, yes. So I thought." Her brows lowered into a frown. "Well, I won't soil your ears with the word I'd like to call you."

"Beth, I've got more important matters on my mind then being branded a harlot."

"Well, it was nice knowing you. Harlot."

Lucy bit back a smile and threw the excess rope at her feet over the side. It was a long line, one which dangled all the way to the sea below, the hemp skipping and bobbing in the wake of the *Revenger* like a kitestring. Lucy eyed it dubiously, then slowly and carefully climbed over the rail.

"*Luuucy,*" Beth moaned.

"It's all right, Beth." But she couldn't stop her arms from shaking as she perched on the opposite side of the rail, her feet firmly planted between two posts. "Don't look so frightened. If I fall, the rope around my waist should stop me before I hit the water."

"Yes, but with your luck it will probably wrap around your neck in the process."

"Beth, really," Lucy admonished. She shook her head, already more nervous than she cared to admit, and the last thing she needed was Beth's pessimistic attitude. Peeking down, she gauged the ledge she was aiming for to be only three feet or so below where she stood.

It was a simple plan, for the row of windows was right

below the deck. Unfortunately—as often was the case with one of her "plans"—climbing to the ledge beneath the windows looked much easier than it actually was. Hanging out over the back of the ship, her posterior bobbing up and down, the roar of the ocean nearly as loud as the roar in her ears, was one of the most terrifying experiences of her life. It didn't help that Beth was peering down at her as if she were about to witness an execution, nor that the wind, as it swooped off the deck above her, kept blowing strands of hair in her eyes. It took every nerve she had—and some she didn't know she had—to pry one white-knuckled hand off the rail, then grab the vertical post beneath it.

Desperate times called for desperate measures.

"Lucy," Beth moaned again as she slowly lowered herself.

"Be quiet, Beth. I'm concentrating."

Pointing her booted foot toward the ocean, Lucy sank lower and lower. Her toes felt around for purchase as both hands clutched the rope.

By the time her feet finally found the ledge, she had to take a moment to calm herself, her breath labored as she hung off the back of the ship like a burr on a dog. Only when she felt sufficiently in charge of herself did she scrunch down a bit to peek through one of the windowpanes. The glass reflected her frightened and pale face before it dissolved into a perfect view of the cabin beyond.

Empty, thank God. She'd not known what she'd have done if she'd found Garrick staring back at her. Probably let go of the rail in fright.

She straightened, her arms already growing strained,

her hands numb, she grasped the rope so tightly. Taking a deep breath, she examined the glass for the best way to break through it.

"Hand me the grappling hook," she called up to Beth.

"Next," Lucy called nearly a half hour later, almost her entire upper body hanging out the window as she waited for another bucket of steaming water to be lowered into her waiting hands.

"Lucy," Beth cried, the thick rope pricking into her skin in a manner which left no doubt she would have blisters the next morning. "This is taking forever."

"We're almost done, Beth. But you must hurry. Garrick could enter at any moment."

Beth stared over the rail, thanking God that barrels blocked Garrick's view of what they were doing. The sun, just about to duck behind the horizon, plainly illuminated Lucy's impatient glare. Beth's own eyes narrowed in frustration. Lucy would pay for making her do this. Somehow, some way she'd make her pay for it all: setting them adrift, their capture by pirates, the dinner with Tully, and afterward, her time alone with that disreputable boor, Ravenwood. She wasn't sure how she'd do it, but she would.

"Lady Beth, might I ask what you are doing?"

So engrossed was Beth in entertaining one notion after another on how to get even with Lucy, she didn't hear Garrick's approach until it was too late. She whirled around to face him at the same time she let go of the rope. The bucket of hot water she'd been lowering dropped into the sea.

"Ouch," came a faint protest.

"I repeat, my lady. *What* are you doing?"

"Garrick," Beth yelled, tilting her head toward the back of the ship. "Good heavens, *Garrick*, you startled me." She placed her hand on her heart, her eyes wide with fear.

He merely stared down at her, his impatience clearly visible, the setting sun glinting off his gold hoop, suspicion clearly clouding the angled planes of his features. She glanced down at the buckets, all of which were empty, thankfully. When she looked back up at Garrick, he'd placed his hands on his hips.

"What, I repeat, are you doing?"

"Well, I'm . . . ahh, I'm . . ." Her eyes fixed on the grappling hook lying next to a bucket. "I'm . . . I'm *fishing!*"

"*Fishing?*"

"Yes, fishing."

He stared down at her for a moment, a very long moment, then he tipped his head, glaring down his aristocratic nose like a papa questioning an errant child. "How?"

"Ahh . . . ahh . . . how?" Beth stalled. That was a very good question.

"Yes, how?"

Her eyes caught on the empty pales. "Buckets! I'm using buckets."

The suspicion in his eyes grew. He crossed his arms in front of him, the look on his face indicating that she better be telling the truth or it would go badly for her later.

For a moment Beth considered telling him everything. Oh, how she wanted to tell him everything, but she knew if she did, Lucy would disown her as a friend. Not that that would be a *bad* thing.

When the silence stretched on, Garrick apparently lost patience, for he uncrossed his arms then stomped over to the rail. Closing her eyes, Beth sent up a silent prayer that Lucy didn't have her head hanging out the window. A few seconds later she gained the courage to open one eye, the other snapping open when she spied Garrick pulling on the rope thrown over the rail. She watched with her heart beating furiously in her chest as he peered over the rail, then turned back to face her.

"There really is a bucket attached."

She pasted a look of absolute and utter innocence on her face. "Mm-hmm."

"But what are all these extras for?"

"For, er, ahh . . . they're for the fish I'd hoped to catch. For storage."

Garrick's eyes lit with something. Humor? "We do have fishing poles."

"Yes, but Lucy said they're terribly hard to use."

She thought she saw something flash in his eyes. Amusement? Whatever it was, it was gone before she could decipher it.

"If you'd rather I use a pole, I can certainly—"

"No, no." He held up his hands. "I believe this method is much safer."

Beth nodded, sweat beginning to bead her forehead. She peeked another glance over the rail.

He shook his head. "Although I don't think I've ever

heard of this technique before."

"I confess, neither have I," Beth muttered.

He ran his fingers through his hair, his expression suddenly growing dire. It was a moment before he spoke again. "Have you seen Lucy?"

"I, well, I think she might have gone below."

"Below?"

"Yes. She, ahh, mentioned wanting to gather some items for dinner tonight."

"I thought Mousad was cooking."

"I . . . He is. She offered to help."

His expression darkened, the setting sun catching the planes and angles of his face perfectly. "If you see her, tell I'm looking for her."

Beth nodded, then watched as he turned and walked away, wondering what was happening between her friend and Garrick.

So engrossed was she in thought that it was a while before she heard a distant "Psst," followed by silence, and then another louder, more emphatic, *"Psssst."*

Beth headed for the rail. Lucy's white face stared back up at her, her aqua eyes wide with anxiety. "Is he gone?"

Beth nodded. "But you'd best hurry. He's looking for you. It's only a matter of time before he gives up and retires to his cabin for the evening."

"Is there any water left?"

Beth shook her head. "That was the last of it."

"Well, thank you very much for hitting me over the head with it."

"He startled me. Are you injured?"

"No. Thankfully it barely touched me. Besides,

'twould take more than that to damage *my* brainbox."
Lucy smiled up at her . . . a small, wistful smile. "Well,
wish me luck."

"Good luck, Lucy." And to her surprise, Beth found
herself actually meaning the words. After her run-in
with Garrick and his glowering expression, she had a
feeling there was trouble on the horizon. She only
hoped Lucy didn't end up with a broken heart. She
would never allow her heart to be captured so easily.

And as she turned away, she wondered why a pair of
dark eyes flashed across her mind and a name to form on
her lips. She scowled. *Ravenwood*. Blast his rotted soul.
He'd be the last person on earth for whom she'd develop
a *tendré*.

20

Garrick paused with his hand on the door to his cabin, wondering if, perhaps, he should scour the ship once more. But, no. Lucy was hiding from him, he was positive of it; there was simply no other explanation for why he couldn't find her.

"G'night, cap'n."

Garrick raised his hand, then opened the door to his cabin, surprised by the light which spilled out to illuminate the deck beyond. Had he forgotten to extinguish a lantern?

Perplexed, he stepped into the room, the door squeaking shut behind him. A slight breeze blew a hank of hair across his eyes. How bloody odd. He swiped at the strands, his confusion increasing.

Something was wrong. There should be no air circulating through the room, and the cabin looked . . . different. Clean. And there was another smell, too. He couldn't quite place what it was, but then it hit him.

Roses.

Gone was the moldering odor of Tully's slovenly cabin; in its place was salty breezes mixed with roses.

Bloody hell.

"'Tis about time, Garrick. I fear my skin shall fall off my bones if I continue to soak a moment longer."

And suddenly the reason why he couldn't find her clicked into place, along with the look on Beth's face when he'd discovered her on the poopdeck earlier, the reason for all those buckets, and Mousad's vague answer about not knowing where sahib was. Blast her eyes, those damn beautiful, conniving eyes.

Anger surged through him as he stepped around the table. But as he strode beneath the skull archway he came to an abrupt halt, stunned by the picture she made.

He took it all in at once: Lucy, an innocent yet brazen expression on her face as she reclined in a wooden tub, her alabaster shoulders rising from the soap as if she were a mermaid. The window behind her was broken, her clothes thrown haphazardly atop the brown coverlet on the bed. Candles were atop every available surface. They rested in holders, leaned against pewter mugs, and nestled within the eye sockets of masks.

He clenched his hands at his sides. He would not be tempted. *I will not be tempted.*

It was an effort to focus his thoughts on something else, but he did, forcing himself by grim will.

How in the hell had she managed to get into his cabin? The lock on Tully's door was like something one would find at Newgate and he'd been standing within eyesight of the door for most of the day.

And then it hit him.

"You didn't?" he said, glaring down at her, all the while fighting the urge to jump into the tub with her.

She blinked up at him with a tentative smile. "I did."

Bloody hell. He couldn't believe it. She could have been killed. Three angry steps and he was by the side of that tub, the pull of her delectable body almost as alluring as the look in her eyes. Somehow he managed to keep his hands to himself, though he was torn between wringing her pretty little neck and yanking her out of the water and into his arms.

"Damn you, Lucy, you could have fallen into the ocean."

"Now, Garrick, don't be melodramatic."

She smiled up at him, though he could see the insecurity in her eyes, the innocence that threatened to override her bold nature. But despite that innocence, she was a sight he'd never forget.

Long ringlets of autumn fire coiled atop her head to spill into the water. She trembled, whether from cold or nervousness or desire, Garrick didn't know. Another breeze blew in from the open window, setting the flames nearest her flickering. And as he stared down at her, for the first time in his life he was tempted to run.

And then he saw her swallow, saw determination light her eyes. She stood, her graceful, delectable body rising like a sea-nymph above the water.

A groan rose low in his throat, his manhood hardening even more. A soapsud clung to the side of her breast, another to her abdomen. He watched, entranced, as it slid ever so slowly toward the ringlets above her thighs.

A few fat droplets of water broke free from her body and plunged into the water below.

He ached to lick that moisture away, yearned for it.

"Garrick," she whispered softly. A stream of rose-scented water rolled past her elbow, navigated the crook of her arm, and glided down her side. He watched it for a second, fought with all his strength to leave it there and not suckle it from her flesh.

"Don't send me away, Garrick."

Oh, how he wished he didn't have to. His wanting was a physical ache, yet more than that. Standing there by her side, he could almost feel the crackling energy which bound them together and entwined them. For the first time in his life, Garrick experienced a want unlike any he'd ever felt. He wanted her now. In the tub. On the floor. Everywhere.

And then she leaned toward him, one wet hand coming to rest against his face. He closed his eyes, knowing he was a doomed man.

"Damn you, Lucy," he groaned just before he crushed her to him.

She raised her head for his kiss, accepted his assault willingly, drew his head down, and twined her hands in his hair. Their lips met, and suddenly everything spun out of control. Her mouth opened and every thought fled from his mind as he flicked his tongue inside her velvety wetness.

Sweet. God, she tastes sweet.

No, warned a voice inside him. *Don't do this. Don't risk it all.*

But he was helpless to stop the explosion of need that burst between them. Wetness crept through his shirt; she moaned and began to undo the buttons. He didn't let her finish; instead, he reached down and scooped her up in his arms, water sloshing from her body, his lips never leaving hers. The kiss turned deep, hot, consuming.

He didn't give himself time to think about his actions. He only knew he wanted her. Heat radiated from her; her upswept hair tickled his chin with its silky softness. She snuggled against him. Never once did she protest nor hesitate, even when he laid her on the bed, her determination and commitment to the course she had chosen so utterly Lucy.

Thunder boomed from above. Lucy flinched.

Garrick paused for a moment, listening. He saw her move, and then a quivering hand stroked his manhood. He groaned, just groaned as if he were a man on a torture rack. He couldn't have her. *Couldn't.* But as her hand glided down his length, every thought, every dire warning he'd received disappeared like flotsam pulled under a wave.

"Lucy," he groaned, ignoring the voice telling him to pull away, the same voice that also warned him of the penalty should he not.

"Love me, Garrick. If not with your heart, then with what you can spare me."

He threw his head back and closed his eyes. Heaven help him, she seduced him with her touch, lured him with each caress.

And he knew it was useless. They were fated to be together. Now. This night.

He sank to his knees. Their bodies met, heart to heart, wet skin to wet skin. He rolled her beneath him, finding her mouth by touch. She opened for him, and what little control Garrick had left vanished as she stroked the velvet of her tongue against his. Long, nimble fingers ignited a throbbing inside of him, a burning need for release such as he'd never known. He moved his hand up the soft skin of her side, then palmed her breast, teasing the nipple into a hard little point.

She groaned again, and an answering moan rose in his own throat: the only thing which penetrated his explosive need for her was the intense heat building between them. He touched her everywhere—the soft flesh of her shoulder, the satiny skin of her sides. And when he caressed the mound of copper curls at the apex of her thighs, she parted for his hand without hesitation.

Lightning flashed into the cabin. Thunder rang out and its resonance rattled every piece of glass in the cabin. She looked startled, but then Garrick covered her lips with his own, willing her to forget as he had willed himself to forget all that he gave up by touching her. Her eyes closed as she gave herself up to him, moaning.

She was wet, oh, she was wet. The rhythm of his tongue matched the stroke of his hand. God, she was fire beneath him, the moans she emitted inflaming him nearly beyond control.

She arched her back and nearly came off the bed. "Garrick," she moaned, grinding herself into him.

Never had he seen a woman so hot. Like bolts of lightning from the heavens above she sizzled for him, dancing beneath his hand.

Higher and higher she climbed, until, in a bunching of spasms, she cried out, "Garrick!" Then she clutched at his hand. Her eyes widened in surprise before she closed them and lost herself to the splendor of her release.

He reared back, tugged off his shirt, released his breeches. He moved to cover her, his whole body trembling with the ache of his own need. Now . . . *now* he would bury himself inside her, slake his thirst. Now he would get his heavenly reward.

But just as he was about to settle himself between her legs, the ship pitched violently to the right. Garrick automatically clasped Lucy to him as he rolled to one side of the bed.

Lucy ended up sprawled on top of him, both her legs to one side, more the pity. Undeterred, he rolled her beneath him. But no sooner had his body rested between hers again than the ship swayed, this time to port.

Two tries later Garrick gave up in defeat.

Arlan, damn his feathered hide.

Resting his head in the crook of her neck, his breath labored, his body shaking from his need to possess her, he knew he'd been beaten. Were he to try again, the ship would undoubtedly roll in the other direction.

"Garrick, the cabin's on fire."

Her voice penetrated the deep fog of unrequited desire that clouded his mind. Fire? Yes, it had felt as if the whole cabin was on fire. Like an inferno. Almost as if the devil breathed fire down their necks.

"Garrick, the flames are getting bigger."

He was big, all right. Big and hard and aching to sink inside of her still.

"Garrick?"

It was the panic in her voice that caught his attention. Panic? Lucy? He drew back.

And that was when he saw it.

"Bloody hell," he cursed, rolling off of her.

A candle had tipped over near the window, the wood beneath it flaming like a hearth. He tried to take a step, realized his legs were effectively shackled by his breeches, and had to hop toward the tub. No bucket. Damn. His eyes searched for something, anything to douse the blaze with. A pewter mug caught his attention. He hopped toward it, grabbed it, then hobbled toward the tub. One scoop later and he was heading toward the flames, the water sloshing out.

Fortunately, or perhaps mysteriously, there was enough water left to douse the flames. They sizzled out, leaving behind a trail of smoke which wafted up and out the window. Slowly, he turned back around to face Lucy.

She stared up at him in dismay, her hand covering her mouth. Then she giggled, the giggles erupting into peals of laugher.

Garrick was not amused.

Damn her. Damn it all. Damn Arlan. Damn Belial. Damn the whole world.

She was still giggling, in between sneaking glances at his privates.

He tossed the mug, the pewter cup landing with a resounding, satisfying clank. Next he pulled up his breeches, feeling as if he were a pubescent schoolboy.

"Oh, Garrick," she gasped. "You looked so silly hopping about like that."

He ignored her.

"Like a rabbit."

He ignored her again.

Her laughter slowly faded.

He headed over to the sideboard. He needed a drink. A *big* drink.

"Garrick?"

Her voice was still tinged with amusement, but now there was a question in it.

But it was only when he'd swallowed a healthy dose of the fiery brandy that he turned back toward her, ignoring her disheveled state. "*What?*"

She looked startled by his terse reply. Sometime during their time together, long strands of her hair had tumbled around her like a molten river. She shoved a hank of it aside and wrapped the coverlet around her. "You're not angry, are you?"

She sounded so completely stunned, so filled with disbelief that he could actually be *mad* at her that his control snapped.

"No, I'm not angry. Not at all. I enjoy vanquishing flames as much as the next man."

Her cheeks filled with color.

"God, Lucy. Can't you even couple with a man without destroying something?"

She stiffened.

He stepped back, though she hadn't physically reached for him, only with her eyes. "Don't," he snapped. "Don't touch me."

"Garrick, what's wrong? What's happened?"

"Nothing has happened, Lucy, except that I've come to my senses."

Her face paled.

"Now. Get the hell out of my cabin."

He stared down at her, those emerald eyes of hers glistening, her lips trembling while she fought to contain her tears. God, what was he going to do? For suddenly he wanted to go to her, wanted to wrap his arms around her and ease the hurt in her eyes, wanted to reassure her that no one would ever say horrible things to her again. But he couldn't. God help him, he had to end this now.

If he didn't, it would be too late for both of them.

"But Garrick, why?"

From somewhere deep inside, Garrick found the strength to paste a look of derision on his face. "Why, look at you. You're no lady, you're a trollop in a lady's clothing."

She gasped. For a moment she looked incapable of words. Then the anger slowly clouded her eyes; it grew and multiplied until it turned into a hurricane of fury.

She slid from the bed and before he knew what she was about to do, she drew back and slugged him. Not a maidenly slap to the face—no, she hauled back and hit him with everything she had. Garrick's breath escaped in a rush.

"How *dare* you?" The words dripped like poison from her lips. Yet beneath it all, Garrick could see the hurt and devastation swimming among her tears. "I'd do anything for you, Garrick Wolf. I love you. And if that makes me a trollop, so be it. I'd rather be a trollop who'd followed her heart than be a *lady* trapped by convention."

And with that she hastily reached down and pulled on her clothes, dressing with sharp, angry motions, all the while refusing to look at him. Every once in a while she reached up to swipe at a tear, the action only bringing home all the more how badly he'd betrayed her.

He forced himself to stand still, even when she left.

"I don't believe I've seen so much white since the Blizzard of '66."

Arlan looked up from his paperwork and resisted the urge to groan at the sight of the red-robed, horned figure standing before him, a figure complete with pitchfork and goatee.

"Good hell, even the chair's white," Belial went on to say.

"What are you doing here?"

"Why, Arlan, what a way to greet a friend. Especially one as old as I am."

Arlan rolled his eyes. "I repeat. What are you doing here?"

"Would you believe I've decided to repent?"

"No."

"Hmm. I didn't think so, but it was worth a try."

Arlan firmly told himself not to let the devil get under his skin. "If you have something to say, I suggest you speak. If you don't, I'll be forced to resort to drastic measures."

"Oooh." The devil pasted a look of mock terror on his face. "Are you going to singe me with a bolt of lightning? Or better yet, make locusts swarm around me? Or perhaps you're going to drown me in a flood?" He pretended to be horrified, before suddenly straightening and waving a hand in dismissal. "No matter. I'm afraid you'll have to do better than that to keep *me* away."

He took a step forward and, before Arlan could stop him, picked up the sheet of paper resting on Arlan's desk, a smile spreading across his face.

"Give that to me," Arlan said, trying to grasp the document.

Belial took a step back, holding the document above his head. His thin lips spread into a smile. "Actually, *he's* the reason I'm here."

"If by that I'm to assume you mean Garrick Wolf, then we have nothing to talk about. Everything is going according to plan. Even your attempts to bribe him didn't work. Now, give that back to me."

"Ahh, but I'm not done bribing him yet."

Arlan released a long sigh of impatience. "Spare me the details, Belial. We've nothing to discuss."

"Care to place a wager on that?"

"No."

Belial arched a pointed brow at him. "Still sore over losing that bet on Lot's wife?"

"Not at all. We warned Lot what would happen if anyone looked back."

"Yes, but you were so sure nobody would. I'll never forget the look on your face when you had to turn his wife into that pillar of salt." He froze, a wide-eyed look pasted on his pointy face, then he dissolved into laughter.

Arlan watched, unfazed. The day was going to . . . well, hell.

"Are you through?" he asked a long while later.

"Oh yes, yes," the devil said with wave his taloned hand. "Thank you. I haven't laughed that hard since I set loose the Black Plague."

"Glad I could be of service."

"Now where were we? Oh yes. About this bet. It's just a simple one. I wager that Garrick will accept my next offer. If I lose, I agree never to bother the man again."

"And if you win?"

"You agree to hand his soul over to me."

"No."

"Come now. Surely your boss won't mind another bet?"

Arlan snorted. "I told you, no. Now, please leave. I've work to do." He leaned over his desk and reached for the document again, but Belial drew it toward his chest.

"But it's such a simple bet, Arlan. A soul for a soul. Either Garrick agrees or he doesn't."

"No."

Thunder rumbled inside the little room and Arlan looked up in surprise. For a moment, he couldn't believe his ears. "You want me to do what?"

The thunder rang out again, louder this time. He looked back at Belial, unable to keep the amazement from his voice. "He wants me to agree."

"Excellent!" Belial applauded, crushing the document. Suddenly, his eyes narrowed. "Why?" he asked.

Arlan shrugged. "Perhaps he's foreseen that Garrick won't agree."

"Hmm, perhaps. But perhaps *I've* foreseen that he will." He waved a hand in dismissal. "No matter. The bet will be that Garrick will accept the standard soul-for-a-soul agreement. *When* he says yes, you will not—in any way—interfere with my taking of it."

Thunder rang out again and Arlan reluctantly nodded. "He agrees, however, one false step and he will force a Moderation."

"Yes, yes, yes. Though I've no intention of getting into a Right to Claim case with you. Hell forbid. No, I'll just be on my way. The goodness floating around this place fairly chokes me."

And with that he stepped back, snapped his fingers dramatically, and was gone.

21

"You bastard!"

It was the next morning, and the heavens were cry-ing miniature tears, the drops falling from the sails above and landing on the deck with soft splats of sor-row.

"Do you know what you've done to her?" Beth con-tinued, standing near the prow of the ship as if she were a figurehead, a wet strand of hair managing to escape from the confines of her chignon to blow about her face. She swiped it away, the motion conveying a crackle of anger.

"She's been crying all night. Lucy, who never cries for longer than two minutes, has been sobbing her eyes out. *All night.*"

Garrick didn't move. Drops dripped off the sheets of canvas to land upon his shoulders and head; a few missed him and splattered against the deck, the sound mixing in with the steady roar of the ocean. Garrick ignored it as he stood in front of Beth. The surging sea exactly matched her rage, rage which grew by the minute like the swell of a wave, especially when he remained silent.

She took a step forward and grabbed him by the shirt. He could have moved away from her, told her to leave, but he didn't. In his opinion, he deserved her scathing antipathy, deserved the scorching anger in her eyes.

"You sicken me."

No more than I do myself.

"How dare you almost seduce her and then discard her?"

I dared because when I looked down at her, I realized I loved her.

"You should be shot."

If only someone would.

"If I was a man I'd do it myself."

And I'd let you.

"Say something, damn you!"

There were tears looming in Beth's eyes now, tears of frustration and anger. That she loved Lucy almost as much as he did was patently obvious.

"Well?"

When all he did was shrug, Beth looked beyond furious. She looked livid. Her cheeks filled with color, her hands clenched at her sides in impotent fury. "You bloody bastard," she spat. "I could just hit you, except you're not worth it. Lucy is better off without you."

Yes, Garrick admitted, she was, but not in the way Beth thought. He had released her from the chains of his love. Now he could leave her knowing she was free to love again. How noble it sounded.

Too bad he felt less than noble.

Beth continued to stare at him contemptuously, her eyes trying to slay him alive. Then she turned away, long hanks of her black hair spinning out like the wings of an avenging angel. He almost laughed at the metaphor. Instead, he turned toward the rail in frustration.

He forced himself to stare out at the waves as they bowed and dipped like dancers at a ball. For years the sound of the ocean as she crashed into the prow of his ship had been a source of comfort; now all he heard was Lucy's pure voice as she proudly stood before him and declared her love.

I'd rather follow my heart. . . .

If only he could follow his.

But he couldn't. He was stuck on his course as surely as a ship sailed up the Thames. But God, she'd been incredible. So fearless, so absolutely unafraid to tell him how she'd felt, even though he knew how much it had hurt her to do so. She was everything he'd ever looked for in a woman and more. If only . . .

If only what?

If only I wasn't dead?

Too late for that. Far too late for that.

His eyes grew unfocused as he stared out at the sea. He had no idea how long he stood there, his mind replaying their final scene over and over again. The cold began to seep into his bones, eating at his soul. He could see the pale outline of England upon the horizon, the coastline peeking between tendrils of mist like a fairytale land of old. The sight gave him little comfort. *Soon,* he thought. *Soon we will sail into Dover. Soon this living hell will be over.*

"Poor, poor, Garrick. You really are feeling sorry for yourself, aren't you?"

Garrick turned toward the voice, the words having whipped over his skin like the forked tongue of a snake. Belial stood only two feet away, a brackish odor rising up around them, whether the sea or the being himself, Garrick couldn't say.

"Tell me, Garrick. Was she worth it?"

He didn't answer, had grown good at holding his tongue and keeping his feet firmly planted to the deck.

"You're a tough one. I'll give you that. I thought I had you in my grasp so many times. So close," he murmured reflectively. "Well, never mind. Now I have a deal I know you won't refuse."

This time, Garrick wouldn't allow himself to be drawn in. Belial could ply him with all the sly innuendoes he wanted, but he'd refuse to bite.

"Aren't you even the least bit curious to know what I've planned?"

What now? Garrick thought, turning toward the rail again. *A sudden squall to sink the ship? The sun to blacken and fire to rain up from hell?*

"Dear me, no. Nothing quite so melodramatic."

Startled, Garrick swung toward him.

"Yes, it's a handy little trick, I admit, being able to read your mind. Arlan can, too, in case you didn't know. Rather unfair of us."

Garrick stared across at him in stunned silence, then turned away, flatly refusing to cowed by such a feat.

"So you think. But I know differently."

"So I think what?"

"That you can resist me."

"I don't think, I *know*."

"Garrick, Garrick, Garrick. When are you going to learn *I* know you better than you know yourself?"

"Go away, Belial."

"But don't you want to hear about Lucy's death?"

Garrick stiffened, then slowly turned back toward Belial.

"Yes, Lucy will die today. Now as a matter of fact. In front of you."

The words hung in the air like the smell of sulfur. Garrick blinked. "You lie," he hissed, but what he saw in the devil's eyes chilled him like an ocean in winter.

"A snap of my finger and it's done."

"You can't."

"Oh no? I believe you've been told 'tis the boy you must help. *He* is the one under protection from angels. I can do anything I want to Lucy."

No. He refused to believe it. "You would have done so before now if it were possible." He said the words as bravely as he dared, though it was hard with his heart pounding like a hammer against a blacksmith's anvil.

Sweat beaded upon his forehead and trickled down the sides. It mixed with the rain as it ran down his neck.

"Perhaps I didn't sense the desperation within you that I do now."

"I'm not desperate."

Turning away, Garrick focused on trying to appear calm, even though the devil's words sent fear skidding through his veins and anxiety pumping into his heart. "I don't believe Arlan would allow you to do such a thing."

"You don't, hmm? Well my friend, look there. The object of our conversation has come into view. Oh, and my, my. Doesn't she look awful? Those bags under her eyes, and that blotchy complexion. She looks as if . . . *No*, it couldn't be, could it? Why, she *is*. Look, Garrick, she's crying."

The rail had become Garrick's anchor in the last few moments. He clutched it now like a man about to tumble overboard. The image of her face as he had last seen it kept clouding his mind. So proud. So defiant.

"You *have* broken her heart, haven't you? Do you think she'll recover? She certainly doesn't look as though she will. Why, I wouldn't be at all surprised if she didn't notice something swinging toward her head, something big and heavy. Maybe a boom—"

"You wouldn't dare." Somehow, the words managed to escape, a hoarse whisper issued from between dry lips.

Belial went on as if he hadn't heard him. "Wouldn't that be sad. Look, she's climbing up to the poopdeck. Isn't that where you almost kissed her? How touching. And she just swiped at her eyes again. Isn't that just the most heart-wrenching thing you've ever seen?"

Still, Garrick refused to turn and look at her, didn't need to, really. In his mind's eye he could see her red hair flying about her face, her eyes—usually so sparkling and filled with life—clouded with tears.

"Come, Garrick. Take a look."

"No." The words were almost a gasp. "And if you harm her I'll—"

"You'll what?"

"I'll hunt you down to the ends of the earth."

"Oh my, there's a threat."

"Silence!" Garrick roared.

"Oh, look, Garrick. She's standing below the mizzen sail now. How careless of her. What do you suppose would happen if the line to the spanker boom broke?"

"Don't you dare," he repeated. He tried to take a step toward the devil, tried to stop the words, but a strange buzzing began in Garrick's ears. He couldn't move. Invisible chains snaked around his arms and ankles and held him firmly to the deck.

Suddenly, he faced Lucy, could see her small form huddled near the back of the ship. She had her back to him, her gray cloak drawn tightly around her. Her shoulders were hunched, as if in defeat. He tried to force her name past his suddenly numb and bloodless lips, to warn her, but no sound emerged. It was as if things were moving at a slower rate of speed. A sound pierced the air, and Garrick tried harder than ever to force her name out, to shout a warning, for he recognized the sound.

A line was breaking.

"You could have avoided this, Garrick. All you'd have to have done was give me your soul."

Lucy! The word reverberated through his mind, louder than the loudest of shouts, but no sound escaped from his throat. He was helpless to do anything but watch as he stood rooted to the deck.

"Behold," the devil taunted. And with a snap of his fingers, the rope snapped.

Lucy whirled toward the noise. Garrick had a perfect view of her terrified expression just before the boom slammed into her.

22

She was going to die.

He'd seen such wounds before.

She was going to die.

The brown coverlet enhanced the paleness of her skin. The ragged gash on the side of her head still pulsed blood.

"'Ere cap'n."

Garrick took the wet rag from Calico without looking up; the hand he used to wipe away Lucy's precious blood shook with emotion. He touched her gently even though he knew she felt nothing. He wiped softly even though she would never know of his tenderness. He caressed her cheek even though she would never sense the love in his touch. Still, some part of him refused to believe it, refused to accept that Arlan would allow her to die.

"It can't happen."

But it could. Keeping Lucy alive had never been part of his mission.

He hadn't known he'd spoken the words aloud until he felt Calico's hand on his shoulder. The gesture was meant to reassure him.

It didn't.

Garrick said nothing; he couldn't have spoken if he'd wanted to. He felt bereft, as if she were already gone, and so guilty for letting her fall into the devil's game for his soul.

The door to the cabin opened and Garrick glanced up.

It was Beth.

"Oh God," she cried, rushing forward when she spied her friend. In an instant she was by her side, tears already making tracks down her cheeks. "Is she dead?" Her eyes held fear and disbelief as they gazed across at him.

He shook his head.

Beth looked back at Lucy, her face nearly as pale as her friend's. Gently, she reached to stoke the side of Lucy's cheek. "She can't die," she said, her blue eyes glistening with tears.

Garrick felt his own eyes burn. Still, he tried to maintain control. He wanted to drag Lucy into his arms, to hold her to him and inhale her sweet smell, except he knew that smell would now be tainted by blood.

He watched as Beth straightened one of Lucy's auburn curls, like a child soothing her favorite doll. The breath she took was ragged, a sound escaping from her that was half moan, half sob. Garrick looked away, but her next words forced him to look back at her again. "This is *your* fault, Garrick Wolf," she spat out. The tears came faster now, the words gasped out. "If you hadn't broken her heart, this would never have happened. She loved you." She pulled her hand away and flexed it into a fist. "Doesn't that mean anything to you?"

"It means everything."

Her eyes narrowed. "Does it?"

It was a moment before Garrick could speak over the lump of emotion clogging his throat. "Yes, Beth, it does. I love her."

She jerked as if he'd hit her, her eyes examining his closely. "Liar."

"Am I, Beth? I wish to God I were."

She stared at him, emotions flicking across her face. And when next she spoke, her voice had gathered fury.

"You bastard," she cried, her hands balling into fists. "How *dare* you say you love her? 'Tis only your guilt which speaks, not your heart."

He couldn't answer her, for how could he begin to explain? Instead, he got up and headed for the door. As he rested his hand on the knob, something made him glance back and he found himself saying, "Believe what you will, Beth, but I do love her." He swallowed, barely able to speak. "I would sell my soul for her."

And with that, he left.

He found Belial where he'd left him. The devil's eyes glowed with unholy glee as he watched Garrick's approach. He leaned back against the rail, his ridiculous red cape glistened with beads of moisture. The rain still fell from heaven like tears from God.

"Why, Garrick. What a pleasant surprise. Imagine meeting up with you here."

Garrick's jaw tightened. "What do I have to do?" he clipped out.

The dark angel feigned a look of innocence magnificent in its understatement. "Whatever do you mean?"

"Cut line, Belial. I'm here to sell my soul."

The devil managed a look of sudden enlightenment. "You *are*? My, my this *is* a surprise."

"*Now*, Belial."

"Oh, but being in such a rush is not at all wise. These things should be heavily considered. But if you insist."

"I do."

"Very well. I guess it's my duty as master of war and pestilence to grant you your wish. It's very simple really. A verbal contract, nothing more. Your life in exchange for Lucy's. The term is for eternity."

"Agreed." Garrick didn't feel a moment's remorse. He turned away, wanting only to get back to Lucy.

"Wait a moment." The devil waited until he'd turned back to him before saying. "It's necessary to tell you a few things before you're allowed to agree."

"Whatever it is, I agree."

"Nevertheless, I must tell you. There are certain rules which govern these sorts of transactions. One wrong move and the powers above"—his lip curled in derision—"will void the contract."

"Can we not deal with this later?"

"No."

"Very well. What are these terms?"

The devil must have read his anxiety. He was reveling in it, really, for he took his time in framing a response, even going so far as to stroke his chin in thought. "Hmmm, let me see. Ah yes. First, I must have your agreement that the term of the deal is for eternity."

"I *already* agreed to that. Do not waste my time."

Belial's eyes narrowed. "You have no choice *but* to listen, Garrick. *I* am the one in charge here, not you. You'd best remember that."

He pointed one of his taloned fingers at him, then crossed his arms, drumming one pointy nail against his red sleeve.

Garrick concealed his frustrated impatience only by focusing on an image of Lucy's face. He was doing this for her, needed to be patient for her. He musn't forget that. Gritting his teeth, he nodded.

Belial looked amused. "Second, you are to agree the commodity is a soul for a soul."

"Done."

"Lastly, we agree that the contract commences tonight at, hmm, say midnight."

Garrick had almost agreed, before the realization sank in that he wouldn't have time to marry Lucy, and suddenly it became vastly important that he should do so. "And what if I don't agree to that?"

"Then the contract is void and Lucy dies."

He almost agreed right then, except suddenly he found himself saying, "I want three days." His heart pounded in his chest. All he wanted was for this to be over, for Lucy to be safe. Still, he held firm. His mission was the boy, and by God, he would finish it. For Lucy's sake.

Belial looked astounded at his tenacity. "Certainly not."

"Then no deal."

"No deal? Have you taken leave of your senses? Lucy will die if you don't agree."

"Come now, Belial," Garrick said, refusing to give in, praying his desperate gamble would pay off. "Surely three days is a short enough time to wait for my soul."

"What in hell's name would *I* have to gain by agreeing to such a thing?"

"My soul?"

"But if you agree, I'll have that anyway. If you don't, Lucy will die."

"Then what else can I trade you?"

Belial stared across at him, looked about to tell him no again, but then he tilted his head and stroked the goatee on his chin. "Now there's a thought. I *could* have you do something for me. Something detrimental to the welfare of other souls I have in my power. Perhaps the duke and his friend the countess?" He straightened and pierced Garrick with a glare. "I have it! Upon arriving in London, you must set Ravenwood free."

Garrick blanched. Before he could stop himself he said, "No. I can't. He's vital to proving Tom's identity."

"That *is* a problem. I guess that means we can't agree." The devil turned away.

"No, wait. Stop." Garrick was nearly frantic now, terrified Lucy would slip away while he stood here squabbling.

Belial turned back to him, eyebrows raised.

"You really are a bastard, aren't you?" Garrick asked.

Belial bowed, his smile as wide as a shark about to gobble its prey. "I am."

"If I agree to this, will you give me the three days with Lucy before coming to claim my soul?"

"I will."

Garrick closed his eyes, both relieved and unsure, torn. He didn't want to let down Tom, and by letting Ravenwood go he would greatly diminish their chance at proving the boy's identity. Then again, perhaps not. If he could convince Ravenwood to aid them of his own free will, perhaps not all would be lost.

Garrick saw the devil's eyes narrow and realized he'd forgotten to shield his thoughts. Not that it mattered. Belial would know what he was up to, anyway. It was like doing battle with the wind.

"We're agreed then. You'll give me three extra days in exchange for Ravenwood's freedom."

"Yes, but now you must agree not to try and talk Ravenwood into aiding you."

"Bastard! That's not what you originally said."

"I know, but I've changed my mind. Best to agree now before I change it again."

For a moment Garrick almost argued the point, but he knew it would probably be pointless. Lucy was waiting. "Very well, I agree. Is that all?"

"No. The final term is agreeing on a time and place for the contract to commence."

Garrick took a deep breath, knowing he had no choice. For the first time in his life he realized what it meant to love someone so completely, so thoroughly, so absolutely, he would do anything for her. And so he said, "Midnight. I'll meet you wherever I am three days hence." ·

Belial smiled, all but rubbing his hands together in glee. "Agreed."

There was no streak of lightning, no clap of thunder, just the normal sound of a ship gliding across the waves. Garrick blinked, amazed that it'd been so easy. When he opened his eyes, Belial was gone.

"He agreed. I can't believe he actually agreed."

Arlan watched from above, a frown clouding his normally sunny features and his wings beating a furious rhythm against the walls of his office as he stared down at Garrick. The view through his office floor was of the ship and the top of Garrick's head as he made his way back to Lucy's side.

"Why did he do it?" Arlan shouted, looking up at the ceiling. "He had to have known Lucy would be well taken care of. Didn't he realize they would have been together again up here?"

In response, thunder vibrated through his little room, the reverberation knocking papers off his desk.

"I know, I know. He felt responsible. But now what are we going to do? We've lost him. And Lucy was supposed to report for duty tomorrow. Instead she's tucked into bed down there, alive as the day she was conceived—"

The sound of thunder rang out again.

"Fine. I won't ask any more questions," Arlan mumbled. "I'll just sit back and trust You know what You're doing."

• • •

Lucy awoke slowly the next morning. The heavy blackness which held down her lids faded into brightness. Two blurry blobs of light sharpened to become lanterns hanging from the skull archway; they rocked back and forth with the ship. Pain pounded in her head, sharp spikes which made thought nearly impossible; the fierceness of it turned her stomach.

A chair creaked. Gingerly, she turned her head.

It was Garrick.

He sat in a chair next to the bed, the lanterns casting a ghostly glow over his haggard features. She tried to smile, but then the thought penetrated that she shouldn't, though for the life of her she couldn't remember why. A memory floated into her mind, one of pain, not the physical kind, but the other kind. Hurt. Betrayal. She tried to hold the thought, but her head pounded too furiously.

"How do you feel?"

She opened her mouth to speak, managed to produce a small gurgle, then swallowed and tried again. "Horrible," she croaked.

He smiled at her, a tender smile full of concern, of love. That struck her as odd, but the blackness was calling to her again. She closed her eyes. Garrick's words forced them open again.

"You nearly died."

She concentrated on his voice, absorbed what he'd said, then nodded, the muscles of her neck protesting the motion. "Feels like it."

His smile wobbled a bit. Again she couldn't squelch the feeling that there was something terribly wrong. "What happened?"

"A boom broke lose and hit you in the head."

She wanted to say something flip, like, "Oh, is that all?" but she didn't have the strength.

"Lucy," he whispered so tenderly. "I love you."

Why did those words strike a cord of anger and despair? She closed her eyes. Words echoed in her mind.

I love you.

I love you, Garrick, she had said. *And if that makes me a . . . Trollop.*

He had called her a trollop. Her eyes snapped open. Everything came back to her in a flash. The bath. Their lovemaking. His horrible words.

"No, Lucy," he said, obviously realizing that her memory had returned. He reached for her hand, clutched at it. "I didn't mean it—"

"Get out," she hissed, the words taking all her energy to force out.

"No. I won't. I know what I did was wrong, but I had to."

She turned her head away, the movement causing a stab of agony to pound into her skull. She didn't want to see him, wanted him to leave. Now. That he would say such things and not mean them made her ill. Why would he do that? To torture her? Probably.

He reached out and grabbed her hand. She tried to tug it back but she didn't have the strength.

"Lucy, listen to me. There were reasons why I said what I said. Reasons I can't explain to you. But I do love you." He swallowed. "I think we were meant to love each other, only I didn't realize it until it was almost too late. Please, please forgive me for what I did."

He grew silent. Lucy refused to look at him, even though every fiber of her being cried out at her to do so. But no. She would not be swayed by his pretty speech. Would not be convinced by the false sorrow in his eyes. He'd hurt her. Never would she forgive him. Never.

Wetness dropped onto her hand. She felt it trickle down her palm.

Still, she refused to open her eyes.

Another drop followed. What was that? Had the roof sprung a leak? She opened her eyes. No. It wasn't the roof.

Slowly, she turned her head, though the motion set pain pounding into her skull. Her eyes fixed on Garrick. Her breath caught. Held.

Garrick, her pirate lord, her warrior, her fearless protector, cried.

Cried.

"Oh, Garrick," she found herself saying weakly, "don't cry."

"I'm not."

The words, so completely untrue, made her want to smile. Slowly her anger began to dribble away, melted by the warmth of his tears. "Liar," she breathed softly.

He blinked, moisture gathering on his lashes. "I know."

And then she did smile, a weak smile, but a smile nonetheless. It cost her to do so. Her head felt as if it would explode, but she felt better for it.

"Can you ever forgive me?"

His eyes were filled with so much longing, so much guilt, Lucy was unable to stop matching tears from rising in her own eyes. She nodded, ignoring the pain in her head, which was easy due to the joy in her heart.

When he observed the motion, his expression changed dramatically. Gone was the uncertainty, gone was the guilt. In its place was a look of so much hope and wonder, Lucy felt her chest tighten with tenderness. Her throat burned, and the tears she'd held back begged for release.

He tilted his head at her, and for the longest moment all he did was stare at her, his eyes filled with awe. "I love you."

She blinked, her smile spreading. "I know."

He released her hand, then caressed her face, wiping at the tears that had managed to escape despite her best efforts. The gesture was tender and reverent, and his eyes so . . . so worshiping.

And finally the tears came, the horror of the last twenty-four hours causing her to break down in sobs. She hardly noticed when he reached out and gently pulled her into his arms. All she felt was the warmth of his body as he pressed it against hers.

It was a long while later before he slowly drew back, but she almost started crying all over again at the look in his eyes.

It was one she'd never seen before.

It was the look of a man who'd come home.

Part 3

For what shall it profit a man,
if he shall gain the whole world,
and lose his own soul?

—*St. Mark*

23

It was twenty-four hours later that Lucy found herself standing on the elegant brick porch of her Aunt Cornelia's town home.

"It's locked," she said, trying the door.

Beth, looking as nervous as a kitten in a room full of dogs said, "Use the knocker," the tremor in her voice clearly evident, her movements agitated as she smoothed her wrinkled gown.

"'An 'urry," Tom urged. "Me balls be freezin' out 'ere."

"Tom!" Beth admonished. Garrick snorted. Lucy turned. He gave her a smile, a smile that touched her with . . . what? She wasn't sure, but her heart melted anyway, her earlier pique over being forced to temporarily leave Prinny aboard Tully's appropriated ship fading. Garrick would relent about the bird, though she had no idea why he'd taken such a sudden dislike to her pet.

"Ahem," Beth coughed, snapping her back to the present.

Lucy blushed before turning back to the door. A few moments later it was opened by a harried-looking Lambert.

"Good morning," Lucy said brightly.

"Miss Hartford," he said in shock. His gray eyes were as wide as teacup saucers. Those eyes only grew more wide as he stared at the four of them.

"May we come in?"

"Oh. Ah yes, Miss Hartford. Of course." He moved aside. The group piled into the hall.

"Lucy?" an incredulous voice asked.

Every thought fled from Lucy's mind at the sound of that very familiar and very dear voice. She looked toward the landing above her.

"Salena!" Tom cried.

Salena stared down at them, her face slowly filling with amazement. Then she was a flurry of movement as she descended the stairs, the blonde curls atop her head bobbing up and down, one hand clutching her mustard-colored skirts, the other the polished rail. When she stepped into the foyer she threw her arms open wide.

Pandemonium erupted, Tom giving out a glad cry as he was enfolded in her arms, everyone speaking at once. Beth hurled questions about her parents at the same time Lucy asked about her aunt.

It was Garrick who put an end to it all by letting loose an ear-piercing whistle.

"Garrick," Lucy chastised, uncovering her ears.

"Please," he said firmly. "I think it would be best if one person spoke at a time."

Lucy nodded, turning back to her friend. "Where's my aunt?" she asked anxiously.

"Lucy, good heavens," Salena said, giving her a hug. "She's asleep, though I'd wager she's awake now."

As her friend drew back, Lucy grasped her hand and squeezed it. "Oh, Salena, it's so good to see you. Whatever are you doing here?"

"I've been keeping your aunt company while we waited for *you* to return. Good heavens, Lucy, where have you been? We've all been so very worried about you. All of London thinks you've been kidnapped."

"Kidnapped! By who?"

"The marquis."

"Garrick? Good gracious," Lucy protested. "Wherever did they get such a silly notion?"

"*I* never thought such a thing," Salena was quick to point out. "Nor did your aunt, not really. 'Twas more believable that *you'd* kidnapped him." She looked at Garrick, a smile spreading across her face. "My lord, 'tis good to see you again."

Garrick nodded. "Your Grace."

"Salena," Lucy said in amusement, "really. I would never kid—"

"*So you've decided to return?*"

Lucy stiffened. There was no mistaking that voice, nor the displeasure in it. She peeked toward the landing above and nearly groaned. Her aunt glared down at them like a curate on Easter morning. "Aunt Cornelia."

Grabbing her black skirt, her aunt took a controlled step toward them, the cane she used thumping nearly as loudly as Lucy's heart as she made her way down the steps. Her mobcap rested slightly off-center—no doubt due to her hasty dressing— and long ribbons of gray hair protested from beneath it. For just for a moment the burning anger Lucy could see glowing from her eyes faded into joy, but then the anger returned full force.

"Lucy Hartford," she said sharply. "This had better be good."

It was. At least Lucy thought it was. Unfortunately her aunt didn't look suitably impressed. She stared across at them as a magistrate might at an uncooperative witness. "You mean to tell me there was no possible way you could turn around?"

Lucy shrugged, her elbow bumping into Garrick, who sat next to her. "We tried, Auntie, but by the wind—"

"We ran into a storm which made turning back impossible," Garrick finished. "By the time we'd sailed through it, we decided to continue on."

Cornelia's eyes narrowed. "Did it never occur to you, my lord, that my niece and Lady Elizabeth would be ruined by not turning back?"

Beth and Lucy exchanged anxious glances as Garrick answered, "It did."

"And still you pressed on?"

"We did, my lady. You see, Lucy and I had decided to marry." That wasn't quite how it had happened, but Lucy wasn't about to complain; at last her aunt finally looked at them with something other than displeasure. Now she stared at them in shock.

"Marry!" she gaped, staring between the two as if they'd suddenly announced their intention to sail to

France in a bathing tub. "But you hardly know each other."

"Time means nothing when you're in love," Lucy sighed dreamily.

Her aunt's eyes widened. "You're in love?"

Garrick's expression was unfathomable as he answered, "We are."

Cornelia grew silent. She looked about to say something, but then her expression closed. "Well, I suppose you are to be congratulated. I must say 'twill be a relief to get the gel off my hands—"

"Auntie!" Lucy cried.

"Heaven knows that takes care of one problem. Perhaps my niece's marriage will be enough to save Beth's reputation, too, though I have my doubts."

Lucy caught Salena's amused expression, then darted a glance at Beth, who looked pensive. "Are we terribly ruined, then?" Beth asked in a small voice.

"Terribly," Cornelia announced sternly. "I don't suppose there was a married lady on board who could have acted as chaperone?"

"No," Lucy answered.

"A maid?"

"No," Lucy said again.

"*Anybody*?" he aunt said desperately.

"Ravenwood," Beth moaned. "Dear God, what happens when they catch wind of Ravenwood being aboard?"

"Ravenwood?" Cornelia asked. "The *Duke* of Ravenwood?"

"Aye," Garrick murmured.

"Good heavens," Cornelia said, wilting back in her chair. "What was *he* doing on board the ship?"

"We took him hostage," Lucy provided promptly.

"Hostage!" Cornelia trilled, sitting back up again.

"Lucy, please," Garrick said. "Let me explain." He turned to her aunt. "We'd only been at sea for a few days when we were attacked by pirates—"

"Pirates!"

Her aunt was dipping up and down like a duck on water, Lucy thought disgruntledly.

"It turned out that the pirates were hired by an agent for the countess," Garrick continued. "The Duke of Ravenwood."

"Good heavens."

"Fortunately, we were able to escape from their clutches, taking Ravenwood as our hostage. Unfortunately, he escaped when we docked in London. We have no idea how, but his escape leaves me with no other choice than to go to Selborne in the hopes of confronting the earl and his countess with what I know. 'Tis the best I can do after having lost Ravenwood."

"Ravenwood. That fiend," Salena shot. "I hope the magistrate catches up with him."

"As do I," Lucy affirmed.

"When will you leave, my lord?" Salena asked, shooting Tom, who sat next to her, a glance.

The boy had been awfully quiet from his position upon the settee, Lucy thought. That worried her, for she knew from experience it meant he was plotting something. This time she couldn't imagine what.

"I shall leave tonight."

"And I will go along." Lucy said firmly, pulling her gaze away from Tom.

"Absolutely not," Garrick said at the same time her aunt said, "No."

Lucy stared between them, amusement bubbling up inside of her. "Why not?"

"Lucinda Hartford, good heavens, I refuse to let you out of this house until your reputation is somewhat salvaged. Besides, it would be just your luck to get yourself kidnapped before I could marry you off to his lordship."

Lucy's smile faded. "But, Aunt—"

"No buts. You are not going with his lordship and that's final."

Lucy wanted to protest, but it was glaringly obvious she would get nowhere with her aunt in her present frame of mind. Not only that, but Garrick was acting as if he'd suddenly lost his hearing.

"Very well, Aunt Cornelia," she said as meekly as she dared, though she had no intention of staying behind. She shot Garrick a glare, which he ignored, then, left with nothing else to do, she got up and crossed to Beth's side. Her friend looked about as happy as a lead player in a Shakespearean tragedy.

"Don't worry, Beth," she whispered, "I'll see to it that matters are taken care of."

Beth raised dazed eyes to her. "'Tis what I'm afraid of."

Lucy heard her aunt snort. She darted her a frown, then patted Beth's hand.

She was about to turn away when Beth's words stopped her. "What if I'm forced to marry Ravenwood?"

"Beth, really. No one would force you to do that," Salena said kindly.

"But if word reaches society that he was on board that ship, we may be forced to wed."

"Nonsense," Lucy said earnestly. "We'll tell people Garrick and I were married aboard the *Revenger*. No one need ever know the truth."

"It won't work, Lucy, and you know it. All anyone has to do is ask a member of the crew. Once *you* marry Garrick, that only leaves Ravenwood. People will naturally assume the worst, that I was compromised by him, murderer or no."

Beth looked so glum, Lucy found herself saying, "*You* can marry Garrick if you like." She was trying to cheer her up, but it fell terribly flat. Beth looked up at her in horror, then flung herself to her feet and ran from the room.

"He's not that bad," Lucy called after her.

"Lucy, really," her aunt admonished when the door had slammed shut. "How could you be so unfeeling? This is a serious matter."

"But I was only joking, Auntie. Come now, you don't honestly think she'd be forced to marry Raven-wood, do you?"

"Well, I should hope not. In any event, the sooner you wed his lordship, the better off she'll be. When do you plan to do so?"

"After we confront the countess," Garrick announced.

"Why not sooner?" Salena asked.

"We would like to, but we're afraid Ravenwood will tell the countess of our arrival. When that happens she'll be quite desperate to get her hands on Tom. Everyone's life will be in danger then."

Salena grabbed Tom's hand, her face having paled. She darted the boy a tentative smile, then said, "Yes. Of course, you're correct. Very well, then. I suppose there's not much else to do but wait."

Garrick nodded, then got up and walked over to Lucy. "Do you promise to stay here?"

Lucy sneaked a glance at her aunt's frowning countenance, then smiled up at him mischievously. "And if I do not promise?"

"Then I shall lock you in your room."

She laughed softly, completely oblivious to the room's other occupants. "A dire threat indeed. I shall have to consider this carefully."

He grabbed her hand, his expression turning serious. "Lucy, please. Stay here with your aunt. 'Twill be much safer."

Lucy firmly shoved aside the sense of guilt which assailed her as she said, "I promise." Clenching her hand behind her back and crossing her fingers, and beneath her slippers, her toes.

"Promise also that you will not leave before me."

She made her expression was as innocent as possible and said, "I promise."

He searched her eyes carefully and whatever it was he saw must have satisfied him, for he chucked her on the chin and said, "Thank you."

24

So she left *with* Garrick. Or at least that was the plan, though escaping from the house had turned out to be much more difficult than expected. Her aunt had way-laid her after dinner, determined to discover if she really wanted to marry Garrick or not. It had taken her nearly an hour to convince her, an hour that ticked away in Lucy's mind like the hands of a clock.

Thank God she'd finally managed to escape, though she could have sworn her aunt kept her there on pur-pose, which was why she had gone to the carriage house immediately. She hadn't even bothered to change out of her peach gown, merely grabbed a lantern and set off.

She was grateful for that lantern when she opened the door of the carriage house, her aunt's elegant landau residing like a giant statue in the center of the aisle. She lifted the light higher. One of the horses nickered softly when it spied her cloaked form.

"Shhh." She raised her finger to her lips, then rolled

her eyes and mentally chastised herself. As if the horse would understand.

Barn dust and bits of straw rose up from beneath her slippered feet as she walked toward the back of the carriage, and more important, to the giant wicker basket strapped to it. The basket was huge, large enough to conceal her small form, though she wasn't looking forward to feeling like a chicken on its way to market during the ride to Selborne Manor.

One must do what one must do, she reminded herself, releasing a sigh of resignation as she hooked her lantern on the rusted nail somebody had pounded into a post. She then blew out the flame. Immediately, darkness enshrouded her like a cloying, black blanket and despite the wool cloak she wore, she shivered.

It *was* chilly out tonight, though she'd wager the reason her blood ran so cold was nerves. She'd best hurry. According to her calculations, John Coachman wouldn't be hooking up the horses for at least another half hour, but she wanted to be well settled before then.

Feeling her way along, she headed toward what she hoped was the wicker basket, but turned out to be a multispoked wheel. As luck would have it, her slippered foot sailed right in between the slats and rammed into the hub with a thud.

"Bloody hell," she cursed, clutching the wounded limb and hopping up and down. When the pain had subsided, she gingerly set her foot down, then limped toward the back of the coach. She felt like a blind man as she ran her hands along the brougham's side, sighing when she found the wicker basket. She moved her hands toward the latch, then opened the lid. Immediately, the smell of sweaty horse enveloped her, which was to be expected since the basket was used to hold horse blankets. Lucy ignored the violent urge to sneeze and gingerly placed a foot inside.

"Argh, me jewels!" a voice screeched.

Lucy jumped, so startled she fell backward. Her breath left her in a rush as her rear collided with the ground. For a moment she just sat there, mentally assessing if she'd broken anything. She could smell a cloud of stable dust rise up around her, feel it land on her cheeks and nose.

A groan.

"Tom?" she asked when she found her voice.

The boy released another moan. Lucy gingerly rose to her feet, placing her hands on her hips, not that the child could see it. "Good heavens, Thomas Tee, whatever are you doing in there?"

"Gettin' me beauty sleep," he grumbled. "Whadda ya thinks I'm doin' 'ere?"

Lucy frowned. "Well, you can't go along."

"Gonna tell on me?" he mumbled testily. "'Ave a fine time explain' 'ow ya come across me 'iding in 'ere, you would."

Lucy's eyes narrowed. He had a point, the little beast. She was just about to threaten him with taking Prinny away when the latch on the carriage-house door rattled. Lucy stiffened. Goodness, that couldn't be John Coachman. But it was. Lucy could hear his obnoxiously cheerful whistle as let himself in.

"Move aside," she whispered as she leapt toward the rear of the coach.

"Ain't no room."

"Move now or we're both lost."

Light spilled in through the doorway. She had a glimpse of Tom's irritated face just before she grabbed her skirts and shoved herself down next to him. "Ouch," he grumbled as she hurriedly closed the lid; the wicker creaked in protest, its ribbed edges hemming her in like a whalebone corset. Tom shifted, his elbow jutting into her side. She cursed him silently, then jumped at the sound of the wide double doors being pulled open. John was hooking up the carriage.

The half moon cast long shadows over the Selborne estate, bright enough to see by, and bright enough to make out the familiar contours of the landscape. Emotions assailed Garrick as he stared at the home—self-loathing, fear, anger—emotions he struggled to seal behind the wall he'd built around his heart, a wall which crumpled more and more each day.

Damn Lucy's aunt and her probing questions.

The lady had been relentless this afternoon, and her final words were that she would speak to her niece before putting her final seal of approval on their marriage. But he would marry Lucy in Scotland if need be, marry her and cherish every precious moment he had left with her.

The carriage shifted, bringing Garrick back to the present. He had a job to do, he reminded himself. One last job. He owed Lucy that much.

There was no light shining through the windows of the estate, which was to be expected given the lateness of the hour. Now all he had to do was find a way inside and be lucky enough to locate the papers he sought.

For once, luck seemed to be on his side, for it wasn't long before he discovered a paneled glass door left ajar. Someone must have forgotten to shut it after visiting the small garden located outside. Garrick hardly dared believe his good fortune as he cupped his hands and peered through the glass. Nothing. Just blackness. He straightened, then gently pulled on the brass handle, watching his reflected shadow as he pulled open the door.

The room was even darker inside. He paused a moment to let his eyes adjust, the inside walls materializing slowly before him: long shelves that reached nearly two stories high, a scattering of furniture, most noticeably a massive desk. It smelled musty, an odor that was at once familiar. Books. A great many of them, if Garrick didn't miss his guess. He'd found the library, or perhaps the earl's study.

Garrick almost smiled. Instead, he paused a moment to ensure there were no sounds coming from outside the room, most especially footsteps. There was nothing but the odd stillness that settled around a house during the night. He permitted himself a small smile. His plan was simple: confront the earl and the countess with the letter still in his possession and hope to God the earl would believe him. Would it work? He had no idea if God still listened to his prayers, but he hoped he would. Hoped for Lucy's sake.

By now his eyes had adjusted enough for him to make out everything but the darker recesses of the room. Feeling more and more confident, he strode forward.

He'd only taken three steps when the hiss of a lucifer flared, the sudden brightness momentarily blinding him.

"Welcome, Garrick."

Garrick blinked to dispel the bright spots, but he didn't need his vision to know who was in the room with him, for the voice had been all too familiar. It was Lucien St. Aubyn, Duke of Ravenwood, aiming a pistol at him.

Lucy peeked out the top of the basket, the evening sky seeming almost bright after the total blackness of her confines.

"Are we there?"

"Yes, Tom, we are."

She pushed herself to her feet and tried not to groan. Her neck felt as if she'd slept with her head on backward and her back felt as bowed as an old crone's. Forcing herself to straighten, she darted a glance around her. John was nowhere in sight. She wondered at that for a moment, then gingerly stepped down. Tom dropped down next to her.

"Where's the coachman?" Tom asked.

"I don't know. Perhaps inside the coach?"

"Nah, we'd a 'eard 'im enter. Probably 'e went ta empty 'is pisser or somethin'."

"Tom," Lucy scolded.

The boy shrugged, and even in the moonlight Lucy could see the mischief shining from his eyes.

"A man's gotta pee."

She ignored him and pulled the hood of her cloak up around her face. "You stay here."

"Not on yer life."

"'Tis safer here."

"I'm goin' with ya," he stated firmly.

Lucy swallowed back her annoyance. If the boy chose to go with her, there was very little she could do about it. It wasn't as if she could tie him down, though the idea was incredibly tempting right about now.

She shook her head and strode toward the house, once again wondering where the coachman had gone to. She had her answer a moment later. They had just gained the crest of the knoll when she looked down and saw John at the bottom of it, his pants around his ankles, the twin cheeks of his rear nearly as white as the shirt on Tom's back.

"See," Tom observed gleefully. "'E *is* emptyin' 'is pisser."

"What do you want?" Garrick all but spat, furious with himself for being caught by Ravenwood. With his black hair, black jacket, and black eyes, the duke looked like the devil himself.

Ravenwood came forward and pulled Garrick's pistol from where he had stored it in his waistband. Garrick's eyes narrowed, watching, assessing for weaknesses. There were none, at least none that he could see. The duke shoved the pilfered weapon into his own waistband then slowly backed away. His eyes looked blacker than coal in the flickering candlelight, the flames gleaming off the barrel of his pistol.

"I asked you a question, Ravenwood."

A voice drifted through the sill. Ravenwood stiffened, crossing the room in three quick steps to shove the pistol in Garrick's side.

"Move," he ordered, pushing the pistol against him until Garrick was forced to walk toward the back of the room and out of sight of the door.

Only seconds later a head peeked into the room, a head with long red hair tied back with a green ribbon and emerald eyes that scanned the room. Garrick nearly groaned. He nearly cursed. He nearly turned to Ravenwood and told him to forget the whole bloody thing. The duke could have Lucy, he could bound and gag her and drag her away—with his compliments.

"Don't make a sound," Ravenwood whispered from behind him, using Garrick's own body to hide behind.

Garrick clenched his hands.

"Why, Garrick, there you are."

At that moment Garrick wanted to ignore the pistol rammed into his back and cross the room to shake some sense into Lucy's mouselike brain. Instead he stayed put, straightening to his full height.

"What's the matter?" she said in the dulcet tones of a person extremely proud of herself. "Cat got your tongue?"

"Garrick, ya should'a seen it," an impish voice said from behind her, and Tom stepped into view.

That was when Garrick *did* groan. "We stumbled upon John coachman emptyin' 'is pisser, we did. Should'a seen the look on Lucy's—"

The boy's words died an abrupt death. Lucy gasped as Ravenwood made his presence known.

"Why, Miss Hartford," the duke said softly. "This *is* a surprise."

"Lucy, run!" Garrick ordered.

"Run and I'll shoot your lover," the duke said quickly.

Lucy pulled Tom up next to her, horror spreading through her. Ravenwood used the pistol to shove Garrick toward her, pulling out another from his waistband. Garrick stumbled, then turned back to the duke, his fist raised.

"Ahh, ah, ah," Ravenwood murmured silkily. "Do that and I shall shoot Miss Hartford."

After what seemed an age, Garrick finally lowered his fist. Lucy felt some of the tension drain from her shoulders, but it returned full-force as Ravenwood turned toward Tom. She didn't like the way he stared at the boy. He looked . . . well, almost triumphant.

"Please, let us go," she pleaded, her heart pounding so hard, her voice came out strangled. She darted a glance at Garrick, whose fists were clenched at his side.

"Sorry, Miss Hartford, but I'm afraid I can't do that." And with those words he aimed his second pistol at Tom.

Lucy screamed as the crack of gunfire filled the room with its deafening roar. "Tom," she yelled, instant, petrified tears rising in her eyes.

"You bloody bastard," Garrick bellowed. He took a step toward the duke, but Ravenwood stopped him by raising the second gun higher.

"'E missed," Tom yelled, patting himself like a blind man. "'E bloody missed me."

"You're wrong, young man. I hit my target exactly." His eyes never left Garrick's. "Look yonder at the candelabra. Particularly the candle on the right."

Lucy turned, then gasped. The candle had been cut cleanly in two. "I don't understand," she murmured.

"You will in a moment," the duke answered enigmatically.

Silence descended, but it was only when a half-dressed servant burst into the room that the realization of what he'd done dawned.

"Fetch the earl and the countess," the duke ordered.

"You *want* the earl present?" Lucy asked as the servant backed out of the room.

"I do."

And Lucy grew even more confused. Ravenwood was evil.

But he'd been kind to her on the *Revenger*.

She nibbled her lip in thought. He'd killed his brother.

Then again, nobody had actually proven that yet. She frowned, thoroughly confused, though that wasn't an altogether uncommon occurrence, she admitted.

Less than five minutes later the door re-opened and a woman who was obviously Melanie, Countess of Selborne, glided into the room with all the dignified aloofness of royalty, but when she spied Ravenwood her regal glide came to a peasantlike halt. "Ravenwood!" she gasped.

"Melanie."

Melanie's gaze swung toward them, her eyes widening. Lucy studied her, curiously disappointed by what she saw. She had expected the countess to look like one of the witches from *Macbeth*—instead she saw a woman approximately ten years older than herself. She had black hair and features which might have been beautiful but for her pointy chin, which spoiled it all. Lucy shivered as she looked into her cold eyes.

"Here now, what is the meaning of this?" asked a man coming up behind her who—judging by the brown and gold dressing robe, and the ingrained loftiness on his face—was undoubtedly the earl. And whereas Melanie's eyes were frigid, the earl's gray eyes were filled with anxiety and confusion as he spied Ravenwood's pistol, then the room's other three occupants. "Who are you and what do you want?"

Ravenwood smiled, an evil smile filled with malice. "I am Ravenwood."

"Ravenwood?" the earl gasped. "The *duke* of Ravenwood?"

He bowed.

"What do you want, you black-hearted devil?"

"I am that, and I'm here to speak with your wife . . . and you."

The earl turned to his wife. "Do you know who this is, Melanie?"

The countess tiled her arrogant nose to an elevated level. "I've never met the man in my life—"

"She's lying," Lucy said, her eyes meeting the evil countess's defiantly. "*She* asked the duke to find us, and he did, capturing us with help from pirates—"

"Who the devil are you?"

Lucy looked the earl square in the eye. "Lucy Hartford. And as I was saying, your wife wanted the duke to kill us, at least, I think she wanted him to kill us—"

"*Kill* you!" the earl boomed.

"Miss Hartford, please," Ravenwood interrupted. "Do let *me* do the talking."

Silenced, Lucy debating the wisdom of complying.

"He wants ta expose the countess, too," Tom exclaimed.

Lucy stiffened. She exchanged a startled glance with Garrick. Wherever could Tom have gotten that idea?

But one look into the duke's diabolically amused face made her realize Tom could be right.

The thought was confirmed when the duke said, "Indeed I do, young man."

25

"Expose the countess?" Lucy gushed, unable to stop herself.

"Indeed, Miss Hartford."

"But why didn't you just confront the earl with what you knew earlier?"

"I needed the boy as proof," the duke answered.

"This is ridiculous—"

"Sit down, Melanie," the duke snapped. He pointed with his pistol to two armchairs whose tall backs were to the dormant fireplace. "You too, my lord."

The earl looked clearly defiant, in his eyes a mixture of fear, anger and confusion. "No."

"*Sit down.*"

The earl jumped, as did Lucy. Then Selborne's eyes narrowed. He straightened his brown and gold dressing robe and with one last look of rancor, placed his hand on the small of the countess's back and guided her to a chair.

"Um, may we sit, too?" Lucy asked.

The duke nodded. "By all means," he announced, indicating a settee opposite the armchairs.

All three of them sat, Tom between Lucy and Garrick. Lucy shifted around a bit, until she realized she was sitting on the spent pistol. She pulled it out from beneath her. Tom snorted in amusement. When she looked up, she found the duke staring down at her with a frown on his face. Ignoring it, she went on to straighten her skirts, then settled back in the settee, impatiently waiting for the duke to begin.

Ravenwood turned back to the earl and after a few moments of contemplative silence finally said, "My lord earl, what do you remember about the death of your firstborn son?"

"I'll not listen to another word," the countess suddenly cried, shooting up from her chair. "Richard, if you do not—"

The duke strode forward, the countess yelping when he shoved her back down. "If you say one more word, Melanie, I will gag and bind you to that chair."

"You wouldn't dare," she huffed.

"Wouldn't I?"

She stared up at him, her eyes cold as tempered steel, her lips pressed together in a thin line.

"Stay put, Melanie," her husband warned.

The countess shot him a glare, then looked at Ravenwood, her expression pure snake venom, but she settled back nonetheless.

"Very smart of you, Melanie. I see you realize I should have no problem putting a ball through that cold lump of iron you call a heart."

"You bastard," she spat out.

"No, my dear, I can assure you I am many things, but not that."

"Is it more money you want? Is that it?"

"No, Melanie. I never wanted the money, I only wanted the letters from you asking—nay, *begging* for my help. But you never mentioned the boy by name. You've no idea of the trouble that caused me. I had to go after the boy myself, my living proof of your perfidy."

"No—"

"Quiet!" he snarled, turning to the earl. "The boy is your first son, my lord. Ten years ago she paid to have the child killed."

"Lies!" Melanie shot.

The duke turned back to her. "Are they, Melanie? I think not."

The countess didn't move.

A slow, victorious smile trickled across the duke's face. He turned to the earl. "Fate has played a cruel trick on your wife, my lord, for the child in question sits over there." He motioned toward Tom. "Say hello to your son, my lord. Your firstborn son. A boy your wife paid to have killed ten years ago."

Lucy waited, hardly daring to breath as she waited for the earl's response. She had it a moment later.

"Preposterous."

Her brow scrunched into a frown. *That* wasn't the response she'd expected.

"Impossible," the earl continued, his eyes latching onto the duke's with the ferociousness of a wild animal. "How dare you, *sir*? How dare you implicate my wife in such a scheme?"

Melanie looked smug now, so much so Lucy found herself saying, "He dares because it's the truth, my lord. The man who was hired to kill Tom was your kennel master."

"Enough," the earl spit out. "You're insane. All of you. Certainly Melanie and I have had our problems, but not even she would be so evil. Besides, I saw my son buried with my own two eyes."

"Did you?" Lucy interrupted. "Did you actually see his body?"

The earl's eyes narrowed in anger, his patience obviously at an end. "No, I did not. Nor would I want to—"

Lucy seized her advantage. "Then how can you be sure it was your son who was buried?"

The earl bristled, the anger rising off him like heat from a fire. "I don't know what your part is in this, madam, but I assure you, you'll pay for your involvement. Whatever it is."

Lucy stiffened and Tom shot up from the settee. "I says we leave 'im to 'er."

"Thomas Tee," Lucy hissed. "Sit down." The boy looked ready to protest until she lowered her tone of voice. "Please," she said softly. "You're not helping matters."

Tom stared hard at her for a moment, but then his shoulders slumped. He turned toward the earl and gave him a glare.

But the earl was staring at Tom as if she'd suddenly sprouted an extra set of arms. "W-what did you call him?" He asked hoarsely, his voice stangely devoid of emotion considering the disbelief on his face.

Lucy darted Garrick a confused stare before saying, "I called him Thomas Tee."

Selborne slowly sat up in his chair. "Where did he get that name?"

"I, well, I don't remember exactly. You told me that was your nickname, didn't you, Tom?"

Tom nodded, then crossed his arms in front of him mulishly.

"Where did you get the name?" the earl repeated, his fingers alternately clutching then releasing the arms of his chair.

Tom shrugged, looked as if he wasn't going to answer, but relented when Lucy tapped his foot with hers. "Been called that since I was a little mite."

"Why?"

Tom was beginning to look rebellious. He darted a glance around the room, his eyes catching upon Lucy's. "Tell him why," she said earnestly, excitement flowing through her. "Tell him Tom, tell him now."

Tom uncrossed his arms, took a deep breath and leveled a glare upon the earl. "It's short for Tom Thumb. Been called that on account of me big toe lookin' like a thumb."

"Dear God," the earl moaned, sinking back into the seat.

"Utter balderdash," the countess said shrilly. "It's not true. They must have heard the tale from somebody."

"But we can prove it, can't we Tom?" Lucy said triumphantly. Tom nodded reluctantly. "Take off your boot."

"Me feet stink," the boy said petulantly.

"Do it, imp," Garrick urged.

Tom shot Garrick a look of long-suffering resignation and then did as he was told. In seconds his left foot was exposed for all of them to see. The earl gasped.

"They don't smells that bad," the boy mumbled.

Lucy laughed. She couldn't help it. She was so delighted. She glanced over at the countess in triumph.

She was gone.

"The countess!"

But Ravenwood already had her, had grabbed her by the back of her dressing robe and tugged her toward him.

"No," Melanie screamed, turning on him with her arms outstretched, her hands curled into claws and confirming her guilt by her very actions. The duke neatly sidestepped her charge, and Lucy tensed as she waited for the crack of a pistol. But it was apparent the duke had other plans for his captive, for he grabbed her and pulled her up against him. She struggled despite the pistol now held to her temple. His head lowered and Lucy had to strain to hear, "I'm looking forward to making you pay, Melanie," he said softly. "Looking forward to it a great deal."

"No," she pleaded, her eyes seeking out her husband's. "Richard, I—"

"Don't," the earl interrupted coldly. "No more of your lies, Melanie."

And for the first time Lucy saw fear on Melanie's face. Loads and loads of it.

26

The next morning Lucy watched, alone, as Melanie, Countess of Selborne, was escorted to the waiting carriage like Lady Jane Grey on her way to the executioner. The image through the glass at Selborne was crystal clear, and so Lucy had a perfect view of Melanie walking toward the carriage, her posture so straight and upright it looked as if she balanced an apple beneath that green bonnet she wore.

It had taken hours to truly convince the earl of Tom's identity. He'd questioned the boy over and over again about his childhood, but in the end it had been the letters that had convinced him, the duke's concern over Tom not being mentioned in them all for naught. Melanie had very distinctive handwriting, handwriting the earl had recognized at once.

Lucy sighed. The sight of the earl's face when he'd realized the truth was one Lucy never wanted to see again. He'd been destroyed. Utterly destroyed.

Shoving the memory aside, she refocused on the scene outside the window again. Ravenwood was helping the countess into the carriage with a smugly superior grin on his face. The countess jerked her arm away, and Ravenwood's smile grew. A moment later he too disappeared. The vehicle sprang forward, the trunks piled atop it swaying from side to side as it rumbled around the curved drive, past some bushes, beyond the fountain, until at long last it crossed between two brick columns and turned onto the road.

And just like that, it was over: the countess was gone and Tom restored to his rightful place as heir to the earldom. Too bad Garrick wasn't here to see it, but he'd gone to London to fetch her aunt, leaving so early he'd missed breakfast. But Lucy was sure Garrick would've liked to have seen the countess being marched from the house like Napoleon on his way to Alba. Perhaps it might have helped to banish the blue funk he'd sunk into, a dark mood she'd no idea how to brighten.

She sighed. Between Garrick's glowering countenance and Tom's obnoxious behavior this morning, she was hard pressed to decide whom she wanted to choke first; Garrick for dodging her questions with the sure-footedness of a goat, or Tom for behaving as if he'd lived in a barn for the past two months. Right now the boy was undoubtedly upstairs, pouting after being forced to take a bath, small punishment indeed for passing gas at the breakfast table.

She turned back to the empty room, the gray light of morning turning the off-white tones of the decor to the color of ash. She was exhausted, the wound on her head still hurt, and she ached for Garrick's arms.

The door clicked open and Lucy turned to see Tom striding toward her with the clomping steps of an outraged general. One look at his attire and she realized it wasn't *her* he was angry with, but rather, whomever had dressed him.

She choked back a laugh. Goodness, someone had forced the boy into a jacket two sizes too small. The arms of the garment ended halfway between wrist and elbow, exposing the cuff of an equally small shirt beneath. Trousers, which very obviously belonged to someone much shorter, rode far above his ankles.

"Look what they done ta me," he cried, holding out his arms.

It was at that exact moment one of his buttons launched itself like a rock from a catapult. She ducked, the button striking the window behind her with a metallic *ting*. It clattered to the floor and spun on the ground like a top.

When she straightened, Tom looked so outraged, so completely belligerent, she couldn't help but let loose with a gurgle of laughter which quickly turned into full-scale chuckles.

Tom was not amused. "They stole me clothes," he gritted out, his little fists clenched in anger.

Lucy laughed harder.

"The earl's man forced me inta this bloody outfit, sayin' it were either that or nothin' at all."

Lucy managed to gasp out, "Oh, Tom. You look as if you got caught in a rainstorm and hung out to dry."

The boy's eyes narrowed. "Never wanted no part o' this bloody scheme anyhow. Everybody tiptoein' around me and callin' me m'lord, as if I were some watch-fobbin' nabob."

Lucy's laughter abruptly faded. Even though the words were spoken bravely, she could hear the underlining note of fear. Sympathy for his plight washed over her. It would be hard to be suddenly thrust into a world that was totally foreign and unfamiliar.

She walked forward and she could see the tears gleaming in his eyes. Placing a hand against his cheek, she watched as his control broke, sobs racking his small frame.

"Oh, Tom," she said softly, drawing him into her arms. "This hasn't been easy for you, has it?"

"I'm scared," she heard him murmur. "Ain't never been so scared in me life afore. Not even o' those pirates."

Resting her cheek against the top of his head she said gently, "Things will work out. You'll see."

"Don't wants ta be no lord's son," he hiccuped. "I want to be your son, or Salena and Adrian's."

She drew back to stare down into washed-out violet eyes. "I'm so sorry, Tom, but it's not possible."

"Then I belong on the streets with the rest o' me mates," the boy continued.

"No, Tom. You belong here, and though you may not realize it yet, in time you will."

"But the man don't feel like me father."

"He will, Tom. One day soon. You'll see."

Just then the door opened, the object of their discussion walking into the room. The earl took two steps into the room and stopped dead in his tracks. "Good God!" he cried. "What happened to your clothes?"

Tom darted a glance at her, then back at the earl, whose uncertainty in how to treat the boy shone in his eyes. Tom didn't make it any easier. He stared at the earl, his eyes declaring war.

"Would you like to change out of that monstrous outfit?" the earl finally asked.

And Lucy could see it for the olive branch it was. Trouble was, did Tom see it?

"I s'ppose anythin's better'n this," Tom grumbled, snapping the branch off. He ignored the earl's out-stretched hand as he walked by.

The earl stared after him, a look of uncertainty on his face.

"Give it time, my lord," Lucy said softly as Tom walked out of the room. "He's been through a lot."

"I understand, Miss Hartford. Believe me."

Yes, Lucy thought. Undoubtedly he did. It must be difficult to lose one's wife and gain a son all in the space of a few hours.

They both looked up at the sound of a carriage wheels crackling down the drive. She turned toward the window, her eyes widening at the shiny black carriage making its way toward the house with all the pomp and ceremony of a coronation. There were two footmen in green and gold livery stationed behind the vehicle, three men riding postilion atop the silver-gray horses, and two outriders. The horses' tack gleamed, even in the gray light, and the black paint on the coach was so shiny she could see the reflection of the earl's green lawn in it. Behind the vehicle rumbled another coach.

Her aunt's.

"Garrick," she breathed.

"So soon?"

"Yes, and unless I miss my guess, the other coach belongs to my friend Salena, the Duchess of Warburton."

"Warbuton!"

Lucy headed for the front door, hearing the earl follow. They reached the porch just as Salena's coach drew to a flamboyant, hoof-skidding halt.

A footman jumped down and placed a small, cushioned step atop the ground so precisely Lucy wondered if he'd been waiting all morning to do exactly that. "'Ere ya go, Lady Salena," he said as he opened the door.

"Thank you, Will," a soft voice answered. A moment later an elegant figure draped in a rose-colored gown stepped down, golden eyes lighting up when they met Lucy's. The feather hat perched atop her wheat-colored curls brushed the frame of the door as she rushed forward. "Lucy, you goose, I can't believe you went and followed Garrick."

"Warned his lordship she would," said another voice.

Lucy groaned as her aunt slowly climbed down from her own coach. "Aunt Cornelia, what a surprise."

"I'd wager it is," she snapped, banging her cane on the pebbled ground like a priest slapping the pulpit.

"This is your aunt?" the earl said from behind her.

Lucy turned. "Er, yes, my lord. Aunt Cornelia, this is the Earl of Selborne, Tom's father."

Cornelia's eyes narrowed. "So it's true, then? Garrick told us you'd convinced the man."

"They have, my lady," the earl confirmed.

"Good, for I don't fancy my niece embarking on any more adventures. Heart couldn't take it."

"Neither could mine," grumbled a feminine voice.

Lucy looked up. "Beth!"

Beth stepped down, her white and blue dress a stark contrast to the black carriage. She looked disgruntled as she made her way toward Lucy, but the look slowly faded into a smile. "Congratulations, Lucy. I knew you could do it."

Lucy felt an answering grin spread across her face. "Thank you, Beth."

"I should hope I helped, too."

At the sound of that familiar and beloved voice, Lucy turned toward her aunt's carriage with a radiant smile. Garrick stared back at her, the most poignant and tender look on his face she'd ever seen. It made her breath catch. The man looked as if he wanted to drag her into his arms and never let her go. And then she caught sight of who was walking beside him. "Adrian!"

An answering smile nearly as bright as the gold watch fob dangling from his tan waistcoat spread across the Duke of Warburton's face. "Lucy, my dear. How lovely to see you in skirts for a change."

She giggled.

"Although considering your propensity for fire, that might not be a good thing."

Lucy laughed again, delighted to have all her friends with her, even if her aunt seemed to have developed a permanent tick in her cheek.

"Where's Tom?" Salena asked.

"We sent him upstairs to change."

"Which reminds me," the earl said. "I offered to find him some clothes."

At Salena's questioning look, Lucy explained as she led them back to the salon. Quickly, she brought them up to speed on the morning's events. By the time she was done, Tom and the earl had joined them. Tom took one look at Salena and flew into her arms. The earl watched, a look of curiosity mixed with longing on his face as, next, the boy hugged Adrian.

"It's good to see you, imp," the duke said. "We were worried about you."

"Ya should'a seen it, Adrian," Tom said excitedly. "There was pirates and a sea battle. And Lucy got the crew sick, an we, Garrick and I, was locked in the 'old, an' we almost died—"

"Ahem," Lucy coughed.

Tom glanced at her, then at the earl. It was to the boy's credit that he actually appeared to realize the effect his words had on the earl. "But we come out all right an' tight, we did," he added.

"My lord," Salena said into the uncomfortable silence which followed. "May I say how glad we are you and Tom are reunited."

The earl nodded stiffly.

"We realize how difficult this must be for you," Adrian added. "My wife thought it might be a good idea to stay with you just until the boy is settled."

Tom looked ready to declare his unwillingness to become "settled" but Salena silenced him with a glare.

"That would be most kind of you, Your Grace."

"Adrian. Please, call me Adrian, and my wife Salena, if you will."

"But Adrian," Tom interrupted. "I wants ta watch Luce and Garrick get leg-shackled."

"Then you must ask your father."

"You're not wed?" the earl said, looking between Lucy and Garrick.

"Er ... ah, no. We're to leave for Scotland today," Garrick answered.

Lucy gasped. "Today! But Garrick, it's so soon."

"The sooner you're wed the better," her aunt harrumphed.

Yes, she supposed that was true. Still, it would have been nice to be sent off in style. She would have liked to have a big wedding, with hundreds of gawking guests and a bunch of little choir boys singing in their pubescent voices, but it looked as if that was not to be.

"I had your aunt pack you some clothes so we can leave straight for the dock," Garrick added.

"You did?"

"And I brought you my wedding gown," Salena said softly.

Lucy's eyes widened. "Oh, Salena. You didn't."

"I did."

"And *I* packed some clothes for you," her aunt said. "Not that you deserve it, you wretched girl."

"Oh, Auntie," Lucy said softly, delight spreading through her. A small wedding would be ever so much fun, she concluded. And in Scotland, too. How scandalous. Pushing herself to her feet, she blinked a few times to dispel the dizziness which had plagued her since her bump on the head, and walked to her aunt's side. "Thank you, Auntie."

Cornelia, obviously in a perverse mood, hardened her jaw.

"You do know that next to Garrick you're the most important person in my life."

"You have a fine way of showing it, gel, gallivanting around as you do."

"But I *had* to go with Garrick. I couldn't let the man I love ride into danger without me."

Her aunt looked as if she was going to be stubborn, but when Lucy reached down and gave her a hug, she heard her say, "Very well. You're forgiven, but only because after tomorrow you will no longer be my responsibility."

Lucy drew back, rolled her eyes, then gave her aunt a kiss on her cheek.

"Well," the earl said into the silence which followed. "Since everything appears to be settled, I've suddenly been struck by an idea. In an effort to repay you for the risks you took on behalf of my son, I insist you take my yacht to Scotland. 'Twill be quicker than returning to London, for as you know, Selborne is only a few miles from the coast. My ship can be ready to sail within the hour."

Stunned silence greeted his words.

"That'd be mighty sportin' of ya, guv," Tom announced.

The earl looked pleased by his son's response, saying, "I do have one request." Lucy nodded encouragingly. "I would like for Tom and me to accompany you."

Tom's eyes widened before he rushed across the room and into his father's arms.

27

They arrived in Edinburgh, Scotland, an hour or so before dusk, and Lucy was so excited she could barely stand it. She had spent the day in the main cabin due to her aunt's dire murmuring about bad luck for the bride to see the groom before the wedding. Lucy hadn't minded too terribly much. Salena, Beth, and her aunt had kept her company, but she would have liked to observe the voyage from the main deck, not the earl's plush cabin. Thank goodness they'd arrived quickly.

"You look gorgeous," Beth murmured, stepping back to admire the sight of Lucy in Salena's wedding gown.

Her aunt, who was busy making last-minute alterations, pushed herself to her feet, her bones creaking nearly as loudly as the ship. "You'll do," she pronounced.

"You look wonderful, Lucy," Salena seconded.

"Yes, but I *do* wish you had more cleavage, Salena," Lucy murmured, glancing down at herself. "I dare say

I'm about to burst out of this thing. Not only that, but this dress is *heavy*."

Salena laughed. "'Tis the pearls."

Lucy glanced down. Pearls, pearls, pearls, she thought. Hundreds of them. The were on her puffed sleeves, on the skin-tight fabric at her wrists, on the bodice, and around the heart-shaped neckline. The gown was so heavy she felt as if she were dragging around the entire crew with her when she walked. She wouldn't be at all surprised if a whale mistook her for a giant clam.

A knock at the door interrupted that dire musing; she heard Adrian's voice saying, "The coachman has returned. Garrick has sent him to fetch you to the chapel."

"Good," her aunt called back, the skirts of her deep blue dress rustling as she cast one last, critical eye over her niece. "We shall be out in a moment."

She turned and grabbed the bouquet of orange blossoms and roses that the duke had been sent to get.

No doubt Adrian had paid a small fortune for them, but Garrick had insisted on roses. Lucy smiled and inhaled their sweet fragrance, sure that for the rest of her life the smell of orange blossoms and roses would remind her of this day.

"Well, are we ready then?" her aunt asked, her eyes suspiciously bright.

Lucy's own eyes welled with tears as she reached out and hugged her. "Oh, Auntie. This is the happiest day of my life." She pulled back and smiled mistily at her friends, the blue dresses they wore shimmering through the wetness of her tears. "Nothing could spoil it. *Nothing.*"

He was going to die. The thought kept pounding into his head with the force of a thousand anvils. Tonight would be his last day on earth. His last day with Lucy.

Garrick stood before the altar of the church, brow beaded with sweat though the day was cool. The black jacket he wore felt tight, and the white shirt beneath it seemed to squeeze the life out of him, as if each breath he took grew shallower and shallower, until at last he would take none at all. But he mustn't think of that. Mustn't think about how horrified the priest behind him would be were he to find the man who stood before him had sold his soul to the devil. Mustn't think about how lately he'd felt a blackness creeping upon him. Most of all he mustn't think about *her.* About Lucy.

"You look nervous, my friend," Adrian whispered, his voice echoing off the beams of the ceiling some one hundred feet above.

"A touch," Garrick murmured, hoping Adrian would leave it at that.

As it turned out, he needn't have worried. A door to their left opened, precluding the duke from saying anything further. It was Lady Cornelia.

"She's waiting outside the chapel door," she whispered, darting a glance at the priest, then at Adrian, who stood next to him. "You look nervous, young man."

"He is, a bit," Adrian answered for him.

"Hmm. Don't blame you. I'd be nervous too, if I was marrying my niece."

"Let us all thank God you are not," Adrian joked. Cornelia smiled, then turned and sat next to the earl.

The chapel door opened and Tom poked his head in. "Are we ready?"

"Aye, young man," the priest answered.

The boy nodded, dipped back outside and said something, then swung the chapel door wide open, latching it into place. When he was done he practically skipped to his seat, looking every inch an earl's son in his dark gray jacket and off-white trousers. The moment he sat, Salena walked through the doorway and the look of love she exchanged with her husband sent a shaft of poignant longing though Garrick. His hands clenched by his side. God forgive him, but he wanted to run, to escape the pain that assailed him.

But he could never escape.

His breath came in ragged gasps as he struggled to contain the multitude of emotions slamming into him with the force of a tidal surge. Longing. Dread. But most of all, fear.

Salena smiled, apparently oblivious to his pain as she took her place next to Lady Cornelia. Beth entered next; the ceremony would be small, but all the more poignant for its simplicity. All too soon the church quieted, so much so that Garrick could hear the priest shift upon his feet; his black robes rustled, the pages of his sermon crinkled.

And then he saw her.

She stood in the doorway, a sudden beam of sunlight emerging from the clouds to illuminate her form. His breath caught. The dress she wore glowed, the pearls luminescent and almost seeming to have an energy of their own. Her hair caught the light, the long tresses hanging loose down her back like a wall of molten flame. Emerald eyes glowed.

Those eyes were filled with love and happiness as she gazed down the long aisle. The narrow, oblong widows lining the walls lit the way like a giant carpet of light as she made her way toward him. Automatically, he held out a hand to her. And the moment she touched him a cloud dipped in front of the sun. Everyone blinked. The priest shifted. Garrick ignored the ominous sign and clasped her hand in his.

"Come," he said, his voice deep and filled with aching tenderness, with the longing of a man who knew he was to die.

She nodded, then followed him to the altar and knelt beside him. From that point forward, Garrick concentrated on speaking the words which would bind her to him until midnight. Every word he spoke was torture, every vow filled him with regret and anguish. And when it was over and he glanced into her loving eyes, he knew with a certainty she would never love another.

"Garrick," Lucy called laughingly after giving her aunt one last tearful hug good-bye. She smiled at her friends, all of whom stood waiting for her and Garrick to climb into the carriage. "Salena and Beth are threatening to sail back to Cardiff with us."

"Are they?" he asked softly.

"Exceptin' we're afraids the ship'll be rockin' too much ta get much rest."

"Thomas Tee," her aunt cried. "What a perfectly crass thing to say."

The others laughed, including Lucy, who allowed Garrick to hand her inside the carriage. It took a moment for her to arrange her tentlike skirts and then for Garrick to settle in next to her. With one last wave they were off, back to the earl's ship, which had been graciously loaned to them for the trip to Cardiff.

Pellets of rice rained down upon the carriage like a winter snow flurry. Lucy laughed and waved good-bye to her friends and family one last time. As they faded from view she leaned back and happily gazed up at Garrick, who stared off into the distance as if trying to peer into the future.

"Good heavens, Garrick. You look so glum."

He glanced down at her, apparently startled by her observation. "Do I?" he asked sharply.

Lucy tilted her head at him. Something bothered him, she was sure of it, but what it was she had no idea. "You seem so quiet."

He stiffened. His face became unreadable, as if someone had drawn a blind over his features. "A lack of sleep, no doubt."

"Are you worried about our wedding night?" she teased.

It was as if someone had struck him a physical blow. Lucy was startled to see a brief flash of pain cross into his eyes. She reached out to clasp his hand. "Garrick, what is it?"

"Nothing, Lucy." He squeezed her hand back. "I've merely a lot on my mind." He looked away, his eyes focused on the passing scenery, but Lucy could tell by his rigid form that all was not right.

"Do you know how much I love you?" she said softly. He flinched, flinched as if she'd suddenly pinched him. It sent fear cascading through her veins. "Garrick, what is it? Please, please tell me."

"'Tis nothing, Lucy." And when he turned back to her his expression was washed carefully clean. She wanted to believe him, truly she did, for the alternative—that something was truly wrong—was too horrible to contemplate. But she knew he lied. She knew him too well to tell when he wasn't being completely honest with her. Still, she let the matter drop, convinced that whatever it was, he'd share it with her when he was ready to.

Reaching up, she gently touched the side of his face. He closed his eyes at the contact. She could feel the stubble of beard which grew upon his face, his skin hot beneath her touch. He inhaled deeply, and when he opened those sea-blue eyes of his, so much love filled their depth that Lucy felt her breath catch with the wonder of it.

"I love you, Luce," he said, gazing down at her as if he never wanted to stop.

Suddenly she reached out and hugged him, burrowing her face into the crook of his neck. The carriage dipped into a pothole, a streethawker cried out his wares, but Lucy hardly noticed. In her eyes there was no one in the world but them.

• • •

It was evening by the time they cast off. The moon, no longer full, was still bright enough to light the coast and the ocean between them as they sailed toward Cardiff. Garrick sighed. The sight of the waves sparkling nearly as bright as the stars above, to Garrick's mind was almost as beautiful as the woman who awaited him in the cabin below. Pain washed over him with the sting of hot pitch as the thought penetrated that his was this last night with her. The fact was undeniable, and though over the preceding hours he had grown somewhat numb, he was determined to prove to Lucy just how much he loved her, would never stop loving her even when he was gone.

He found her in the cabin, the multitude of candles she'd lit setting her skin aglow as she lay atop the brown coverlet, its folds alternately shielding and revealing her perfect, naked body. He stopped midstride, his mind focused only on her.

"I promise not to catch the cabin on fire this time," she teased impishly, breaking the spell.

Garrick remembered the night he'd called her a trollop. What a fool he'd been. If the pain she felt that day was a tenth of what he felt at the prospect of leaving her tonight, he deserved his fate.

"Garrick," she whispered softly.

He wouldn't do it, wouldn't dwell on the fact that he'd sold his soul. He'd done it for her, her reminded himself. He'd do it again. Swallowing his anguish, he forced himself to walk toward her, though he lacked the strength to muster a smile. Forced himself to undress, though he wanted nothing more than to hold on to her for dear life. Forced himself to act as if he was a man sailing toward the rest of his life, not one fated to "die" at the stroke of midnight.

She smiled and opened her arms, the fabric of the coverlet parted to reveal her white breasts. Garrick needed no further urging. Even so, he took his time, preferring instead to study her as he would always remember her: hair tousled from their trip to the dock, the dusky contours of her body. Like a man in a trance, he slowly moved forward and when he could stand it no longer, lay down beside her. Savoring each moment, he allowed their lips to meet. This, too, he memorized. He kissed her gently, lovingly, longingly. Her lips parted for him, and Garrick closed his eyes and savored the taste of her, the delicious, achingly sweet taste of her own desire.

It was Lucy who broke the kiss, Lucy who drew back and framed his face with her hands, gently stroking back the hair which she'd released from his queue. For the longest time she simply stared at him. Desire flickered in her eyes; it lingered, then was replaced by a look of such complete and total love, Garrick's breath escaped in a rush.

A coldness settled around his heart, a coldness borne of pain. He tried to keep it at bay by covering her lips with his, then assaulting the sensitive cords of her neck, his tongue gently licking the salt from her skin. He tasted her, relished in the spicy scent of her.

One last time.

She moaned, a deep moan that sent a streak of longing through Garrick. He would spend the rest of eternity remembering that sound. He wanted her, hardened with anticipation, wanted her even though it was all he could do to keep the agony at bay.

"Garrick," she moaned.

But he would not rush this, would not spoil her first time because of his nearly uncontrollable need. Even with the heat of her body nearly scalding him, he refused to give in, preferred, instead, to lap at her ear.

She writhed in his arms—he could feel her toes curl, her legs brush against his—but he held back, some inner strength forcing him to take his time, to worship her, revel in the power of their desire for each other.

For the first time and for the last time.

Down the side of her neck his lips trailed, halting at her collarbone to place a tender kiss against the pulse beating above it. She arched into him, rubbing her butter-soft thighs against his and pressing herself against his hardness. For a moment he lost control, nipping her flesh. She groaned. He nipped again, taking his time as his lips traveled toward her nipple. When he took her between his lips, he tasted her.

One last time.

He allowed her to shift beneath him so he could memorize the feel of legs against his, the satiny touch of her inner knee, the heel of her foot as it brushed against his calf. Once again he began to kiss her, memorizing the soft touch of her tongue against his, the heat of her thighs as she parted for him, the sound of her sighs.

She brushed up against him, her body urging him closer. But he refused to enter her. Instead, he started a new kind of assault. Slowly, he moved his hips, using the tip of his erection to trail up her wetness. It was paradise.

It was hell. He heard her breath catch. Then she breathed his name against his mouth. Closer and closer he brought her toward fulfillment. Tremors racked his body as he fought to hold back, but still he didn't enter her. Dear God, how he wanted to.

"Garrick, please," she begged.

And this, too, he committed to memory. The husky sound of her voice, breathless with need. The frenetic movement of her body as she tried to coerce him inside her. And when the torture grew too much to bear, he trailed his lips down the cords of her neck again, nipped the small indentation next to her collarbone, swirled his tongue down toward her navel. She arched into him, parted wider, and he took what she offered. He drank of her, lapped at the flesh between her thighs. Moisture flooded his mouth. Her cries grew louder. She pressed herself against him, and he drank until she cried out his name, pulsed against his lips.

"Oh, Garrick."

But he wanted more, wanted to give her all he had to give, and then some. He rose above her and slowly, gently sank into her willing sheath. He felt her barrier break, heard her soft moan, then released his own sigh of pleasure and pain as he entered her fully.

Finally, they were one. The love that shimmered between them was all the more poignant for its power. He knew he would lose control soon, but he couldn't stop his own answering moans as he slowly slid in and out of her. His chest hair brushed against the swell of her breasts, exciting him more. Still, he held back. One more time. He needed to hear her moan with sweet release one more time, wanted to close his eyes and recall the sound for all eternity.

"Gar-*rick* . . ."

And there it was. The sound he'd been waiting for. Her body spasmed around his and he let himself go. Just closed his eyes and moved in and out of her faster and then faster still. He savored the feel of it, the warmth of her, the sweetness of her, until finally, all too quickly, his body pulsed its own sweet release.

"Lucy," he whispered. "My sweet Luce."

Her arms wrapped around him. He could feel her warm breath as she nestled her head against him. Slowly, he returned to earth.

For the last time.

His eyes burned as he held her close. God, how he loved her. Would always love her. She was the light in his darkness. Heaven, in his hell.

"Garrick?"

He didn't want to move, didn't want her to see his torture. But soft hands clutched at him, forced him to look at her, and when their eyes met, hers widened.

"Oh, Garrick. You're crying."

It felt as if he were dying. Still, the minutes passed, dropping away one after another until only moments remained.

Garrick made love to her twice more during the night. Now, as the time for him to leave drew nearer, he was tormented by the thought of doing so.

She was nestled against his side like a child, her

breathing even, her arms wrapped around his shoulder. Beautiful even in her sleep. Her hair lay tossed around them, like a silken cloth. Her skin glowed in the lamplight, and the single sheet that covered them tangled about her legs. Never would he forget. Not the way she felt against him, not the smell of their spent passion, not the way she looked while she slept. Not a thing.

"Do you know how much I love you?" he asked softly. The fear returned; it clutched at his insides and clasped itself around his heart. He must go, though he was terrified of what awaited him beyond; go because if he didn't, Lucy would pay the price.

His throat clogged with emotion as he stared down at her, so peaceful in sleep, so completely unaware of what he was about to do. "I'll miss you, my love." His hand trembled. A feeling of helplessness assailed him. He swallowed and then bent down to lightly kiss her forehead, inhaling her sweet fragrance. Roses. He committed it to memory, vowing never to forget.

Closing his eyes, he forced himself to let go, to break contact with her. First his legs, then his body. His arms were the hardest for they felt leaden, shaking so terribly now he could barely force them to work.

The ship began to pitch wildly, making it hard to dress. As he turned to leave he knelt down beside the bed. Gently, he stroked the side of her face. His legs began to feel weak, his eyes to burn. "Little angel." Tenderly, he leaned over and lightly kissed her forehead. "I love you."

When he drew back, a slight smile creased her lips. He committed the picture to memory.

The ship rolled violently. She grumbled in her sleep.

Garrick stood, barely noticing the yaw. His hand fell limply back to his side.

It was time.

The breath he took was nearly a gasp, his feet not wanting to move, but he forced them to. One last look of longing and he turned away; the door seemed to him as frightening as the very door to hell itself. And when he touched that door, was it his imagination or did it feel hot? He rested his forehead against the wood. He couldn't do it. Jesus, it felt as if he were being torn in two. Squeezing his eyes closed he took several deep breaths, then forced himself to turn the knob. He had to, for Lucy's sake.

The moment the door was open, rain hit his face like small pebbles. The door was pulled from his grasp by the wind, the wood banging against the outer wall. Papers he'd left on the table blew behind him.

"Garrick," Lucy cried.

He paused, the wind whipping wildly about him. His tears mixed with the rain. Hot rain. Nearly as hot as the sting of pain which filled his insides, his mind, and his heart. He took a step.

"Garrick," she called again.

He took another step. God help him, he couldn't turn to look at her, knowing if he did, he'd never leave.

"M'lord," a man yelled from behind the wheel only a few feet in front of him. "I never seen nothin' like it. It comes out of nowhere."

Garrick registered his words only distantly, moving past the man, heading for the ladder that led to the upper deck. It was as if he were being compelled to move forward, drawn by a force he could neither see nor feel. Stinging rain lashed his face, falling into his eyes with pelting force. The world became a washed-out blur. It was black, blacker than the deepest part of the ocean. Salt filled his mouth, burned down his throat, stung his eyes. Still, Garrick climbed slowly, one foot at a time. The sails crackled with a simmering energy, the very air itself felt charged. It was time, he thought. Time to leave. Time to leave Lucy.

"Welcome, Garrick," a voice said. Strangely enough, he could hear that voice perfectly over the element's rage. "I see you've kept your part of the bargain, though you're a bit early."

Belial.

Even against the backdrop of blackness, Garrick could see his darker than midnight form.

"Garrick?"

Garrick jerked as if he'd been struck. The voice, so cherished and dear, called over the scream of the storm. Lucy.

"Such a brave thing, she is," Belial said with mock pity.

"Don't touch her," Garrick warned. He turned. God help him, he turned.

Bright red curls bobbled into view, then the pale oval of Lucy's terrified face. The sheet she had wrapped around her was a splash of white as she struggled to climb. Thunder boomed above, and lightning flashed in the same instant. Garrick's heart stopped. It had grown strangely quiet, a quiet he had heard only once before.

He tried to cry a warning, but he was too late.

The wave, when it hit, knocked him off his feet and sent him skittering like a rock toward the rail. He clawed at the deck, his terror for Lucy giving him a will he hadn't known he possessed. Pain sluiced through him as his back made contact with the thick oak rail. For a moment he couldn't breathe, the weight of the wave and the freezing cold knocking the breath out of him. Then he was clear. The water rolled off him, leaving foam in its wake. The ship rocked, but he clung, his thoughts centered on one thing.

Lucy.

"Gaaarick," she screamed.

There was terror in that voice, terror such as he'd never heard. Nearly blinded by the salt and wind that filled his eyes, he crawled toward where he'd last seen her, climbing up the rail.

Laughter echoed around him, taunting, triumphant, terrifying.

"Gaaaariiiiick."

He pushed himself to his feet; the wind ripped at his clothes and hair. He found her hanging half-on, half-off the deck. One more wave and she would be swept away. Panic made him lunge toward her.

"Garrick," she cried.

"Take my hand," he called.

It took two tries for her hands to meet his over the rocking of the ship. She was icy-cold in his grasp. He pulled, slowly lifting her.

Evil, mad laughter filled the air.

They landed, sprawled upon the deck. Hands fumbled for him, making their way toward his face. He blinked rapidly, trying to clear the stinging rain from his eyes.

A pair of cherished green eyes peered into his own. "Oh, Garrick. Thank God," she gasped.

He wanted to touch her, to kiss her and never let go, but once again a sudden, ominous quiet filled the air. His heart stopped beating, then resumed at a furious rate. Lucy seemed oblivious. Using the last vestige of his strength, Garrick rolled atop her. She looked startled, then smiled.

"Hold on," he cried.

Her look turned to one of confusion. He bent down and kissed her.

A last kiss. His last taste of heaven.

"I love you, Lucy," he called over the howl of the wind. "Never forget."

She seemed startled by his words, but then his body was pulled away from hers as a giant cauldron of water rammed him like a charging horse. He heard a tremendous crack and knew the rail had broken. Blackness descended, a feminine scream filled his ears, and then he fell, fell as if he'd never land, fell toward the churning mass of angry sea.

28

He was dead. Lucy lay on the sandy beach, the sun making prisms on the waves like glass in a kaleidoscope. The steady roar of the ocean filled the air, the smell of brine and the buzzing of sand flies creating its own peaceful melody.

Lucy was oblivious to it all as she sat on the sand, her eyes staring sightlessly out at the horizon.

He was dead.

She took a deep, shaky breath, trying for the thousandth time not to cry. It didn't work. The tears managed to escape anyway. They fell, unchecked, down her cheeks, the wind that always seemed to whip over the shores of Garrick's estate picking them up and tugging them toward her jaw. A gull cried overhead, the sound as lonely and raw as she herself felt. Pain intensified, doubled. She inhaled deeply, and her breath caught on a sob.

Concentrate, Lucy. Concentrate on the black fabric of your dress. Concentrate on being strong. Concentrate on the ocean

Garrick loved so much. You may be a widow, but you can be the bloody finest widow Cardiff had ever seen.

Cardiff. So beautiful with the granite castle stretching high on the cliffs behind her.

She squeezed her eyes closed, knowing one of the staff watched her from the parapet behind her, yet the tears managed to escape anyway. She inhaled a ragged breath. A tear trekked down her cheek and she wiped it away with a grainy hand, uncaring that she left a streak of fine grit behind.

They had searched for him for days, which had stretched into a month, and then two. The magistrate had told them they would continue to watch the beach. Sometimes they'd wash ashore, he had told her. *They*, the man had said. As if Garrick was nothing more than a piece of flesh, an empty shell to be found. Bile rose in her throat at the image of him being found. No. She would not think of it. She would remember Garrick as he was, vibrant, his sea-blue eyes full of life, his smile filled with love.

Her hands clenched into fists, her shoulders hunched. She was going to break down again; she could feel the storm of tears building inside of her, could feel the emotion clogging her throat, plugging her nose. She squeezed her eyes shut, but it didn't work. Her next breath was a sob and when she opened her eyes, it was through a sheen of tears.

She cried.

Cried for the love she had lost.

She sobbed.

Sobbed for the pain she saw in her friends' eyes every time they looked at her.

She mourned.

Mourned for the child who would never know its father.

She lay down on her side, uncaring that sand tangled in her loose hair. Her body shook with the force of her emotions. Their child. A child conceived in love, a child Garrick would never see, never teach how to sail, never grow to love.

Everyone told her that it would be all right, that she must go on. But it would never be right. The man she loved was dead, taken away by her own carelessness.

"It's in, they've decided!" yelled a white-robed, dark-haired figure with the face of an angel—which he was.

The door to Arlan's office banged open so hard, the brass nameplate with A. H. SHUCK inscribed on its surface clattered to the marble floor.

Arlan looked up, excitement caused his wings to quiver. "When?"

"Just now. They're about to read the verdict. Hurry."

Arlan shot up from his chair and raced around his desk. His friend turned, his wings swatting Arlan across the face and giving him a mouthful of feathers. Not that he cared. He had waited months for this moment, months during which Garrick's soul had been in limbo, and Lucy, poor Lucy, had nearly died of a broken heart.

The counsel room bustled with activity, those from the upper regions sitting on his right, their wings furled behind them. On his left, those from the lower regions sat, a forest of pitchforks rising from their masses.

Arlan ignored it all and kept his eye firmly focused on the raised dais in front of him, or more importantly on the gray-bearded, silver-headed moderator who sat upon it. It was impossible to glimpse anything in the man's brown eyes. His bushy brows shielded them from the light, but his lips pulled into a frown as he glanced first at Arlan, then at Belial, and then looked away.

A bailiff opened the gate separating the masses from those defending the case. Arlan took his seat, refusing to look at Belial and the devil's counsel, Dameon, who had argued the case. No doubt both were looking smug, which was to be expected given the moderator they'd drawn. It was an established fact that although moderators had a vested interest in being neutral, many had a tendency to vote more frequently for one side or another. Even moderators would one day try to earn their wings. When that time came, who wanted an angry devil trying to foul them up?

"Quiet, please," the bailiff ordered.

The din faded into silence, pitchforks lowered, wings fluttered, throats cleared.

"You may read the charges," the moderator said.

"Case number 100923. Wolf vs. Belial. Charges filed on behalf of Wolf by A. H. Shuck."

The moderator inclined his head. "Let the record state that counsel for both parties are present."

The bailiff began to read. "The charges filed by Mr. A. H. Shuck on behalf of the Plaintiff state that the Defendant, one Belial, aka the Devil, aka Beelzebub, aka Old Scratch, etc., did knowingly enter into a standard soul-for-a-soul contract with Plaintiff, one Wolf, and that the aforementioned Contract should be considered null in that upon execution of said Contract, Exchangee's soul, Exchangee being one Lucy Hartford, was in reality *two* souls, in that Exchangee was carrying Plaintiff's child.

"Plaintiff also argues that the Defendant did knowingly and willingly change a soul's Time of Death in order to coerce the Plaintiff into said Contract. Said T.O.D. has now changed the course of history in that it has been foreseen that Exchangee's child, a child who was never supposed to be born, will affect future world events." The bailiff lowered the paper he was reading from and looked at the moderator.

"Let the record state that the charges have been read," the moderator announced.

Arlan tensed. This was it.

"Let me preface my decision by saying that this was one of the most difficult cases I've ever had to moderate. Not only did I have to consider the T.O.D. issue, but I also had to consider the Exchangee's health and happiness, as well as that of the child she carries." He paused, piercing Arlan with a stare. "I have decided in favor of the Plaintiff."

The crowd gasped, pitchforks banged on the floor, angels applauded.

Belial slammed his fist on the table, letting out a screech of rage which echoed throughout the room.

Arlan shot from his chair. His wings quivered in excitement.

"Further," the moderator went on, much to Arlan's shock, "in light of the child and the health of the

Exchangee, I have decided to invoke the Right to Release Act."

Another gasp came from someone in the room.

"Therefore, at oh-eight-hundred earth time, the Plaintiff's memory of his time with us will be erased, whereafter he will be returned to earth and his Lucy."

Thunder boomed into the little room, the thunder of God's laughter.

29

The horse and rider were a tiny speck on the horizon when the servant first spotted them from the granite parapet. He raised a hand to shield his eyes, the glint of the sun sparkling off the sea making it hard to follow the rider's progress. Closer and closer they drew, galloping at a breakneck speed toward the castle, the rider seemingly oblivious to the sheer drop to his right, a drop which fell over a hundred feet to the ocean below.

The servant watched, heart in his throat, as the horse and rider materialized into two separate beings, the horse's rhythmic blowing audible now. White flecks of foam fell from its mouth and onto its chest and legs, its hooves pounding the soft dirt and sending up puffs of dust. Soon man and horse clattered beneath him and into the courtyard below, the horse skidding to a halt on the polished cobblestones. Sparks shot out from beneath its dancing hooves. The man didn't seem to notice. He dropped the reins.

"M'lord," the servant gasped.

Garrick froze, then tilted his head back, his hands automatically grabbing for the reins again. His horse, impatient with the sudden loss of movement, spun beneath him and tossed its arrogant head.

"Mother o' God, we thought you dead."

"So I've heard."

"Her ladyship—"

Garrick stiffened. "Where is she?"

The servant straightened, seemed to recover himself, then said, "Down on the beach, m'lord."

Garrick jerked his horse toward the road.

"'Tis good to 'ave you 'ome," the servant called after him, making the sign of the cross.

Garrick was oblivious to the man as he spurred his horse back toward the coastal road and the path which led to the beach. It was a narrow trail hewn into the rocks from generations of shoes, but never had Garrick guided a horse down it, nor would he now if the gelding he rode had any say in the matter. The animal balked, but Garrick's sheer determination forced it to obey. He must see Lucy. For the past three days since his memory returned, the thought had burned in his mind.

He kicked the animal forward and the horse tossed its head in protest. Garrick's eyes alternately scanned the beach below and the path before him as they picked their way over clumps of shale and overgrown sea grass. His leather breeches scraped the side of the cliff, but he didn't care.

Then he saw her.

Her body was still, so motionless at first he thought it was a piece of driftwood discarded by the churning sea. But when he glimpsed a flash of red hair and a glint of pale skin, he knew better. Panic choked him, fear sent a chill over his flesh. The waves broke terribly close to where she lay.

He kicked his horse forward again. The gelding arrived by her side in moments, kicking sand upon her. Still she didn't move.

Flinging himself down, he quickly crossed to her and gazed at her pale and drawn face, a face clouded with pain even though she slept. The ravages of her grief where plainly visible. Dark circles lay beneath her smoky lashes. Her skin, once so vibrant, looked as colorless as the shale which dotted the cliffs behind him. He reached out to stroke that flesh, first her arm, just barely visible beneath the thick cloak she wore, then her cheeks. So soft, those cheeks, so familiar.

"Lucy, my love," he groaned, unable to keep his throat from tightening with tears. God, how he loved this woman. He would move heaven and earth for her, storm the very gates of hell if need be.

A pair of green eyes slowly opened, eyes as beautiful and pure as spring, eyes which were filled with a pain so deep Garrick felt his heart clench.

"I'm home, Lucy."

But instead of snapping awake she closed her eyes again and whispered, "Dream."

"No," he said softly, swiping away a lock of hair which tugged across her face.

She opened her eyes again. "Don't wake."

He grabbed her hand and squeezed it softly. Then, unable to bear the distance a moment longer, he scooped her up in his arms, burying his nose into the waterfall of curls and inhaling her sweet fragrance: roses and tears, sand and sorrow. "God, Lucy, I love you."

He drew back and kissed her forehead, then dropped kisses on her cheek, her lips.

A gentle finger touched his face. "Tears," she said softly. "I feel tears."

He kissed the side of her neck, then her left ear.

"And breath. I can hear someone breathing."

For a long moment she said nothing, but he could feel her trembling as he gently caressed her ear. "It can't be," she said softly.

"Oh yes it can," he said gently, trailing his lips toward hers. Her lips were cold and she tasted of salt and sunshine, of fear and disbelief. She was unyielding at first, but then suddenly she clutched at him, her nails digging into his arms. Her mouth opened and he kissed her, kissed her as he'd dreamed of doing for the past three days, kissed her as it was his fate to do from the moment he'd met her.

A long while later he drew back. A grin spread across his face at her look of wonder and tender joy. "There. Have you ever been kissed by a dream?"

"Yes," she said on a sigh. "His name was Garrick."

He drew her to him again, hugging her tightly, but she wouldn't let him for long. Instead she pulled back. And like the first rays of morning sunshine he saw the realization dawn. Finally, she seemed to accept that he was really there beside her. A multitude of emotions traipsed across her face: disbelief, wonder, hope.

"Garrick?" she asked.

"Yes, Luce, it's really me."

She shook her head and for a very long moment simply stared. Her hands reached for his arms, clasping them, her grip growing tighter and tighter until, suddenly, she began to shake him. She did a poor job of it, her own body rocking harder than his own, her red hair flying about her face. The look in her eyes grew intense, as if she were almost angry.

"Garrick Asquith-Wolf, where have you been?"

He chuckled. This was the Lucy he remembered. "Luce, my sweet Luce. I've been recuperating."

Instant concern crossed her face, her eyes roving over him. "From what?"

"Relax, my sweet. Just a small knock to the head. My memory only returned three days ago, it took me that long to get to you."

She lapsed into silence again, her gaze never wavering. Then her eyes began to glisten, to well with tears. "Don't you ever leave me again," she mumbled in a tear-clogged voice. "When I saw you fall overboard. . . ." She stopped talking, as if she couldn't go on.

He gave her a smile, one to reassure her, one meant to tell her without words that she could go on, with him by her side. "Never, Luce. The fires of hell couldn't pull me away from you."

And when he said the words, a niggling memory tugged at the edges of his mind. It bothered him for a moment, but then he forgot everything as he observed the love and tenderness captured in the sparkling depths of her miraculous emerald eyes.

"Garrick," she said softly.

"Lucy. My angel." He bent down and kissed her again.

Neither one of them noticed the wave which promised to douse them.

Then again, chances are they wouldn't have cared.

　　　　　　　　cᗕᗷᗳ

The red-haired boy stared down the snow-carpeted
mountain with a look of excitement on his face, the
makeshift sleigh cold beneath his breeches-clad bottom.
It's time, Robert thought. After three days of waiting for
the snow to stop falling over Cardiff, it was time to
embark upon his great adventure, an adventure he'd
been planning for nigh on three months, the Grand
Adventure.

For a brief moment he let himself admire the view.
Gray streamers of smoke rose from the chimneys of the
home he'd been born in. Their wispy tendrils blended in
with the gray sky and silver ocean beyond. From a distance the house looked tiny, instead of the castle it was,
but it could have been a dog house for all Robert cared.
What mattered was the coming ride. Once again, he
smiled and then settled himself more firmly atop his
great-great-grandfather something-or-other's battle
shield. He took a deep breath, releasing it in a steamy
column of mist. Gingerly, he shoved off.

Nothing happened.

Frowning, he ignored the sting of cold through the fabric of his mittens and gave himself another shove.

Still nothing.

Frustrated, he got up only to have the shield begin to move without him. He flung himself atop it, a smile lighting his face as he began to slid down the hill.

The sound of metal scraping over snow rang through the air. Soon he slid down the hill with the speed of Mr. Hanford's new thoroughbred. His hands clasped the cold edge; his body vibrated. His eyes began to water. He hit a bump, giggling hysterically as the breath was knocked out of him. Next he hit a pit, sailing out of it like a ship jumping a wake. With a war whoop of delight, he glided down the hill, heading directly for the back of the castle.

It was only as he reached the bottom of the hill that he realized he had a problem. It wasn't a miscalculation on his part, really; it was more of an underestimation of his body weight.

He had assumed the meadow was of sufficient length for him to glide to a gradual stop. Unfortunately, he was clipping along at a rate of speed far greater than he'd anticipated.

It was with a sense of doom that he found himself heading for the stable yard and the clutch of chickens newly liberated from their coop.

"Shoo," Robert called, waving his arms to get their attention. Next he tried to alter his course.

No luck.

"Shoo," he called again.

Still no luck.

He collided with them at full speed. Feathers flew through the air and the birds squawked as loudly as a rusty butter churn. One smacked into his chest; he was blinded by red-brown wings as the shield was launched off a mound of snow. Heart in his throat, chicken screeching madly, he braced himself for impact.

He landed on a pillow.

At least it felt like a pillow.

It was only as he lay there, gasping for breath, the chicken who had ridden upon him clucking in fury as it ran away, that Robert realized he'd landed upon a pile of hay.

He giggled.

What luck. What complete and utter luck. Closing his eyes, he ignored the sting of cold and relived every moment of his spectacular ride.

"Did we have fun?" a stern voice asked.

Robert's eyes snapped open. He pushed himself to his feet and flung himself at his father. "Did you see it, did you see it? I came all the way down that hill. I hit a hole and . . . and a bump, and I probably would have smashed into Cinder's stall if that mound of snow hadn't . . ."

Garrick Asquith-Wolf stared down at his son and silently cursed. No, he wondered if he *was* cursed. Not that he cared, mind you. No, he loved his son more than life itself. It was just that from the moment he'd been born, it had been one calamity after another, starting with the doctor he'd watered down not five seconds after he'd been lifted from his mother, right up to the time Garrick had caught him jumping off the barn with makeshift wings attached to his back. He sighed. Much as he loved his child, the boy took after his mother, even sharing her propensity for falling out of trees. He smiled as he remembered that long ago day, the day he'd met his wife, the day an angel had fallen from the heavens and into his arms, his angel.

My fallen angel, he amended.